Book 1

ALONE

BY J.D. CRIST

Dedication

To my family, who have always stood beside me and encouraged me to take this step. You all have served as inspiration throughout this entire process. To my dad, I have kept my promise. I wish you could have been here to see this.

Trigger Warnings

This book contains several themes and topics that some people may find uncomfortable. These include:

Domestic Abuse (Mental)

Death

Zombies

Killing

Blood

Attempted Rape

Use of Crude Weapons (crowbar, screwdriver, etc.)

Dead Children

Strong Language

If you are unable to continue, I understand. But if are, welcome to the world of The Dead Flash.

Chapter 1

The first morning of summer was waking up outside, and the world was full of life. Inside the suburban house, it felt as if the energy was being drained out of Emily. It was a morning like any other as she stood at the range where the hot plate sat cooking scrambled eggs. The stove had gone out four years ago, and they had still not found a way to replace it. Emily watched as the eggs finished, and she turned off the hotplate. It was then that the toast popped up. The toaster was the only thing in the kitchen that worked. Emily divided the eggs between two plates and set to work buttering the toast.

As she was finishing, her husband, Chad, entered the kitchen. He was, as usual, wearing designer clothes and sporting an expensive haircut. Emily could not help but glance down at her worn second-hand blouse and faded blue skirt. He always got upset when she did not dress as well as him. But he told her she was greedy if she asked for more of a budget for her clothing. Emily glanced back up at Chad and could tell by the sour look on his face that this outfit was not up to his standards. Emily had long gotten over any feelings of embarrassment on this issue. She continued to make breakfast and pretended not to notice.

As Chad sat at the table, Emily grabbed a cup of coffee from the counter and turned to give it to him. She set it on the table in front of him with a warm, "Good morning, dear," that Chad responded to with only a grunt. She chose to believe it meant "Good Morning." She then turned and put toast on the plate with the eggs. As she gave Chad his breakfast, he took a sip of the coffee. Emily was able to move out of the way just as he spat it across the kitchen.

"What the hell, Emily?! Is this instant coffee?! What is wrong with you?!"

Emily stood as tall as she could as she replied," It's the only option. The coffee pot went out, and we do not even have the ten dollars to buy a new one. Unless you are willing to cut something out of your budget..."

Chad interrupted before she could finish. "I should cut something out? You're the one who spends our money. Tell you what, Emily, until you learn to handle the budget better, I will buy coffee on my way to work. You can suffer from this crap!"

Emily nodded and placed the plate on the table in front of him. She knew better than to argue when he was like this. Chad had never laid a hand on her, but his words could hurt a lot worse than a slap if pushed when he was angry. Emily didn't mind her "consequences;" she would drink her morning coffee at work for free. She instead turned and finished making her plate. They sat in silence as they ate breakfast. When they finished, he left, no goodbye or anything. Emily had expected this as he was still upset, and it didn't bother her. She set to cleaning up from breakfast with a smile.

Emily took her time and ensured to clean up all

the coffee he had spit at her. When she finished, she
glanced down at her watch. With a gasp, Emily
realized that she should have left the house ten
minutes ago. She ran to the living room, where her
keys and purse waited. Emily gathered them in a flash
and was soon in her car, driving fast down the roads.
She had not been late once in five years; she was not
going to change that now. There was no traffic on the
road this morning, and she made it to the office with
two minutes to spare.

Breathing a sigh of relief, she walked towards
the doors of "Everett's Landscaping." The crews
would not be here for another half hour, but she had
plenty of work to do until then. It was early June and
their busy season. She turned on the lights while
walking toward her desk. As she sat down, she saw the
company logo flashing on her computer screen. She
pressed the space bar to wake up the computer as she
put her purse away. Turning back to the computer, she
saw it was asking for her password, which she had
entered. She then proceeded to print the work orders
and schedules for the day. The crews would be busy,
so she would likely spend the rest of the day alone
once they were on their way.

The printer finished as the crews began coming
in the door. There was the everyday small talk and
grunts as they reviewed the orders and schedules for
the day. Each foreman asked, "How could you do this
to me, beautiful?" or "And here I thought you loved
me." She smiled and joked with them all. But, by
eight, they were all gone, and the office was silent
once again. Everett would most likely not be in today.
He hated office work and preferred to be in the field.

Everett relied on Emily to handle everything at the office. Emily took the quiet time to check the few voicemails and the next day's schedules.

When she looked at the clock on her computer, she noticed it was time for lunch. She reached down and opened her bottom desk drawer but saw only her purse. Emily began cursing to herself under her breath. With all the excitement of that morning, she had forgotten her lunch. She slammed the drawer closed and looked around. Everett had told her she could close and go out for lunch any time. But, after the fight with Chad this morning over money, she felt this would cause more issues.

She decided that skipping lunch would help her keep her trim figure. Emily set back to work and tried to ignore her stomach. She frequented the water cooler many times to refill her cup. She hoped it would help keep her stomach from complaining too much. But this led to more trips to the ladies' room, and she hated to keep getting up. With all these interruptions, Emily's afternoon flew by. By the time five came, she felt relieved to be going home. According to her pedometer, the only good thing about her day was that she had reached her step goal. Emily shut down the office and locked the front door. The crews would not be back for at least another hour, but they parked the work trucks and went home without needing her to stay.

Emily tried to find ways to get the money for a new coffee pot on the drive home. The coffee pot would make Chad happy, and her evening would be better than the rest of her day. But it was impossible to

turn the two dollars in her purse into anything more.
She accepted defeat as she pulled into the driveway.
Chad was not home yet, but he would be by six-thirty.
Emily headed up the front walk and unlocked the door.
She set down her keys and made her way straight to
the kitchen.

She walked towards the refrigerator and opened
the mini-fridge on the counter next to it, yet another
thing that she should figure out how to replace. With
such a small fridge and only the hot plate to cook with,
Emily had gotten creative over the years. She was
proud of the meals she was able to put together.
Tonight, she made fried pork chops and fried potatoes,
two of Chad's favorites. The potatoes had finished as
she heard the front door open.

"Emily! Emily! Where are you?!"

Emily could hear the excitement in his voice.
He was definitely in a much better mood than he was
this morning.

"In the kitchen, Chad! Dinner's almost ready!"

Emily had set the plates on the table as he flew
around the corner with a grin so big one would think
he had won the lottery. Emily stopped in her tracks,
shocked that he was this happy. After glancing at the
table, Chad looked confused as well as happy.

"How did you know?"

"Know what?" Emily replied. "I wanted to
make your favorite foods to make up for this morning."

Chad's grin spread even wider. Emily could swear she could see his wisdom teeth.

"It's finally happening!" He exclaimed. "Mr. Harrington came to me today and said I was the perfect fit for the launch. He wants me to be in charge of everything!"

Emily could not help but gasp with excitement. Chad worked at a video game development company. He had been trying for years to get this chance. His ultimate goal was to take over for Mr. Harrington one day. She felt the excitement that his dream was coming true and about the pay raise he would get. Money was a source of most of their fights, and she would be glad to see it end.

Chad took giant steps across the room, wrapped Emily in a hug, and kissed her. This was the first time they had kissed in a month. Emily kissed him back; she felt they were the couple they used to be for the first time in years.

"My new pay raise starts on Monday, and we will have no more money problems. Everything is finally going to be how I want it."

With that, Chad turned, sat at the table, and began making his plate. Emily stood for a moment while the weight of his words sank in. While it was a simple enough phrase, he had said how "he" wants it, not how "they" want it. She thought about saying something, but decided against it. Instead, she did what she thought a good wife should. She smiled and sat down at the table. She ate while listening to him go on about the promotion and his plans. Chad spoke of everything he wanted to get for himself and sounded like a kid at Christmas.

For an hour, she listened, and never once did he mention fixing things around the house. He did not even talk about a new coffee pot that had been the end of the world this morning. Emily could feel her smile fading and the flush of red in her cheeks. She couldn't believe that they were finally on track to be happy, and he was thinking of only himself.

"Emily, are you feeling alright?" Chad asked, sounding concerned. This caused her temper to relax somewhat, but then he spoke again. "You can't afford to get sick. The co-pays would kill you since you aren't even able to buy a new coffee pot."

"I can't afford a new coffee pot!" Emily felt the rage starting to spill out of her, and she searched for a way to stop it. "I pay for everything around here and get nothing in return! We could have a decent home if you weren't such a selfish son of a bitch. I wouldn't have to shop the thrift store rejects, so you can have your designer clothes! We could have an actual refrigerator and stove, but your haircut is more important! For God's sake, we can't even get a new coffee pot, but you can buy designer coffee on your way to work!"

Chad sat for a moment from the shock that she was speaking to him this way. Emily was always the perfect wife to him. Emily never yelled, complained, and did everything she could to make him happy. Emily had no idea she could speak to him like that, and he seemed as shocked as she was. She did not give Chad time to regain his equilibrium and fight back. She couldn't hold this in anymore and couldn't stop it from coming out.

"You can't afford the fucking haircut you get every three weeks or the car you had to have. I have to pay for all those things, and then you say I can't afford to take care of myself. I don't understand why I have to suffer while you get to act like a rich asshole. None of what you get do you need." Emily could tell by the look on his face that he was already thinking of an argument. "Please, Chad, explain it to me! Explain how a new car will help you make video games. Please explain how a three-hundred-dollar haircut will help you be successful! I'm listening. Please tell me!"

She paused to take a breath, and Chad jumped at the chance to speak. "You are an idiot! If you want to succeed, you have to look the part. Do you think I want to be like you?! Drive a ten-year-old car and dress like a bag lady?! No wonder you will never be more than a glorified receptionist. Why would I give a shit about this house?! It's not a home; a home is for a family! You screwed that up, so why should I give a shit?!" Chad's face showed that he knew he had gone too far. He recovered and was back to looking angry in a few moments.

Emily sat for a moment to allow his words to sink in. They were fighting about him being selfish, and he was now finding a way to blame her. She knew what he was talking about when he said she screwed up making them a family. They hadn't spoken about her miscarriage since it happened because he refused to. Having him bring it up out of anger was more than she could take.

"I am done with this shit," Emily said in almost a whisper. She felt her pain turn into anger. She looked up at Chad and felt the words explode out of her. "I am done with you and your bullshit! You can buy your fucking coffee pot, pay your fucking car payment and pay for your shit! I thought we still had each other, but I'm not good enough for your royal highness! You can go fuck yourself and make your own family."

Emily stood from the table, slamming her chair into the counter behind her. She stormed down the hall and could feel her anger radiating from her body. She reached the bedroom and slammed the door shut behind her. She felt her energy leaving her body as the thud echoed through the house. Emily did not know what came over her there, but she would not apologize. Instead, she headed for the shower to wash away the pain of the day. As she cleaned, the memory of the miscarriage came crashing back to her. She stood under the warm water for several minutes and allowed the tears to flow. She looked down at her stomach and rubbed where a growing baby had once been.

The doctors had said that it wasn't her fault, but she blamed herself from the moment it happened. She remembered Chad telling her in the hospital that it wasn't, but now she knew how he felt. Emily turned off the water and dressed for bed. Her emotions drained her energy, and she crawled into bed at eight-thirty. As she lay there, she heard the front door open and close and Chad's car start. Right now, she didn't care if he came back. She wanted him nowhere near her. She felt the tears come over her and was asleep before they had stopped.

Emily's alarm went off right on time, and for a moment, she had forgotten the events of the night before. But, as she turned off the alarm, it all came rushing back. She looked to Chad's side of the bed to see that he was not there. Perhaps he had left her, she thought as she drew back the blankets and proceeded to get dressed for the day. Once dressed, she headed towards the kitchen for a quick breakfast and decided to go to work early. She didn't want to be in this house a minute longer than she had to.

When she opened the door, she found the smell of food cooking and fresh coffee. She stood frozen in the doorway and pinched herself to ensure she was awake. She walked down the hall and stood in the kitchen doorway. She found Chad cooking what appeared to be French toast. But her eyes were more drawn towards the counter, where a brand-new coffee pot sat. She had no idea what he paid, but it was the most beautiful thing in the world to her. As she stood there, Chad looked up from his cooking.

"Sit down, Em; everything is almost ready."

He had not called her Em in years, and she did not know how to react. She moved across the kitchen and sat down in her chair. As she sat, Chad placed a cup of hot coffee in front of her and, a few minutes later, a plate of french toast. He sat down across from her and began eating. Emily sat in silence, not touching the food in front of her. She couldn't believe that he wanted to have breakfast and pretend nothing had happened. Chad looked up at her with a confused look.

"You have to be hungry, Em," he sounded like he was concerned about her. "Please, try to eat at least a little bit."

Emily slowly picked up the fork and took a bite. She couldn't help the surprise she felt that it was good. She continued to eat but kept her eyes on her plate. She could not bring herself to look at Chad. As soon as she finished, Chad picked up the plate in front of her and began washing the dishes. She could not remember Chad doing the dishes the entire time they were married. Emily turned in her chair and looked at him, trying to figure out what game he was playing now.

"So, is the food supposed to make me forget about last night, or was the coffee pot supposed to do that?" she spoke to the back of his head.

Chad breathed a heavy sigh and shut off the water. He walked back around to his chair and sat down across from her.

"I shouldn't have said what I did about the miscarriage. It wasn't your fault, and I'm the one who said I wasn't ready to try again. I was hurt, and I wanted to hurt you. I'm sorry, Em, I should have never said it." Chad took a breath and looked deep into her eyes. Emily was reminded of the man she married and felt like he was finally returning to the surface. "You were right, you do pay for the extras around here, and it's time I take on my fair share. I will take some time today and put together a priority list. We can go over it together if you want and figure out how to make it all work."

Emily sat listening to every word he said. He had not talked to her like this in a very long time, and she felt he was sorry. She was not ready to give up on her marriage. She wasn't the type who was okay with divorce. She took her wedding vows to heart, and if they could figure out how to make it work, that's what she wanted to do. He showed that he was willing to let go of his anger and try to change. She should try as well.

"I can't live like this anymore," she finally spoke. "I want us to find a way to make it work, to be there for each other. I just can't.." Emily felt the tears coming once more and couldn't finish.

"I understand, and I want you to know that I am going to make more things about you. I tried to start with the coffee pot in case you didn't notice," Chad teased.

Emily turned and looked at it on the counter. It was nice and appeared to have more functions than she would ever need. Yet, she didn't know how this was supposed to show that more things would be about her. He was the one who made a big deal about not having one, not her. She turned back to Chad with a forced smile, trying to think of something to say.

"It's red, your favorite color," Chad spoke before she could.

Emily looked back at the red coffee pot once more. Chad was trying, sure, but he had been so selfish for so long that he didn't even realize his mistake. Her favorite color was green, and Chad's was red. Emily considered pointing this out to him, but decided this was not the time. They were on shaky ground as it was, and he was trying. She made a note to find a way to bring this up later, but she wanted to hold on to the hope she had right now.

"Thank you, Chad," she said as she turned back to him. "It is lovely. We have a lot of work to do, but I think we are on the right track."

Emily watched as a smile spread across his face.

"Why don't you head on to work, and I'll finish the dishes? I know you have a lot to do with the launch and the promotion," Emily smiled back.

"Are you sure? I want to show you that I am willing to take on my fair share around here."

"I'm sure. We are supposed to support and help each other, right? she smiled at him.

"You're the best, Em. I'll be home by six-thirty."

With a quick kiss on the cheek, Chad was out the door. Emily finished cleaning up the kitchen and headed to work. She was early again but had a weird feeling in the pit of her stomach. She felt like she had forgotten something. She checked to ensure she had her lunch and remembered locking the front door. She decided to ignore it and headed into the office. Once inside the building, she went about her routine as usual. She had to ask Steve, one of the foremen, to change the water bottle for her. She had nearly emptied it yesterday. He did it with a smile, asking her if the office had turned into a desert the day before. Emily laughed with him and thanked him as he left. The rest of the day was business, but the feeling that she had forgotten something remained.

As she headed home, the feeling continued to grow, and she could not shake it. She decided she probably felt out of sorts because of everything at home. She assured herself that everything was fine as she arrived home. Emily turned the handle, and she found that the door was locked. There was nothing left that she could have forgotten to do today. She took this as confirmation that she was right about everything and unlocked the door. Once inside, she headed to the kitchen to decide what creation she would make tonight. But, a note on the mini-fridge caught her eye. She walked over and grabbed it. Her eyes moved over the words that Chad had written:

Sorry, Emily, my boss invited me out to dinner to celebrate. I would have loved you to join us, but it's a guys only thing. I noticed nothing in the fridge for tonight, so I transferred $10 to the joint account. Would you please get yourself something to eat on me? I left all the information on what my new raise will be and the things we should do in my office. It would be great if you could look at it and start making a plan. I will be home late, so don't wait up.

I love you,
Chad

Emily placed the note on the table and stood for a moment in the empty house. He was trying and making changes. This was the first time he had transferred money to the joint account in years. She felt her stomach rumble and realized how little she had eaten over the past few days. She pulled out her phone and began to look at "Freno's", her favorite pizza restaurant website. She found they had a couple's special going on for eight dollars. While it was more than she would normally eat, she decided to go with it and treat herself. She called the restaurant and placed her order. She felt a little bad that she wouldn't have much of a tip, but there was nothing she could do about that now.

Emily decided to look at Chad's list; it was sure to lift her spirits even higher. She headed to his office and found the red folder on his keyboard. She took it back to the kitchen and began to look through it. His raise was more than she could have imagined. He was going to be making three times as much as she did. She quickly found the list he had made, excited to see where he wanted to start.

Yet, as she looked through his list of priorities, she felt the red returning to her cheeks. All the hope and happiness she felt was ripped from her, and she was back to anger. She couldn't even manage to feel any sadness as she read through it.

1. New car for me this year, new car for you next year.

2. Personal Shopper - you do so much already. Having someone else to shop for me would give you time to find clothes for yourself.

3. Teeth Whitening - we can get you one too if you want.

4. New Monitors

5. Rolex

6. Second hot plate

7. Household repairs ($500, we won't include the hot plate or the coffee pot)

The words on the paper began to blur as Emily's rage filled her. He tried to make it seem like he was changing, but she saw right through it. They could afford a new stove with his raise, but she got another hot plate while he got a personal shopper. She crumpled the paper in her hands and threw it into the trash. She felt like he just did not want to lose his human slave. She was nothing to him, and he just wanted her to shut up. It was almost like someone else had taken over as she logged into her bank accounts. They each had a personal account and a joint account. They each said they would transfer funds into the joint account. It was for household costs, but only Emily ever did it. She had her account set up to move all her paychecks into the joint account every time she got paid. She felt like she was watching someone else control her body as she clicked through the screens. She watched as she canceled her transfer for the next day and all future transfers.

As she finished and logged out, she heard a

knock on the door. She searched through Chad's desk and found his emergency twenty. She went to the door to find a teenager with her order. He seemed less than thrilled about his job but perked up when she tipped him the twenty. She took her feast to the bedroom and set a picnic on the bed. She then turned on the small TV to watch her show. She ate while watching and was shocked that almost nothing was left. As the show ended, she cleaned up the remains of her meal and got ready for bed. She crawled between the blankets, still high on her newfound confidence. She had no idea how Chad would react and she didn't care. She felt strong right now and wasn't going to back down. She wouldn't fall for his act again, and he would learn the hard way.

Chapter 2

Emily awoke the following day with a clear mind, ready to face Chad about how he was behaving. She glanced next to her to see that he was already up and gone. Emily dressed and headed toward the kitchen. Emily opened the door, part of her hoping for the smell of fresh coffee to fill the house. Yet, the house was quiet, and it was apparent that Chad had already left for the day. Emily made her way to the kitchen and could not help but stare at the coffee pot on the counter. It was several minutes before she noticed the note hanging from the mini-fridge. Emily read the message and could not help but laugh at how self-entitled Chad was.

I left early. We decided to take a trip over the three-day weekend to celebrate. I will be back on Monday night at around five. I found my list in the trash. We will talk about this when I get back. Also, something is wrong with your paycheck. It is not in the joint account. It would be best if you had this fixed immediately. I don't want to look poor on this trip.

Chad

Emily ripped the note from where it hung, crumpled it, and threw it in the trash.

"I'm sure we will," Emily said to herself.

A glance in the mini-fridge reminded her that there was nothing left. She closed the door and headed to the living room. After gathering her keys and purse, she ran out the door and climbed into her car. She drove to her favorite drive-through and ordered a breakfast sandwich and coffee. Paying with her debit card felt strange as she could not remember ever using it, and it still looked brand new.

She arrived at the office half an hour early. She decided to go ahead and enjoy her breakfast at her desk. Emily unlocked the front door and turned on all the lights on her regular route to her desk. Once there, she pulled the food out of the brown paper bag and in front of her. She enjoyed the silence and her disobedience of Chad's rules as she enjoyed her breakfast. As she finished and disposed of her trash, she heard her cell phone ring. A glance at the Caller ID showed it was Chad. He must have been upset that she had not transferred the funds. Emily considered answering it for a moment, but it was time to start work according to the clock. She pressed the silent key and dropped it back into her purse.

Emily set to work while her phone was vibrating in her desk drawer. Emily could not help but laugh and let the phone remain in her purse. She couldn't help but be extra cheerful with the crews as they came in for their morning assignments. Fridays were always crazy, and she was sure to have plenty to keep her busy. Soon, the crews were all gone, and Emily began her Friday routine.

The usual Friday phone calls started from upset crews and needy customers. Emily handled them all with the most grace she had ever shown. By lunch, the phones were silent, except for her cell, which vibrated in the desk drawer. With no food left in the house, she did not have anything to bring for lunch. She took Everett up on his offer and closed the office to go out for lunch. There was a little cafe a few blocks away that she loved. She only went there on her birthday with her sister once a year. Yet today, she decided to go celebrate her newfound strength.

She arrived in a few minutes and requested a table on the patio. It was a lovely day, and she did not want to be penned up inside anymore. She placed her order with the waitress and began sipping her water. She then remembered her cell phone and realized it had been quiet since she arrived. She decided to ensure she had missed nothing important and took it out. Even she is shocked by what she sees. There are sixteen missed calls from Chad and twenty text messages. She can't help but be impressed by his persistence.

She only glanced over the texts but got the gist of what he was upset about in moments. The money was still not in the account. How dare she ignore his calls? He would come to her job if he remembered where she worked, blah blah blah. She decided to put down the phone without listening to the voicemails. Today was her day, and he was not going to ruin it. As she was about to slide the phone back into her purse, it began to vibrate.

"Really!?" Emily breathed to herself.

Resolved to put it away, she barely saw the name on the Caller ID. It was her sister Rachael. Emily pulled the phone back up and answered the call.

"Hey, Rachael."

"Don't you hey Rachael me? I wanted to make sure you were alive after you stood me up!" Rachael tried to sound angry, but Emily could tell she was more playful.

"I didn't stand you up," Emily replied, uncertain what her sister was talking about.

"Yes, you did. I sat at the cafe for two hours yesterday. I would have called you, but I figured you went out with Chad or something and forgot about me." Rachael then added a few fake sniffles, but Emily could hear the playfulness in her voice. Emily remembered the feeling the day before that she had forgotten something. That something was her damn birthday!

"Oh my God, Rachael. I am so sorry. I completely forgot."

"Well, you need a break if you can't remember your birthday. Is Chad out of town or something? I know he makes a big deal out of it." Emily had been lying to her sister about this for years. Chad had not celebrated Emily's birthday since right after they were married.

"No, he must have forgotten. You know how life can get sometimes." Emily did not feel like getting into the details right now. Not until she was sure what was going to happen to herself.

"Well, I'll forgive you this once. I can't be mad

at you at the party. Mom and Dad would kill me!"
Rachael said very casually. But Emily felt her heart
jump into her throat, and party was not a word she was
expecting.

"What do you mean party?" She asked, trying
to hide the concern in her voice.

"The one you couldn't say no to because you
stood me up yesterday. Mom and Dad are insisting.
We are going to come to your place on Saturday
around noon. We can talk and catch up, and then they
will take us all out to dinner. You guys don't have
plans, do you?"

Emily knew that this situation would be
complicated. Though her parents only lived twenty
minutes away, Emily only saw them once or twice a
year, and she always went to them. She didn't want
them to see the house, her struggles, or that she and
Chad were having issues. But she knew there was no
getting out of this, and she would have to play the part.

"Chad is out of town until Monday, so I am
free. But I could meet you guys at the restaurant
instead. Things are crazy around the house right now."
Emily could not help but cross her fingers. Hoping
that her sister would bite the hook, she was dangling.

"Crazy! Try having three kids under the age of
five. That's crazy. I'm sure everything will be fine,
Em's. We will see you on Saturday. I've got to go for
now. Take care, and I love you."

"I love you too." Emily chimed back, hoping

she sounded as cheerful as she wanted.

She slid the phone back into her purse as the waitress reappeared with her order. She found it hard to be as excited about the meal and ate half of it. She gave the woman a generous tip and drove the few blocks back to the office. Once inside, she decided not to think about it. She worked through the afternoon and kept herself busy. So busy, she did not notice the cell phone vibrating in her desk drawer. Soon it was five, and Emily closed up for the weekend and headed for her car. She considered checking her cell phone, but was not in the mood. Emily had a lot to do before her family arrived. She had to try to save herself some embarrassment, and dealing with Chad would make it worse.

The whole way home, Emily could do nothing but think of ways to hide all the broken things about her home. She could put the mini-fridge in Chad's office and pretend the refrigerator worked. The hot plate could slide into the oven. They would not be cooking at the house anyway. The broken floorboard in the hallway, she could not think of a way to hide. She had no idea how to fix it and had to pray no one stepped on it. The thoughts were still running through her mind as she pulled into the driveway.

Looking at the house, she realized that she could not tell it was anything but a beautiful home from the outside. Everett had offered to do her landscaping a year after she began working for him at no charge. Her car had broken down again, and he had given her a ride home. The yard at the time was like looking at an abandoned house. Chad did not have time for such a thing, and she tried but struggled to make any headway with it. She would never forget the day she came home to see it all beautiful. Everett still had a crew come by once a week to mow the yard and maintain the flower beds. Emily had saved for months to buy enough paint to repaint the door and the shutters. She borrowed a power washer from work to clean the siding. Chad had called it a waste of time, but she loved the outside of their home.

Even as she walked up the steps, it was still her favorite part of her home. It hid the truth that everything inside was rotten and broken. Once inside the door, she put her keys and purse down and looked around. The couches were stained and ripped. The carpet in the center of the room was missing. Chad had wanted to see if there were hardwood floors underneath. The answer was no, but the hole had been on the carpet for years. The paint was peeling or even missing on sections of the walls. This is where she would start doing what she did best, hiding the truth.

She had put an area rug down in the bedroom last year because she could not stand to walk on the bare subfloor anymore. She went to the bedroom, rolled up the carpet, and took it to the living room. It covered the whole carpet nicely. A good vacuuming and her floors would look decent. She then moved the few pictures on the walls to cover the worst of the failing paint job. A quick trip to the closet allowed her to find a few blankets that looked decent enough to cover the couches. By the time she had finished, the living room looked halfway decent.

Next, she headed to the dreaded kitchen. She

began to move the makeshift appliances as she had planned to make it look like everything worked. As she carried the heavy mini fridge into Chad's office, she felt the anger crawl back inside her soul. This room had new flooring, a fresh paint job, a new light fixture, and only the best of everything. Anyone who came here would think they had their life and relationship on track. They would never know how selfish he was unless they saw the rest of the house.

She put down the fridge, slammed the office door shut on her way out, and headed back to the kitchen. Four chairs sat at the table, but they would fall apart if anyone touched two of them. She started to make a list in her head of things she could buy cheaply to make the house look presentable for her family. Superglue, flowers, and placemats made the list. She wiped down everything in the kitchen and tried to make the broken counters look like they could be a style. As she cleaned around the coffee pot, she thought to serve everyone coffee while they were there. She then remembered that she only had two coffee cups. According to Chad, only two of every dish and utensil are needed because dishes are a waste of money. She hated that these thoughts kept creeping in while she worked. She added four more coffee cups and drinking glasses to the list.

She wiped down the inside of the broken fridge as she did every week to keep it from developing a smell. She decided that she could put a few bags of ice in here to cool some soda. It would help to sell the look that the refrigerator worked. She added these things to her growing list. She then glanced up at the ceiling. The water spots were not glaringly obvious from the roof leaking every time it rained, but they were there. She sighed as she decided there was nothing she could do about those except hope no one looked up.

The bathroom would be the last stop on her fake-it train. Standing in the doorway, she saw how little she could do to fix this room. There was no way to hide the cracked mirror above the sink, the door was missing on the cabinet, and the towel on the towel rack looked like it had been around for fifty years. It was so full of holes. The worst part is that it was her best towel. She added two new towels to the list, a shower curtain to hide the bathtub, and a new bath mat. She set to work wiping down everything she could to make it look as good as possible.

Once done, she stepped back out into the hall. Looking to her right, she could see Chad's office door. Nothing needed to be done in there. To her left was the master bedroom—no sense in trying to fix it up. No one would see it anyway. The door in front of her was one she could not stand even to open. Emily discovered she was pregnant when they had only been married a few months. Chad had been so happy, and this was when their marriage was at its best. He had painted the room a soft yellow, put down a new carpet, and even a new light fixture. They had even begun to buy the baby furniture. Behind that door, she would see a crib, a small dresser, and a rocking chair. Everything had been perfect, and she could not have been happier.

This was when tragedy moved into the house and never left. At five months, something went wrong.

Emily knew the doctor had explained it, but she could only focus on what he said. She had lost the baby. The doctor had put her on medication to help her and said they could try again in a year. Chad would not even look at her for months. She knew he blamed her and was angry. He had shut the door when they got home from the hospital that night, and it had not been opened since. She would not change that today, not with everything else she had to deal with right now.

Emily headed back to the living room and grabbed her purse and keys. It had been a long time since she made a shopping trip like this, but she could not find it in herself to be excited. This was a mission to hide how bad things were from her family. Once in the car and driving towards the store, she heard her phone vibrate again. She never talked on the phone while she drove, so she resolved to ignore it once more. This time, though, it did not stop. The phone would only be silent for a few moments and then start again. This continued as she pulled into a parking spot at the store.

Emily took a few moments and steadied herself as she pulled the phone from her purse. Chad's name was shown on the Caller ID, and she could almost see the anger on his face. She had avoided his calls all day but figured it was time to talk to him. He still thought he was in control of her, and she was ready to tell him how wrong he was. She pressed the accept button on the phone and put it to her ear.

"Hello," she said in a cheery voice that even shocked her.

"Are you fucking kidding me, Emily?! I have been trying to get a hold of you all day. Where the hell have you been?!"

"I've been busy. You know I had to work today, and then I had work to do at home. We had no food at the house, so I just pulled up to the grocery store." Emily spoke like it was just any ordinary day. She ignored that she had denied him access to her paycheck and had been ducking his calls.

"Don't give me that shit! You have been avoiding me, and I have had enough of it! After everything I did for you yesterday, this is how you repay me! We will handle this when I get home! Right now, I need you to call the bank because they say you didn't transfer your check, and I need that money now!"

"Oh, I'm sorry. You weren't home this morning, so I didn't get a chance to tell you. After looking over your list last night, I had a thought. If you can have such a list, why can't I? So, I didn't transfer the money. I paid all the household bills last week, so there are none of those left. I decided to keep the money I earned and start marking things off my list."

"Who the hell do you think you are?! That is my money, you crazy bitch! I put up with your shit every day and ask nothing from you! You will transfer that money now or so help me…". Emily was done hearing what he had to say. Instead of yelling back, though, she replied with a smile.

"So, help you what, Chad? I said no, and that

was my choice. You got paid today as well, and there are no bills this week you need to contribute to, so use your own damn money! I have things to do right now, and I am sure you do as well. If you want to talk about this when you are done celebrating, I will make sure I'm home on Monday."

With that, Emily hung up the phone and dropped it back into her purse. As she headed into the store, she realized she was returning to her old self. Back before the miscarriage, back to before Chad had to be the top priority. She had been a strong person who would say or do what she had to. Chad could either accept that or not. It wasn't her problem. The house was in her name, not his, and even if a judge said she had to buy him out, she would. She let her newfound confidence guide her through the store. She even stopped to look at things she needed to make permanent repairs to the house once the weekend was over.

When she returned home, she put the things she had bought in place. She sat for half an hour, gluing the chairs back together. They would work for tomorrow, but she was resolved to buy new very soon. She would need to remember to go out in the morning to buy fresh ice for the fridge to keep everything cold. She heated the meatloaf dinner she had purchased at the store in the microwave and sat enjoying her meal. By the time she was done, the sun had long since gone down, and she felt exhausted. She forced herself into the shower and then straight to bed. Sleep came quickly, and the thoughts of the day melted away.

Chapter 3

Emily woke peacefully. She thought she had woken before her alarm, but the sounds outside told her that morning was well underway. Emily glanced at the clock to see that it was nearly ten. She overslept and had so much to do. Emily jumped from the bed and began to curse the hard subfloor under her feet. She would have to move the rug back that night. She quickly made the bed and headed to the closet. She decided to go simple and wear a pair of jeans and a light dress shirt. Soon she was in the kitchen and had a pot of coffee brewing. She would need to make another before her family arrived, but she needed the pick me up right now.

While she waited for the coffee, she ran through the house, freshening it up. With a cup of hot coffee, Emily headed to the car to get a few more bags of ice. The trip was uneventful, and it was eleven-thirty when she returned home. She pulled out the empty bags from the crisper drawers, emptied the water into the sink, and slid the new bags of ice into the drawers. The refrigerator is surprisingly cold, and she can't help but think she might pull this off. She washed the coffee pot and put on a fresh pot. She began to walk to the hallway to see if she could figure out something with the floorboard. A knock at the door froze her where she stood.

She finally managed to free herself from where she seemed trapped on the floor and made her way to the front door. She reached up and quickly straightened her hair, and then reached for the door handle. The handle seemed to take forever to turn and was much heavier than it had been that morning. As the old door finally swung open, she was greeted by nothing but smiles. A cheer of "Aunt Emily" rang out as her nieces and nephew rushed to put her in a hug.

"You guys are getting so big!" Emily exclaimed while hugging them back.

"Alright, kids, we have all day. Don't kill her in the first five minutes," Rachael stepped through the door after them.

The children scattered into the living room as their mother entered. Emily hugged her sister and stepped aside so that she could join her children. Next at the door were Emily's parents, Charles and Christine. Christine wrapped Emily in a hug, and Emily could feel in it how much her mom had missed her.

"Hey, Mom, it's good to see you," Emily whispered.

"I half expected you not to be home with as busy as you always are." Emily could hear the pain in her voice.

"I wouldn't do that to you. Please, come in." Emily saw that her father was still looking at the yard.

"Looks like a professional job out here," he said with very little emotion. This was the first time they had been to the house that Emily knew of before today.

"Yes, my boss makes sure it gets done for me as a thank you for all my hard work." Emily knows that this is the only truth she can tell her dad about her life.

"Well then, you must be damn good at your job." He finally turned to face her, and Emily could have sworn that she saw tears in his eyes. "It's good to see you, kiddo."

"It's good to see you, too, Dad."

Emily wrapped her father in a hug and felt safe for the first time in a very long time. She also couldn't help but be glad that Chad was not here. He would find a way to rob her of this moment, and she did not want to lose a second of it.

"I hope you don't mind, but we had a party crasher that insisted on coming."

Emily let go of her father and looked at him with confusion. Charles nodded his head towards the driveway, and Emily's gaze followed. Standing next to a small black hatchback was Joseph, Emily's younger brother. His hands were in his pockets, and he smiled at her as she looked at him. Emily had not seen Joe in nearly four years.

"Well, it wouldn't be a party without a crasher or two," she quickly quipped back at her dad.

Charles laughed and headed inside to join everyone else. Emily then turned her attention back to Joe. Their fight had been pretty epic, and, in the end, they decided not to speak or see each other ever again.

Emily remembered the details of the fight like it was yesterday. She had tried to confide in him about the struggles between her and Chad after the miscarriage. Joe had listened and been there for her as she cried. But he concluded that Chad was a "piece of shit," and he had insisted that Emily leave him. As she thought back through the fight details, Joe had been right about everything. But she was still not ready to admit that to him or anyone else. But she also did not want him to disappear again, either.

"You still driving that death trap?" Emily yelled across the yard while looking at Joe's car. She could see him visibly relax, and he began to walk toward her.

"Hey, don't knock my baby. She may not be fancy, but she has character".

"Well, you'd better get inside. I'd hate for it to blow up and us still be out here." Emily laughed as she walked back through the door and shut it behind Joe.

As the door shut, Emily felt her tension rise and hoped her plan would work. Everyone sat and talked; her mother even complimented the blankets she had put on the couch. Emily felt that perhaps she had been over-prepared.

"Where is the bathroom?" Rachael asked while everyone was telling stories and enjoying a good laugh.

"Down the hall on the left," Emily replied without thinking.

Christine was talking about Emily's Birthday,

where Emily had wished Joe had been a girl. It was embarrassing because she had done it out loud in front of Joe while blowing out the candles. They all were laughing as the crunch sound and a cry came from the hall. Emily's heart dropped, and she took off at a run. Her sister had stepped on the floorboard. She had completely forgotten about it. As she reached Rachael, she was pulling her foot up out of the hole in the floor.

"I'm okay. It scared me more than anything else," Rachael said as she heard Emily behind her.

"I'll get some ice," Christine said as she turned to the kitchen.

Emily did not have time to react, and how would she explain that it was in the crisper drawer? Everything was falling apart, literally. Emily and Joe helped Rachael back to the living room. As they did, they heard Christine yell from the kitchen.

"Charles, could you come here, please?"

"She must see something in there that she wants in our kitchen," Charles stated as he left the room.

"Doubtful, unless she likes the coffee pot," Emily thought.

Once they had their sister settled on the couch surrounded by the kids, Emily headed to the kitchen. Her parents were standing close to each other and whispering. Her dad looked angry, and her mother could not hide the look of worry on her face.

"Emily, are you okay?" her mother finally spoke. Emily knew what she thought, that she and Chad were having financial problems. Which, in a way, was true; she earned enough to keep up with the house, but Chad spent it all on himself.

"Yes, Mom. You know how busy my life gets; sometimes, things get away from us. We bought a new fridge, and it will be here tomorrow." It wasn't a complete lie; they did buy the mini-fridge, and she would have it back in here tomorrow.

"And what about your stove? I assume it's broken too since it's not even plugged in." Charles chimed in.

Damn them for having to be so observant. When her father looked up, Emily was trying to think of something to say that wouldn't be a complete lie. Why did he look up? He grabbed one of the freshly glued chairs and pulled it over to stand on to inspect the ceiling closer. Emily did not trust the glue that much and finally decided to tell the truth.

"Stop! Just stop," she was nearly crying by the end of the last word. "It's barely glued together, and I don't want you to get hurt, too."

Charles stopped and stood looking at Emily. She knew that look from when she was growing up. He wanted to know the truth, not parts of it but all of it, and he wanted to know it now. Emily knew she would later regret opening her mouth. She had been having issues with shutting it once she opened it. But she could not hold it in anymore.

"It's all broken. The fridge has been out for I can't even remember how long. We have a mini-fridge on the counter, but I hid it in Chad's office. There is a hot plate in the oven that I set on the stove to cook. The chairs are falling apart, the roof leaks all the time, and if you turn the kitchen sink above a dribble, it will flood the kitchen floor. The kitchen window is barely in place and mostly held by tape."

"Emily, how long has it been like this?" Joe asked from behind her.

"Years. I didn't want you guys to see it until I could at least make it safe to walk to the damn bathroom." Emily watched as her father inspected the window and her mother pulled the hot plate from the oven.

"What else?" Charles asked.

Simple yet to the point as he always was. Emily proceeded to walk her family through her house of shame. She showed them everything wrong in each room. She went into every room except for two, Chad's office and the nursery. Her mother was the one who stopped in front of the nursery door.

"What about this room?" she asked while reaching for the handle. Emily felt herself nearly jump out of her skin at the thought that the door could open.

"That room is perfect, except I caused it to be empty." Emily felt the tears welling up in her eyes. "Please, don't open it."

Joseph leaned over and whispered to their mother, who let go of the handle. Emily could tell by the look on his face that he knew it was the nursery. They walked back down the hall and stopped at Chad's office.

"Well, let's see what needs to be fixed up here," Joe said as he opened the door. He could not hide the anger on his face. His eyes darted all around the perfect room filled with everything a gamer could ever want. "Well, I guess Chad's doing okay for himself while my sister lives in a home she calls a death trap!"

Emily could not take any more. She felt her legs begin to run towards the front door. Once outside, she allowed the tears to come. They had seen, and now they know about the house and Chad. She should have said no or just not been home when they arrived. Why did she have to try to make it work? Emily sat in the soft grass for a long time, resolved not to go back into her death trap. She was running out of tears when her family came out the door. They were all smiling and seemed happy. Now, even they were enjoying her pain.

"Aunt Emily, don't cry. We will fix it." Jr. ran over and wrapped his arms around Emily. She hugged the three-year-old and didn't even realize what he had said until he let go.

"What do you mean you will fix it?" she asked. But the little boy just smiled and ran back to his mother.

"Sorry that took so long, but the guy at the

hardware store must have been new. It took forever to place the order," her father said. "I think it's about time we head out for an early birthday supper, as we all have a busy day tomorrow."

"Wait, what are you talking about, Jr? What order and what is going on tomorrow?" Emily had to try hard not to yell. She wasn't mad at them, but she hated being confused.

"Look, Em, I'm sorry about that comment inside. I haven't exactly been around to help either." Joe sat down on the grass next to her. "But we all talked, and if the house is what keeps you from being able to be around or makes you unhappy, we want to fix it. Dad placed the order for the materials and called in a few favors to get a roofing crew out tomorrow to fix the roof. We will help you get this done before dinner on Monday." Emily could only sit and stare at her brother. Was this real or another joke?

"And don't worry about the cost. We have it covered. The store has my credit card on file, so you will need to go tonight and pick out your new appliances, paint colors, and flooring. A few lights need replacing, so go ahead and get those and the bathroom mirror. Everything else is already ordered and will be delivered in the morning." Charles smiled, and Emily knew he wanted her to be happy.

"This is too much, you guys: the cost and the work. I'll get it done. I don't want to put you out."

"Hey, I know you are a hard worker, but you will not get it done faster or better than all of us will

together. We got you, girl." Emily could tell that
Rachael was not going to budge on this issue.

"Now, if you don't mind, I am starving!"
Christine announced. "Can we please go to dinner?"
They all shared a good laugh, quickly organized into
two cars, and headed to the restaurant.

They all enjoyed a fantastic meal and shared
stories that made them all laugh. Dinner ended with
the staff singing a loud and very off-key rendition of
"Happy Birthday." Soon they were back at Emily's
house and saying their goodbyes. Emily promised her
parents she would make it to the store that night to
pick up the needed things. Charles made her promise
she would get the right stuff and not shop cheap.
Emily waved goodbye as her sister's minivan and
parents' truck pulled away. The day had not gone
according to plan, and she had very few secrets left.
However, she had not felt this happy in years. She
could not help but rethink the philosophy that secrets
are needed to be happy. As the cars pulled out of view,
Emily could feel that someone was still standing
behind her. She turned to see Joe standing next to his
hatchback, looking at the sky.

"You don't have to worry. The house is not
going to explode during the night. Your car, on the
other hand..."

"Hey now, I told you she's sensitive." Joe
laughed. "I thought I would go with you to help you
pick out stuff. After all, I'm not sure you know how
refrigerators work. You probably would have put the
ice in the freezer if you did. It would have kept

everything cold, and Mom would have never noticed."

"I did not know that," Emily laughed. "Maybe I could use your help after all."

"It will also give me a chance to show you that my old girl will not explode." He joked. "Come on; the store closes in a few hours."

Emily walked over to the small car and opened the door. This thing had not changed since he was in high school. As she climbed in and shut the door, Joe started the car. The seat belt automatically went back over her shoulder.

"See, she wants you to feel safe."

"Or to keep me from escaping," Emily shot back.

Soon they were at the store and shopping. Emily worked her way through her dad's list, asking Joe for his opinions on each thing. They finished just as the store was closing. Joe confirmed with the clerk that everything would be delivered in the morning, and they were back in the car. Emily hated to admit it, but this car had a better ride than hers. She watched as the city flashed by out the window. She suddenly realized that they were not headed back to her house.

"Are you kidnapping me?" she asked Joe.

Joe laughed and replied," Yes, and there is torture planned. You have to pick a flavor of ice cream AND eat it."

Emily pretended to be suffering, but could not help but laugh. Joe pulled up to the drive-through window and waited while she chose strawberry and ordered chocolate for himself. They received the ice cream and sat in the parking lot to eat their cold treats. Joe suddenly stopped eating and stared at the steering wheel for a long time.

"Everything alright? Did you get a brain freeze or something?"

"No, my brain is fine. I want to say I'm sorry, Em. All those years ago, I should not have tried to push you to leave Chad. While I may not like the guy, it is obvious that you love him. I was not there for you, and it's kind of the one thing I am always supposed to do as a brother." She could tell he was struggling not to talk badly about Chad and that his apology was genuine. "I still don't like the guy, but you are my sister. I can keep my mouth shut about those things if you let me back into your life. If I'm pouting like a three-year-old, I can't be there for you. It's your life, Em's, your choices, and your happiness. I just don't want to have to go away again."

"I don't want that either. I miss being able to talk to you." Emily fought back the tears, trying to find their way out of her eyes. "Let's just move forward and eat ice cream." Joe laughed and took a few more bites. When they were done, he took the empty cups to a trash can, and they headed back to Emily's house. Emily was so exhausted that she wanted to go to bed for a week. Joe walked her to the door and promised to see her in the morning. She waved as the little hatchback disappeared down the street. Once inside,

Emily ensured the door was locked and slipped into a sleep shirt. She had no time to think about the day as she fell asleep when her head hit the pillow.

Chapter 4

A banging on the front door ripped Emily from her dreamless sleep. She cursed whoever it was as she pulled herself out of bed and walked to answer it. Even half-asleep, Emily remembered the hole in the floor and could step over it. She fumbled with the lock for a few moments and could hear voices outside laughing and talking. She was too tired to be perky with salespeople this morning. As she opened the door, the previous day's events came flooding back to her. There stood her sister, holding a cup of coffee out to her.

"Well, now I owe Joe five bucks. Take this, drink it, and put on some real clothes." Rachael laughed.

As Emily closed the door, she saw Rachael hand Joe five dollars. He must have bet that she was still in bed. She went down the hall and helped herself to a few sips of coffee. A glance at the clock showed it was seven in the morning. She pulled out a pair of old jeans and the t-shirt she wore while she painted the shutters. It already had paint spots on it, so it was perfect for a day's worth of work. She returned to the living room, where her family had let themselves in. They were already moving things out of the way. The plan looked to be to take all the furniture out front. New couches and a dining set were on the list her dad gave her yesterday. She was sure the old ones would be taken for recycling and never returned.

"There are doughnuts on the counter if you're hungry. We are going to be starting in the kitchen, so eat while you can," her mother chimed while carrying the coffee pot into Chad's office. It could stay there for all Emily cared. Thinking of Chad made her realize that he had not called back or even texted since she hung up on him. She quickly checked her bank account to ensure he had not found a way to get to the money. She breathed a sigh of relief when everything was how she had left it. She made her way to the doughnut box and chose a glazed one. She was eating it when a man walked in that she did not know.

"Good morning, miss. The name's Steve. Your dad asked us to climb up on the roof and see if we could do something about the leak. I've taken a look, and I have good news and bad. It would have been a simple fix if someone had been called right away. But it looks like it's been leaking for a while. It will take my boys all day to get it repaired, but on the good side, the rest of your shingles are in great shape. Your dad says the bills are on him, so there is no need to worry about that. I just wanted to make sure you are okay with us banging around on your roof."

"Welcome to the construction zone." Emily laughed. "It's perfectly alright. If you can stop the leak, you can stay up there all night if you need to."

"Well, that is not plan A, but if you're good with it, we will get to it immediately."

"Would you like a doughnut before you go up?" Emily asked.

"Don't mind if I do." Steve grabbed a doughnut from the box and headed outside. In moments, Emily could hear footsteps above her. Just as she finished her last bite, Joe came into the kitchen and laughed.

"Thanks for helping with the money this morning," he patted his pocket.

"No problem. What else are sisters for?" She wiped her hands on her jeans and looked around. "So, what should I do?"

"Well, Dad and I are going to start removing the big stuff from the kitchen. But Mom and Rachael are ripping up the carpet in the living room and hallway. I think they want to get the painting started. I would head in there and give them a hand."

Emily walked into the living room to find her sister cutting the carpet into strips and her mother rolling it.

"I got that, Mom," she stated as she walked over and began rolling the new strip of cut carpet.

"Perfect, then I will get to work taping so we can paint it soon." The carpet removal went quickly, and soon the bare subfloor was all that could be seen. Emily had glanced up a couple of times to see her old kitchen appliances leaving. Her mother had the paint cans all set up and the rollers ready to go.

"I'm just going to get a glass of water quickly. Does anyone else want one?" Emily asked as she walked towards the kitchen.

"There's bottled water in the cooler outside," her mother replied.

"It's okay. I got it." Emily stopped in the kitchen doorway. She had expected the appliances to be gone, but the room was empty. There were no cabinets, counters, or even a kitchen sink! Her father was even removing the linoleum from the floor.

"Don't worry. Everything will work when we are done."

Emily did not know what to say and instead just turned to walk outside for the cooler. She grabbed three bottles of water and took them back in. She was not mad but shocked. She would have been over the moon just to have new appliances, but they were replacing everything. She felt out of place, a little like this wasn't happening. She set to work helping to get the first coat of paint done while Joe worked on cutting out the rotted piece of sub-floor in the hallway. They would be able to paint it once he was done. They took a few minutes just to relax on the living room floor while he finished. It didn't take long, and he came down the hall with an "All Clear" to tell them it was good. The hallway was fast to paint, and soon they were done. A glance at her watch told Emily that it was only nine. They had accomplished so much in just two hours. She could still hear the footsteps on the roof, showing that the men were still repairing the leak. She was pulled back inside by her father's voice.

"I've repaired the pipes and electrical. If you lovely ladies could start with the paint, me and my oaf of a son will start on the bathroom. It shouldn't take too long in there. So, Em, if there is anything in your bedroom you don't want us to see, you better move it now," he teased.

"Nope, it's all good. I moved it all already," Emily teased back.

The work continued nonstop until lunch. The old floorings had been removed by then, the walls had all been painted, the broken cabinets had been removed, the electrical switches had been repaired, and the windows were fixed. Emily barely recognized the house as they all headed outside to enjoy lunch. Her mom had brought deli sandwiches for them all, which tasted like they were from a gourmet restaurant. They even invited the workmen on the roof down to join them. After lunch, it was back to work. The new cabinets were installed in the kitchen and bathrooms, the new lighting fixtures were in, and the sink flowed cool water that stayed in the sink and off the floor. She had chosen laminate flooring for the kitchen. Joe had tried to talk her into the tile, but she liked the look and feel of the laminate better. Joe and Charles made short work of the kitchen floor, and soon Emily watched as a new stove and refrigerator were brought in and put into place.

"Well, that's all for us in here. The rest is up to you, ladies. We will get to work on the living room floor."

Emily knew it would take them longer as she had chosen a wooden laminate that would have to be pieced together. She worked with her mother and sister to carry in the new table and chairs, carefully trying to stay out of the guy's way when they walked through the living room. Next were brand new small appliances that Emily did not remember picking out. She helped unbox a stainless-steel toaster and microwave. However, it was the coffee pot that gave her pause.

"I know how you like things to match. I thought the red one could go to Chad's office." Her mother stated after seeing her stare at it for a moment.

Emily wrapped her mother in a hug. While she knew her mother might be confused, it was nice that someone knew her well enough to know which coffee pot she would like. They continued to work and put away the dishes and silverware that her sister bought her, so there would be plenty for family dinners. They were putting the final decorative touches on the kitchen when the footsteps on the roof stopped, and Steve entered the kitchen.

"That should do it, miss. If you have any issues, give me a call, and I will be straight out to fix it". Emily reached out and took the card from his hand.

"Thank you so much, Steve. You have no idea how much this means to me."

"Anything for Charles's daughter. I mean it, any issues, please let me know. I will visit yearly to inspect and ensure everything is still up to par." With that, Steve turned and left. Emily heard him say goodbye to her dad and the sound of the work trucks pulling off.

"Well, I think we are all done here," Christine

said while looking around. Emily looked around and could hardly believe she was standing in her kitchen. Everything was so beautiful. She walked to the refrigerator and was greeted by a cold gust of air. She smiled and walked to the stove. She turned on a burner to watch it turn red from the heat. If they had done nothing else, these two things were life-changing. She turned the knob to click off the burner and turned back to her mom.

"You deserve it all and so much more, honey. I don't hear banging anymore in the living room. Let's go check on their progress."

Emily nodded and followed her mom back to the living room. The floor was done in both the living room and the hallway. It was beautiful, and Emily could not help but stare at it. When she looked up, she saw her dad and brother carrying the new couches. They were a lovely cream color and looked so comfortable.

"We've got just a few more big things left, and then it's up to you ladies. We will head to the bathroom next, and we should be able to finish it by dinner. Not bad for a day's worth of work. Don't worry, Em. We will return to finish your bedroom and the other bathroom in the morning."

"I'm not worried. If you don't have time to come back, that's fine. I am so happy with everything that has been done already." Emily could feel the tears stinging her eyes.

"You know what Dad says." Joe puffed out his

chest and began to speak in a deep voice, "A job doesn't count unless you finish it all the way. Half-assed work makes you an asshole." The three siblings began to laugh together.

"Well, you guys were listening," their father chimed in. "Come on, son. You don't want to be an asshole."

Once the two were working in the hall and bathroom, the women began working. Emily's mother and sister helped her decorate and arrange the living room in a way she never thought possible. As they were finishing, a knock came at the door. Emily answered to see that one of her parents must have ordered pizza for them all. Her sister stepped forward, paid the tip, and helped carry all the food to the kitchen. The men could smell it at the back of the house and appeared before everything was set out. Soon all five of them were gathered around the table, enjoying a well-deserved meal.

Emily remained quiet while they all talked and laughed. She had been having a thought most of the day that she had kept to herself. She had held her paycheck from Chad. Perhaps she could set up a payment plan with her dad to pay him back for everything he had bought. She knew he got significant discounts as he owned a construction company, but she felt wrong letting him pay for everything. At the same time, though, she knew that he would probably be insulted if she tried. She struggled with the thought and decided to sleep on it. She moved the dishes to the sink and turned on the water to begin washing them.

"You did realize we installed a dishwasher, right?" Charles asked from behind her. She looked down at the cabinets, confused, and was surprised that she had not seen it earlier. She had not had a dishwasher in five years.

"Did you install any trap doors I should know about?" she asked as she opened the dishwasher and began loading the dishes.

"Maybe." Charles laughed. "We will lock the rest of your stuff in the trailer for tonight. You can come home with us if you want, since your bed is not set up."

"I appreciate it, Dad, but I want to stay here tonight. I'm still trying to convince myself that this is not a dream."

"I thought you would say that. We will be back early in the morning. Do you need anything else before we take off?"

"I wanted to talk to you about something, but I don't want you to get mad." Emily found herself staring at her feet as she spoke the words.

"You're not paying me back for any of this if that's what you want to talk about. Instead, take the money and promise me you will buy yourself a new car. That thing is leaking oil everywhere, and I know the heat didn't work in it last Christmas. Let me know you will be driving something safe, and we will be even". Emily knew that there was no changing his mind on this. Instead, she said, "I promise," and hugged her dad. She waved goodbye again as her family left and grabbed some blankets from the closet. She set up a bed on the new couch and then went to the shower.

She had not seen the bathroom since the guys were working here and was surprised when she walked in. The bathroom was just as beautiful as the rest of the house. She took a long, hot shower and felt relaxed as she made her way back to the couch. She allowed herself to slip off to sleep. The following day, Emily woke at about six-thirty. She folded the blankets and put them back in the closet. She then made her way to the kitchen, brewed a fresh pot of coffee, and sat at the kitchen table, slowly sipping it. Once she finished her cup, she rinsed it and placed it in the dishwasher. She then headed to her closet to find an outfit for the day. It seemed like another pair of blue jeans and a t-shirt kind of day. She had just made her way back to the living room when there was a knock on the door. She opened it and immediately heard Rachael yell," I win!" Emily watched as Joe handed Rachael five dollars. She could not help but laugh.

"If you three are done with your games, maybe we can get some work done," Charles stated as he worked his way into the house. "I'm sure Emily would like a bed to sleep in tonight." With that, they all set to work. By mid-morning, the flooring was done in her bedroom and bathroom, and furniture started moving in. Everything was going much faster than she could have imagined.

By lunchtime, everything was done. Emily couldn't help but walk back and forth in the house, ensuring everything was real. Her family was gathering in the kitchen, preparing for lunch, and letting her do her own thing. Once she had convinced herself that it was real, she joined them. She was beginning to get used to these family meals. She was already planning to make sure that this became a regular thing. They had just finished cleaning up from lunch when she heard the front door open and slam shut. She was pulled back to the reality of her marriage, which she had avoided for two days. Chad was home, and he was not happy. Emily watched as her dad and brother started to make their way to the living room and barely heard herself ask them to stop. Even more surprising was that they did. She stood tall and walked out to deal with Chad. As she entered the room, she saw Chad standing right in front of the door.

"What the hell, Emily?! Is this what you did with the money instead of making sure I had what I needed?! You are so selfish! Sometimes I wonder what I did wrong to get stuck with a selfish bitch like you!!"

Emily knew that the kitchen would empty as soon as the word "bitch" was said. She heard the angry footsteps coming through the house, and before she could speak, her brother and dad stood between her and Chad.

"You must have lost your damn mind if you think you can talk to her that way," her father yelled back at Chad.

Her brother kept making sure that Emily was safely behind him. Emily knew they were trying to protect her, but she was tired of being treated like a china doll. She felt the words boiling up in her chest.

"What the fuck is wrong with you, Chad?! Everyone has been working all weekend to give us a nice home, and you walk in yelling like an asshole! I'm so sick of this shit. You have everything and want to call me selfish! You can take your pity party to someone else! I am done with this shit!"

As she finished, she noticed everyone staring at her in surprise, including Chad. Except for Joe, who wasn't even trying to hide the smile on his face. Emily decided to carry on and not let go of this strength.

"Thank you, everyone, for fixing up our home. It means the world to me. Daddy, I will keep my promise. I will probably give you a call in the next week or two, and we can go car shopping together. As I'm sure you guys can see, I have a problem to take care of right now. But I will call you tomorrow to let you know I am okay. I also want to set up a family barbecue before the end of summer. I promise not to disappear again."

Joe looked at her with concern, and she could tell he was about to argue to stay and ensure she was okay. But she shot him a look that convinced him she would be fine. She hugged them each and walked them out the door. Once they had pulled away, she shut the door and looked back at Chad. She decided that she would speak before he could.

"I may be a bitch, but I don't know how I got stuck with such a selfish prick. That would have been for us if I had spent the money on the house. You wanted it for you. My family paid for everything you see. And my paycheck, it's mine. I've made my list and am buying myself a new car." She took a breath and saw he wanted to talk, but she wasn't done yet. "You decide what the hell you want, but things have to change. You can either get the hell out, or we can do things differently that are not about you! You decide!"

She stood there feeling light-headed but strong. Chad stood a moment in silence. She could tell what he was deciding to do. When he finally spoke, it was not the response she was expecting.

"You're right, Em. Things do need to change. I think we should start going to counseling, and you are right. Your check is for you to spend. For now, let's do it how you want, and we will ask the therapist how to proceed. I don't want to lose you, Em." She could not tell if this was real or another of his acts to get her to back off. She wanted to believe him, but did not want to trust him.

"I'll call and find us someone tomorrow. Tonight, I think you should sleep on the couch. I'm going to go do some grocery shopping." With that, Emily grabbed her keys and purse and left. Chad helped unload the groceries and put them away when she returned home. She decided to go take a shower, and when she came back, he had made pasta for dinner. She finished eating and loaded the dishwasher.

"It's been a long day, and I'm going to bed. Good night."

"Good night, Em. I love you."

She still believed she loved him, but right now, she could not say the words. She simply turned and left the kitchen. Once in the safety of her room, she texted her family that she was all right. She told them they were taking some space and would get some help. She would call them all soon, but she just wanted to sleep. With that, she climbed into bed. Sleep did not come easily that night, but it did eventually come. Emily felt change around her, but she had no idea the changes coming in the next few months.

Chapter 5

Two months had passed since the big fight, and much had changed in Emily's home. They found a therapist to help them with couples counseling. Their therapist suggested that they should keep their money separate. Sharing funds took more trust than they had right now. While working on their relationship was important, Emily wanted to improve herself. She was doing individual sessions as well as couples therapy. This is what led to the new addition to the family. Her therapist helped her realize that Chad had been starving her emotionally. While he was working on those issues, she needed someone ready to support her immediately.

Enter an emotional support dog named Marley. They had given her some recommendations, but this guy just spoke to her the most. While a bullmastiff is a lot of dog, he was what she needed. He was always there, and they never yelled at each other. Step two of the healing process was turning the nursery into a guest bedroom. According to the therapist, leaving the room set up for something that was not happening kept the pain of that night fresh in their minds. They had taken down the crib and painted it a new white color. They put in a queen-size bed and only left the small dresser. The door to the room stayed open now, so they could see that they were moving on.

Emily woke that morning but lay in bed looking at Chad for several minutes before waking him. Every morning, she took this time to remind herself of why she married him and how much she loved him. He woke with a good morning, and they went about their usual morning routine. Emily dressed and then returned with Marley to let him have his time. When they went back in, Chad was getting breakfast on the table. She gave Marley his breakfast and sat back down at the table. They each cooked one meal a day now. Chad had breakfast, and she handled dinner.

They looked like a couple who had it all figured out to an outsider. But their troubles would have been apparent to anyone who knew about therapy. They used all the "tools" their therapist gave them almost daily. It was like learning to work your way through a minefield. He had warned them that it would not be easy, but if they truly loved each other and wanted to stay together, it would be worth it. Emily believed they were on the right track. Chad even moved back into the bedroom last month, and they had been intimate a few times since.

Emily couldn't help but feel excited for that afternoon as they finished breakfast. They had invited her family over for dinner. It would be the first time they had all been to the house at the same time since the night of the big fight. Chad had agreed to cook on the grill, and Emily would handle the appetizers and sides. Not their normal division of cooking, but Chad loved to grill. Emily cleared away the morning dishes as Chad headed out the back door. She knew that he would spend most of the day setting up and getting things ready for that night.

In truth, she was glad to have the kitchen to herself. She felt like a master chef with everything she could make in her kitchen since everything now worked. She pulled fruit and vegetables from the refrigerator and chopped them for the trays. Marley had settled on the kitchen floor and watched her as she worked. Once the trays were finished and back in the refrigerator, she set to make a chocolate cake and cupcakes for the kids. She took her time with them and tried to make them taste good and look amazing. By the time the cakes were finished, it was already afternoon. She pulled the stuff for sandwiches out of the refrigerator and made a couple. Emily then took both plates outside to have lunch with Chad.

"I thought you might be getting hungry," she mused while walking down the back steps.

Chad had set up several chairs and a new fire pit in the center of them. There were also several strands of white lights hung over the chairs.

"This looks great!" Emily could not help but be surprised at everything he had done.

"Thank you," Chad said as he took the plate, "On both accounts. I even managed to clean up the mess that the dog leaves behind. I swear, people would think we were keeping a dinosaur back here."

"I appreciate that. I was coming out to clean it up in a little bit." Emily was genuinely grateful that Chad cleaned up after Marley. She usually does it every afternoon, and Chad takes no responsibility for the dog. Marley is here for her, and she is the one who should handle everything to do with him.

"I know, but I wanted to help out and show appreciation for everything you are doing to help out today."

Another one of their tools. They were not supposed to assume that the other person knew they appreciated them, but show them and say it.

"Thank you for your appreciation," Chad replied.

Simple, but it was the best line, according to their therapist. Emily wished they could talk to each other like ordinary people, but they had problems with that. They needed the script, at least for now.

"What time did you tell everyone to be here?"

"I told them five, which means my parents will be here at four-thirty, my sister at five, and my brother at five-thirty."

"Sounds about right. I will start the meat at about four, then. It will take at least an hour."

"Sounds like a plan. Do you need any help with anything? I don't want to make you feel like you're on your own." Yet another tool.

"I appreciate that, but no, I do not need any help. I will let you know if I do because I know you are there for me."

That was about all Emily could stomach of these scripts for now. She called for Marley and headed back into the house. Once inside, she changed into shorts and a tank top. It was warmer outside than she had expected. She ensured the house was in order and prepared a few dinner sides. She was just about to sit on the couch when there was a knock. Marley jumped up, barked twice, and then stood by the door, wagging his tail. He already knew who was on the other side. Emily walked over to open the door, and sure enough, her parents were standing there smiling.

"Hope you don't mind, but I wanted to contribute," Charles handed Emily a six-pack of beer.

"Ah, Dad, you shouldn't have!" Emily exclaimed while looking at the beer like he had given her a dozen roses.

"Well, what's a father for if not to spoil his daughter?"

"Are you two finished?" Her mother sounded exasperated, but the look on her face told Emily she enjoyed the exchange as much as she and her dad.

"Probably not, but we can pick it up later." Emily stepped aside so they both could walk in. "Chad is in the backyard if you want to head out. I'll be right behind you."

"Um, I think we will wait for you." Emily could tell by the look on her dad's face that he had still not forgiven Chad for the fight he had heard about that night. He was willing to be civil, but he was afraid of what he might say if Emily was not around.

"Alright then. You guys can help me carry some stuff out if you want." Emily walked towards the fridge, suddenly remembering the six-pack in her hand. "Here dad, you take the precious cargo, and Mom, would you please carry this tray?" Emily grabbed the second tray and led them out to the backyard. The smell of cooking meat was already filling the air. Chad turned at the sound of the door opening and closed the lid on the grill.

"Hello there, you two. Great to see you both again." Chad sounded truly happy.

"The place looks great. It's come a long way since I first saw it."

Charles could not help himself. He was sounding nice, but was still going to get his shots in. Emily decided it was best just to smile and move on. Chad had expressed concern about this in the therapy session. The doctor had said that he couldn't hold Emily responsible. Chad had hurt other people who would be a part of their lives. He had to listen to what they said and felt, accept it, and work to find a way forward. Chad's smile, which looked like it belonged on a Mr. Potato Head, told Emily he was struggling with this tool.

The next hour went by fast as her brother and sister both arrived. Rachael's kids took off running and playing with Marley. Her husband, Greg, hugged almost everyone but shook Chad's hand. Emily could tell he was not completely happy with the situation, but they would all accept and support her decision. She couldn't ask her family for more than that. She was still working through her issues with Chad. Soon the food was ready, and they all settled down to eat.

As the meal went on, Emily could feel the tension begin to melt away from the situation. Everyone began to talk and laugh. The children ate quickly, with the help of Marley, and were soon off to play again. Before she knew it, the sun began to go down, and the little ones were rubbing their eyes. Emily was not ready for the night to end, but knew they would need to lie down soon, or things would turn ugly.

"Rachael, we could lay the little ones down if you want?"

Emily was hopeful that suggesting it before her sister said they would have to leave would provide her with more family time.

"That would be great. They are normally sweet, but their inner demons start to surface when they get tired." Rachael laughed.

Rachael called the children over, and Emily followed them inside. She followed them down the hall as she noticed Rachael had walked past the guest bedroom. Her sister was unaware that this room had changed and was heading for the master bedroom.

"They can lie down in here. It's the most comfortable bed in the house and deserves to be used."

Emily saw the confusion on her sister's face as she looked through the open door. The kids walked in without hesitation and climbed up on the bed. Rachael moved in behind the kids, and in just a few minutes, the kids were tucked in, and they were closing the door.

"I guess many things have changed," Rachael commented once the door was closed.

"Big changes are what we needed. We still have a long way to go, but we are working on it." Emily tried to sound upbeat, but the thought of all the work she and Chad had left to do made her feel exhausted.

"Well, you have my support. If there is anything I can do, sis, please do not hesitate." Emily could see the sincerity and concern on her sister's face. She knew she had to lighten the mood, or she would start to crack.

"Well, if you're offering, I don't want to handle all these dishes..."

"Anything but that." Rachael interrupted with a laugh.

The two walked outside to join the rest of the family around the fire pit. The conversation never died down, and Emily felt normal for once. She and Chad did not have to use their tools, and everything was perfect for the first time in a very long time. Rachael got up every fifteen to twenty minutes to check on the children, but other than that, no one moved or talked about wanting to go home. Joe would not speak directly to Chad, but Emily was sure they would never be close. Joe disliked Chad before the big fight, which would not change anytime soon.

Charles was telling a story from his childhood when it happened. The only light in the yard was the fire and the dim glow of the lights overhead. But all at once, the sky filled with a bright white light. It was bright enough that you would think that dawn had come. The backyard fell silent. Emily could not even hear the sound of the fire crackling anymore. Just as suddenly as the light came, it was gone. The sound of the fire came back, but everyone sat in silence. No one knew what to say or do at this point.

After a few minutes that seemed to take forever, Christine stood up and gathered things to carry inside. Emily and Rachael jumped up almost by instinct and followed her lead. The boys set to work putting out the fire, cleaning up the grill, and turning off the lights. Soon they were all inside and standing in the kitchen. Yet again, in complete silence.

After some time, Charles walked to the living room and turned on the television. They all followed like a herd of sheep and watched as he flipped through the stations. Most of them were black, indicating that the stations were offline. Usually, there would be a message saying "Technical Difficulties" or something similar. The nothingness made it feel like they were utterly alone. After several minutes, the screen suddenly became a bright red color. The color offered comfort initially, but the white words quickly took that away.

PUBLIC ANNOUNCEMENT

**MANY RESIDENTS SAW THE
UNKNOWN FLASH IN THE SKY AT 9:32 PM.**

**THE ORIGIN AND CAUSE OF THE
FLASH ARE UNKNOWN.**

**SOME CITIZENS ARE EXPERIENCING
ADVERSE SIDE EFFECTS FROM THE LIGHT.**

**ALL CITIZENS ARE NOW ORDERED TO
STAY INDOORS AT THEIR CURRENT
LOCATION.**

**ALL TRAVEL IS FORBIDDEN UNTIL
FURTHER NOTICE.**

**ANYONE TRAVELING WILL BE
DETAINED BY THE US MILITARY.**

**MORE INFORMATION WILL FOLLOW
AS IT BECOMES AVAILABLE.**

As Emily read the final words, she could not help but let the worry and fear wash over her. It made no sense. She could not understand what adverse side effects could cause them to be locked down where they were. She looked around at her family and saw them all feeling the same.

"At least we are all together," Christine said. "I know we might not want to, but we should try to get some rest. Rachael, you and Brad should go lie down with the kids. When they wake, they will think this was a fun sleepover." Rachael nodded, and she and Brad walked back to the guest bedroom. "Emily, you and Chad should head to bed as well. Don't bother arguing. Your father and I can take the couch, and I'm sure Joe will be fine on the floor."

"Yep, a few blankets, and it's one of the most comfortable beds I have ever slept on," Joe said as he took off down the hall to grab some of the spare blankets.

Emily wanted to argue that Christine and Charles should take the bed, but the look on her mother's face told her that would be a mistake. She turned to look at Chad, but he was halfway down the hall to the bedroom. Chivalry was not his strong point. Emily hugged her parents and headed down the hall with Marley behind her. Once inside the room, she saw Chad was already lying in bed doing something on his phone. She proceeded to get dressed for bed without a word and slid into the bed next to him. Chad clicked off his phone screen as she did so.

Emily turned to face the wall. Chad was not good at comfort, and soon she could hear the sounds of him sleeping next to her. She could not help but feel frustrated with him. She was scared; none of them knew what had happened, and he fell asleep fast. She stared at the wall, knowing it would not be any time soon if she found sleep that night. Emily felt a cold nose touching her toes from under the blanket. Somehow, Marley always knew when she needed to be distracted from the thoughts inside her mind.

Emily put one of her hands over the side of the bed and soon felt the touch of his soft fur on her palm. As she pets the dog, she reminded herself that Chad was trying. Neither of them was perfect, and they had things they needed to work on. Then she remembered that the message on the television had said that the light had affected some people. Chad could have been affected somehow, or maybe he was just freaked out. Either way, Emily could not blame him for what he was going through.

Emily felt herself releasing the tension she had built up and petted Marley on the head. With that, the pup lay on the floor next to her. Emily pulled her hand back under the blanket and made herself as comfortable as possible. She did not want to toss and turn and disrupt Chad. Soon, she was as comfortable as she could be and was back to staring through the darkness at the wall. Sleep would not come easily, so she would have to lie here and wait for it to find her.

Chapter 6

Emily lay in the dark for what seemed like hours. Every time she closed her eyes, she was back in the yard, looking at the bright light that filled the sky. She couldn't push it from her mind and had to open her eyes to see the darkness surrounding her. Suddenly, she felt Chad move in the bed behind her. He had been still since she lay down and was not known for tossing and turning during the night. It felt like he was sitting on the edge of the bed when he stopped moving. Emily felt confident now that he was struggling with what had happened just as much as she was.

Emily was getting ready to roll over and talk to him about it. Just as the thought crossed her mind, a soft light shone from where Chad was sitting. Emily knew that the glow was from his cell phone. However, whom he would be trying to call, she did not know. He had no family to speak of and was not close with anyone. Emily did not know why, but lay still and pretended to be asleep. Emily listened as Chad clicked on his phone, and then the light dimmed as he put it to his ear. Emily's heart sank as Chad began to speak.

"I know it's late, but I had to ensure you were okay. Don't worry. She's asleep."

Emily continued to listen to his conversation as tears began to flow silently down her face and onto her pillow.

"You know I am only here to make sure I don't lose everything. You know how I feel about you."

Emily continued to lie still, even though it felt like her heart was breaking in two.

"As soon as this craziness is over, I'll end it. It will be you, and I like it should be."

Emily found that she did not have the strength to move or even say anything. Chad hung up the phone and lay back in the bed behind her. Emily listened as he fell asleep as if the conversation had not happened. Emily replayed all the talks they had over the past few months and all the times he said he wanted no one but her. Who was this mystery person he knew he was supposed to be with? It was as if something else had taken over her body. She watched as she folded back the blankets and slid out of bed. She stood for a moment, looking at Chad in the dark to ensure he was asleep.

Once she was sure he was asleep, she walked gently to his side of the bed and took his phone from his nightstand. Once she had it, she slipped out of the bedroom and into the bathroom. Inside, she unlocked the phone and looked at the name last called "Veronica." Emily tried hard to remember anyone named Veronica but came up with nothing. She began to scroll through his call log, and the tears started to well up once more. Chad was calling this one at least once a day. She quickly clicked over to his text messages and found Veronica there once more.

Emily sat on the bathtub's edge and began

reading through the messages. The tears started to flow freely as she read. The conversations were more personal and warmer than anything he had ever said to her, even before they were married. There were several messages where Chad stated that he was only pretending to want to be with Emily to talk her into adding his name to the house to get to keep something in the divorce. He had already met with lawyers and picked the one he wanted to handle his case. The lawyer said he would get more if he went through the counseling steps.

Emily closed the text messages and opened his photos. She scrolled through all the pictures, and there were many of Chad with a blonde woman. Emily knew that it must be Veronica. Emily began to grow angry with herself. She loved and trusted Chad so much. These same qualities had allowed Chad to get away with doing this. He was not even trying hard to hide it. Emily closed the photos and clicked the phone, so the screen turned off. She sat and allowed the hot tears to run down her face without end.

All at once, the tears disappeared, and the anger took over. This was not her fault, and she will not blame herself. He had treated her like shit, and she had stood up for herself. She had opened her heart and given him a second chance. He had played her, and she wouldn't let him win. She walked to the sink and washed her face with cold water. After drying her face, Emily turned off the light and walked back into the bedroom. She returned the phone to Chad's nightstand and headed for the bedroom door. As it opened, she felt a cold nose touch the back of her leg. She had forgotten that Marley was in the room. She opened the door and held it open to allow him to follow.

Emily made her way down the hall in the dark. She stopped at the closet and grabbed a blanket. The house was pretty much packed with her family, but she could not lie in the same bed with that man. She made her way down the hall and walked into the kitchen. Not the most conventional sleeping room, but it would do. She lay down on the floor and stretched the blanket out over herself. When she went to put her arm where her head would be lying, she touched soft fur. Marley had lain right where he knew she would place her head.

"Good boy," Emily whispered as she ran her hand over his fur.

After a few moments, she lay her head on his belly. For a moment, she thought she would begin to cry again, but instead, she lay listening to Marley's breath and feeling her head gently lift up and down. Before she knew it, she was asleep, and thankfully, it was a dreamless sleep.

"Wow, I didn't think you'd feel the need to guard the kitchen. I know I can be a pig, but I think I deserve a little more credit than that, Em."

Emily opened her eyes to see Joe standing above her.

"Trust is something that I give too freely, it seems," she replied as she stood up from the floor.

Joe was confused by her comment, and he just

stood silently as she folded her blanket and placed it on the table. Emily then walked to the back door and opened it to let Marley out. She was not ready to talk about Chad's affair just yet. Joe could tell that something was wrong, though. As Emily walked out the door, she saw him heading to the living room, probably to tell her parents about what she had said.

Emily stood on the porch and allowed the cool morning air to wrap her up while Marley walked around the backyard. Marley seemed to enjoy being out here, and Emily was in no hurry to go back inside the house. Emily walked into the backyard and sat in one of the lawn chairs. She had been out here for quite a while when she heard the back door open. Emily turned to see Joe coming down the back steps towards her. He looked visibly flustered, which changed to surprise when he saw her.

"Em, what are you still doing out here?" he asked as he rushed towards her.

"I needed some time alone," Emily quickly responded and turned away from him again.

"It's not safe out here," Joe answered. Emily turned back towards him and could see him looking around with worry on his face.

"It's fine. Marley is here, and the only neighbor who didn't go on vacation is Ms. Tilly. I don't think she is a threat." Emily turned back in her chair and closed her eyes.

"Do you guys have anything like a crowbar or

tire iron?" Joe quickly asked.

"If we do, it's in the shed. What do you need it for?" Emily was caught off guard by his question, but didn't turn to face him.

"We'll explain inside," Joe said as he turned and headed for the shed. "I'm going to go look, but when I'm done, you're going back in with me," Emily closed her eyes to show him that she wouldn't be moved. "You're going if I have to throw you over my shoulder and carry you."

With that, Joe headed into the shed. Emily opened her eyes once she was sure he was gone. She kept hearing him say it wasn't safe out here, but what could be dangerous, she didn't know. Just then, she caught sight of her neighbor, Ms. Tilly, walking towards the fence line. She laughed at the idea that the old lady could be dangerous.

"Good morning, Ms. Tilly," she called out.

Ms. Tilly did not respond and appeared to stumble and grabbed onto the fence to stabilize herself. Emily jumped up from her chair and ran towards Ms. Tilly.

Emily reached the fence in seconds and began to reach for the old lady to check on her. Suddenly, Ms. Tilly turned and grabbed hold of Emily. Emily could not even scream as she tried to get the older woman's hand off her. Ms. Tilly's once blue eyes were now white and cloudy; she had open cuts on her face, and Emily could swear that she was trying to bite her.

Marley was barking and trying to attack Ms. Tilly through the fence. Emily struggled with the older woman as a crowbar swung down and hit Ms. Tilly on the top of the head. The older woman's grip released, and she fell to the ground, lifeless.

Emily looked back to see Joe holding the crowbar. His face was pale white, and he was visibly shaking. Emily could not find the words to say to him. Instead, she reached out and grabbed his arm, which was still holding the crowbar, ready to swing again. Joe looked like she had shocked him out of another place as he looked at her and lowered the crowbar.

"You killed her," Emily muttered as she looked down at Ms. Tilly's body.

"No," Joe responded firmly. "She was already dead, Em." Emily looked at him and felt herself take a step back. Joe had just killed a sweet old lady, and now he was talking like they were in some horror movie.

"What are you talking about, Joe? She was a person, not a…."

"Zombie," Joe cut her off. "Yes, she was Em. She was a damn zombie.

Emily looked down at Ms. Tilly once again. Remembering the cloudy white eyes, the cuts on her face, and that Ms. Tilly had been biting at her. Emily would have been screaming at herself that it was a zombie if this had been a movie. But this wasn't a movie. This was real.

"How did you know?" Emily asked while continuing to stare down at the corpse.

"Dad and I stepped out front to talk about me finding you on the kitchen floor and what you had said. I didn't want the kids to hear. We saw someone walking up the road, and Dad tried to greet them. You know how he is. A few moments later, a woman across the street came out of her house and started to run at us, screaming for help. Dad and I took off, but the stranger on the road got to them first. They started eating her Em like it was Thanksgiving dinner. They started chowing down." Emily looked back at Joe and could see the tears in his eyes. "I pulled the stranger off the woman, but it was too late. There was so much blood, and the woman was already gone. I checked for a pulse myself and swore she was gone."

"So, this led you to believe it was a zombie that attacked the woman and not just some crazy person?" Emily could not understand.

"No, my first thought was that the person was crazy. That they must have been affected by the flash, like the announcement warned. But then the woman who was killed started to move Em. She started to stand, and her eyes were milky white, just like this woman's." Joe motioned towards Ms. Tilly's corpse. "I tried to help her; I did. But when I reached for her, she started trying to bite me. Dad ran to the truck and hit her several times with a jack handle, but she wouldn't let go. The one I had knocked to the ground joined, and they both were trying to bite me, Em! They didn't stop until Dad hit them in the head. Tell me what else it could be!?

Emily stood silent for a moment, studying Joe's face. Everything he described sounded like a zombie movie, but zombies weren't real. They couldn't be.

"It's okay if you don't believe me," Joe spoke, "I don't know if I believe it. Dad sent me out to look for weapons. Let's get back inside."

With that, Joe turned towards the back door, and Emily felt herself follow him. Marley stuck close to her as they walked into the kitchen. Emily closed the door behind them and saw Chad heading into the living room.

Emily searched for something to do. She walked over and grabbed Marley's bowl. She knew she was useless, but she could still make sure that Marley was taken care of at least. She filled his food and water bowls and set them down when everyone began to file into the kitchen. Chad was with her family, a look of shock on his face. He walked around everyone and headed straight for her. She recoiled from his touch as he reached out to touch her to pretend he cared and loved her. Marley looked up from his breakfast and let out a low growl. Chad took a step back, looking between her and Marley. Once he was far enough back, Marley returned to enjoying his breakfast.

"So, whatever is going on has driven the dog insane as well?" Chad's pointed question was more than Emily could take at this point. "We should put him down before he starts trying to eat people."

"No, he just doesn't want a piece of shit like

you near me, and I agree with him." Emily suddenly remembered the children and looked toward her family. She breathed a sigh of relief to see they must still be in the living room. "No yelling," she told herself, "They don't need this right now."

"Look, Em, I know you have been through a lot this morning, but I am not the bad guy." Chad sounded like he was speaking from the heart, but Emily knew the truth. With everything going on, this was not the time, but she could not hold it in any longer, or she would explode.

"Why don't you go check on Veronica?" she responded.

The look on his face told everyone what was going on. The shock was more about what she knew than anything else.

"How do you, I mean, what are you talking about, Emily?" Chad clumsily muttered.

"You are only here to make sure you can say you did everything you could and get the most out of a divorce. I'll tell you what, as soon as the world is working again, I'll gladly sign the paperwork, and you can go to hell."

"I can go to hell?!" He began to yell, making Emily angrier because now the children could hear. "You want to play the victim here, Emily? You could have played the role of a good wife. You could have given me everything that a wife is supposed to. But instead, you chose to make everything about you. You couldn't even carry my child into this world. Veronica she gives me everything, including a son."

Emily's heart stopped. She played back the pictures she had looked at on his phone in her mind. There was one taken a few weeks ago that looked strange, but she had not thought much about it at the time. There had been a picture of Veronica standing sideways with her shirt pulled up, exposing her stomach. There was no noticeable baby bump, but it was apparent now that he was taking pictures to watch the baby grow.

"You are a bastard." A weak response, but it was the only words she could find. She watched as Joe began to take giant strides across the kitchen. His purpose was clear. Chad was going to feel real pain. But before Joe could reach him, Charles stopped him.

"This is not the time. We need to get somewhere safer. Once we are there, you can kill each other for all I care."

Charles's words echoed through the room. He had not yelled, but he had used his dad's authority to make them all stop in their tracks.

"Finally, someone in this family has a damn brain in their head." Chad cheered, thinking that Charles was defending him in some way.

"Don't get me wrong, boy. You will pay for what you've done. I want to ensure the dead walking outside don't hear you scream."

Emily had never seen Charles look so angry, even when he caught her smoking when she was seventeen. Chad suddenly realized that no one would stand next to him in this situation. Emily watched as his shoulders dropped in defeat and finally stayed silent.

"We should see if there is any update," Christine suggested and ushered everyone back to the living room.

Emily followed and sat on the arm of the couch next to Rachael as the television came to life. The screen from the night before appeared, but the words had changed.

FINAL PUBLIC ANNOUNCEMENT

THE ORIGINS OF THE FLASH ARE STILL UNKNOWN.

THE FLASH APPEARS TO REJUVENATE DEAD TISSUE.

THE REANIMATED CAN AND DO TRANSMIT THE CONDITION THROUGH THEIR SALIVA. SYMPTOMS BEFORE THE CHANGE INCLUDE FEVER AND DECREASED MOTOR FUNCTIONS.

TO END THE REANIMATION, THE BRAIN TISSUE MUST BE DAMAGED.

PEOPLE ARE ENCOURAGED TO STAY IN A SAFE LOCATION UNTIL A CURE IS

FOUND.

MAY THE GOD YOU CHOOSE TO OR CHOOSE NOT TO BELIEVE IN HAVE MERCY ON YOUR SOUL.

Emily finished reading the message and sat in silence. The words might not have said it, but Emily knew. They were on their own, and there was nothing anyone could do about it. She watched her family and could see on their faces that they all thought the same thing. She could not even bring herself to look at Chad. She really couldn't care less about how he was feeling.

"We can't stay here. Too many people live around here. Let's gather what we can and go to my hunting cabin. It's in the middle of nowhere, and we would be safer." Charles was surprisingly calm, and no one questioned him. Instead, the family started to move and gather what they thought they would need in the house. Joe and Charles trip to the shed out back to grab what "weapons" they can find to protect themselves.

Emily clipped Marley's leash to his collar when they walked back into the living room. Joe walked over to her, took the leash from her hands, and handed her the crowbar. He must have cleaned it while he was outside, as there were no signs of it having killed Ms. Tilly. She nodded at him and reached to take the leash back. Joe pulled it back from her hand.

"Your hands need to be free just in case. He's a good boy, though, I think we can tie it around your waist, and it will be fine."

Emily nodded and raised her arms as Joe secured the leash. Marley seemed to understand and stood close to Emily's side. As Emily looked around the room, she looked at Chad for the first time. She felt a hatred that she expected but also a concern that she did not understand.

"Chad, you should try to call Veronica and see if she can meet us to make it to the cabin." Emily could see the shock on everyone's faces as she spoke the words. Even Chad stood motionless, obviously caught off guard.

"Look, I may hate him for what he did, but I can't leave a pregnant woman alone to die. Chad, make the damn call."

Emily was proud of herself and watched as Chad dialed his cell phone. While she may be the bigger person, she could not stand to listen to him talk to that woman. She began singing show tunes in her head to drown out the noise.

"She only lives about a mile from here. It's on our way out of town, and she says she will be ready."

"Well, we should get going then."

Charles would not let anyone make a big deal out of this. If it was how Emily wanted it handled, he was on board. Emily stood with her mother and sister while the guys ran the few supplies they had to the vehicles. Once it was all loaded up, they returned.

Charles, Greg, and Joe each picked up one of the kids to carry to the van. Emily took her place at the end of the line. No one argued with her choice to go last. Emily believed that she looked so determined that no one wanted to stall them with an argument.

Emily watched as the front door opened and her family began the run to the cars. Emily followed Joe out the door, and the bright sunlight clouded her vision for a second. They had the windows closed inside to keep from being seen, and the sun seemed overly bright today; as Emily stepped out on the porch, habit kicked in out of nowhere. She turned to close the front door, and by the time she turned back, she could see that Joe had already reached the van. All the kids were inside, and Charles was sliding the door shut as Joe looked back at her.

She watched as Joe turned back to her, and his face dropped. He looked to be screaming as he ran toward her, but Emily could not hear anything. Emily began to turn to look behind her as a white-hot pain filled her shoulder, right next to her neck. She reached for the doorknob and turned it back inside, but the zombie's grip was too strong to move as the door swung open. Emily's gaze turned to her family, frozen where they stood. To yell a single word, Emily fought the pain, "RUN!!!"

She then looked up at the sun as her eyes closed and the darkness took over. She could feel the tug at her waist as Marley tried to fight whoever had her. Poor Marley had to die with her. He deserved better than to be tied to her corpse forever. She wished she could untie the leash and free him from her fate. But she had nothing left and felt the cool pavement as she hit the ground. The sound never returned to the world as her thoughts drifted to nothingness, and she let go of everything.

Chapter 7

Thump, thump, thump...

It had to be the final heartbeats she was hearing. Emily lay still and listened to them pass by.

Thump, thump, thump...

Emily forced her brain to think clearly. It was not her heartbeat she was hearing. The pain in her shoulder suddenly shocked her back into reality. She remembered leaving the house, her family's faces, and the pain. She remembered the cool pavement under her face as she let the darkness take over. Then, she realized she was no longer lying on the pavement. Emily forced herself to open her eyes as much as she could, although she didn't want to. She saw that she was lying on the wooden floor of her darkened living room.

Thump, thump, thump...

Emily placed her hands on the floor and forced herself to sit. She tried to look at what must be a bite mark, but could not see it. She reached her hand up, and when she drew it back, it was covered in a rust color. Emily wiped it on her jeans and looked around. Her family must have listened to her final plea and left. She was alone but could not figure out how she got inside.

Thump, thump, thump...

There was that noise again. Emily looked behind her to see that the front door was opening only an inch or two and then closing again. When the door was closing, it was not quite latching. Her gaze traveled to the floor in front of the door. Lying there was Marley. He appeared to be exhausted but was using his size to keep the door from opening all the way. Emily suddenly remembered Ms. Tilly and the events by the fence that morning. She sprang from the floor and ran the few short steps to the door. She shoved the door violently closed and locked it for good measure. She then reached down to untie the leash from her waist. When she pulled the leash away, she could see its outline in her shirt and skin.

Emily looked down at the poor pup that now lay at her feet. He must have dragged her inside before the dead could make a complete meal out of her. The poor guy was trying to save her and did not realize that she was already dead. She allowed herself to slide down to the floor next to Marley. She ran her hand over his soft fur. Emily knew there was no way to tell him that he should run; even if there were, he would never leave. She didn't need Chad; she had Marley.

After several minutes, Emily stood up and made her way to the kitchen. She could hear Marley stand and follow her, but not with the usual energy he would have. She rummaged in the cabinets for a while and eventually found a small bag of puppy chow she had bought just in case of an emergency. She pulled a couple of bowls from the cabinets and gave Marley food and water. He ate slowly, but the water went very fast. She refilled the bowl and set it back on the floor.

While Marley continued to eat, Emily made her
way to the bathroom. She left the bedroom door and
the bathroom door open as she went. She knew that
when Marley had his fill, he would come looking for
her. Once inside the bathroom, she stood in front of
the mirror. She found it difficult to raise her eyes to
look at it. After several minutes of arguing with
herself, she finally took a look in the mirror. The sight
shocked her, but not in the way that one might expect.
There was a wound where her shoulder met her neck,
but it was not nearly as bad as she had expected.
Emily looked at it for a few minutes and pulled her
hair from the drying blood.

"Well," she said," I am not going to be one of
those dead things walking around looking like hell. I
might as well try to clean this up."

With that, Emily moved toward the shower and
turned the knobs to the perfect temperature. She then
began to remove her clothes and tossed them in her
hamper. Emily pulled back the shower curtain and
stepped under the warm water. Emily stood under the
gentle waterfall, allowing the water to wash away
everything that had happened. Once the water began to
run clear off her body, she washed and scrubbed until
she felt squeaky clean. She washed thoroughly yet
carefully around her wound, as it was very tender. She
felt a pain of sadness as she reached down to turn off
the water. She was safe here, and nothing outside
existed, but all good things must end.

Emily pulled open the shower curtain and saw
Marley sleeping on the bedroom floor. She reached for
a towel and wrapped her long hair in it. She then

grabbed a second and, after drying her body, wrapped the towel around herself. She stepped out onto the bathmat and positioned herself back in front of the mirror. She ran her hand over the glass to clear away the steam and get a second look at her wound. It was a bite mark; she could see the teeth marks where they had broken the skin. It was no longer bleeding like crazy and appeared to be clotting. Emily reached down and grabbed the first aid kit from under the sink. She was sure everyone had tried antibacterial ointment to cure the bites, but she would use it anyway. She placed a generous amount on the bite and then taped a square gauze over the top.

"Might as well try to take care of myself. Just because I'm going to be a zombie doesn't mean I have to look like hell. I refuse to walk around covered in blood with only one slipper on."

She could not help but laugh at the mental image she had created for herself. She headed to the bedroom to pick out the outfit she would wear while hunting for brains or human flesh. She chose a form-fitting pair of jeans but decided against the belt. It could get caught on something and leave her looking like the dumb zombie in the group. She then chose her black boots and a novelty shirt that said "I'm not in the Mood," which seemed fitting for what she would be doing. Once she was dressed, she headed back to the bathroom. She decided against makeup; it would only run the first time it rained, and she would look like a box of melting crayons. She began working on her hair and decided on a tight, high bun. It would be less likely to get snagged while she roamed. Emily looked herself over in the mirror and smiled. She then turned back to the bedroom and looked at Marley.

"What do you think?" she asked. "Am I the best-dressed zombie ever or what?"

Marley wagged his tail and came to sit next to her. Emily patted the dog's head and headed back to the living room. She could only hope that when the change happened, he would be able to tell and run. Emily did not want to hurt him, but she wouldn't have any control at that point. Emily sat on the couch and began to play with her hands. She could see through the cracks in the curtains that the sun was almost entirely set. It should be happening anytime now. Suddenly, she felt Marley jump up on the couch next to her and lay his head on her lap. Chad had made it clear that the dog would never be allowed on the furniture. Well, it was his turn to be wrong about something. Emily began to pet the pup's head, and before she realized it, she fell asleep.

The sun breaking through the cracks in the curtains woke her the next day. As she began to stir on the couch, she felt Marley fall to the floor. Emily stretched and looked down at him. The poor boy had probably been waiting for hours to use the bathroom. Emily forced herself to stand and walk towards the back door. As soon as she opened it, Marley shot out like it was the start of a race. Emily stepped out on the back porch just like she would any other morning to wait for him. Once out there, she could see the body of Ms. Tilly next to the fence. Emily reached up for the bandage on her neck. How was she still herself? Ms. Tilly had changed overnight, and Emily had been bitten almost a day ago. Marley pawing at the back door pulled her out of her thoughts. He was done and ready for his breakfast.

Emily headed inside and gave him the last small bag of puppy chow. Marley began eating his breakfast, and Emily started to see if anything was left for her to eat. She managed to find one package of breakfast pastries in the cabinet. She opened the package and decided against the toaster and just began eating them right out of the package. She finished her small meal in minutes and tossed the silver wrapper in the trash. Marley was still enjoying his meal, so she decided to check out the bite while he finished. She headed down the hall and went into the bathroom. Carefully, she removed the bandage and began to examine the bite. She pulled herself as close as possible to the mirror and looked at it from every angle she could manage. Emily could not believe what she was seeing. It appeared to be healing.

Emily looked at the bandage and saw very little blood on it. Every zombie movie she ever saw never took someone this long to turn into a walking corpse. People turned quickly, even in what she had seen, yet here she was. Emily reached down and dug through the drawer until she found the thermometer. She pressed the button to turn it on and placed it under her tongue. She waited for an eternity until it beeped, signaling it was done. She pulled it from her mouth and looked at the digital display, 98.6. Even the announcement on television had said that people infected would develop a fever. Emily placed the thermometer back in the drawer and looked at her bite again. She could not even believe that she was allowing herself to think that maybe she would not turn. Of course, she would. Emily made herself a new bandage and placed it over the bite. She could not stand to look at it anymore.

She headed back down the hall just as Marley walked into the living room. He seemed to be happy and full. Emily knew that would not last forever, as they both were out of food. She could feel her stomach growling as the Pop-Tarts were not enough to make her feel full. Looking around the house, she knew that there was nothing left. They had loaded everything to take to the cabin, which was an hour away.

"I guess we will have to venture out, boy, unless you have decided to stop eating?" Marley licked his face while wagging his tail. "I'll take that as a no," Emily laughed.

She headed back down the hall and grabbed a duffel bag from her closet. She quickly put a few changes of clothes into the bag and headed to the bathroom. Once there, she packed the first aid supplies and a few toiletries she thought she needed, including a couple of rolls of toilet paper. She then returned to the living room, where Marley was already taking a nap. She grabbed his leash beside the door, stuffed it into the bag just in case she needed it, and grabbed her purse from the rack. The purse was all on instinct. Indeed, she would not need money or credit cards in a world like this.

However, Emily held on to it anyway. She walked past Marley and headed towards the kitchen. As she walked past her bookshelf, she glanced down at the only photo album she had. The few pictures she had of her family in happy moments were in it. She knew it would not help her survive outside this house, but for some reason, she had to have it anyway. She grabbed it and stuffed it into the duffel bag as well. She then turned and patted her leg, signaling Marley to follow her. Marley stood from his resting spot, stretched, and followed her into the kitchen. There was nothing left in here for Emily to take, so she headed for the back door. She grabbed her crowbar tightly and placed her hand on the door handle.

"Stay close to me," Emily warned Marley, hoping somehow he understood her.

Emily then opened the door and headed towards the fence. Emily saw that Ms. Tilley's body was still lying on the ground and chose a spot a few feet down the fence line. She hadn't jumped a fence since she was a child, but she will try it again today. She placed her hands on the fence and, with ease, lifted herself to the top. She jumped to the other side. She turned to see Marley standing on the opposite side of the fence. He had begun pacing and whining, not sure of what to do. Emily backed up a few steps and called out to him.

"Come on, boy! You can do it! Come on now!"

Emily watched as Marley backed up a little and ran at the fence. She watched as he jumped, clearing the fence with ease. As soon as he landed on the other side, he ran towards her, excitedly wagging his tail.

"Good boy!" Emily praised him.

She then turned towards Ms. Tilly's backyard and started walking towards the back door. Ms. Tilley had always prided herself on her garden, and Emily could not help but admire all the hard work the older woman had put into it as she walked through. She noticed that one of the side gates was open and pulled it back to its closed position. This would probably have something to do with what happened to Ms. Tilly.

Emily was near the back door when she saw another body. It appeared to be their mailman, and he had a garden trowel buried in his skull. It looked like Ms. Tilly had been working in her garden when he attacked her. The older woman had put up a fight, though, and taken him with her. Emily stepped over the body and soon was at the back door. She turned the handle and sighed, relieved that it was unlocked. She opened the door, and once she and Marley were inside, she locked it behind them. Then there was no time to waste. She made her way through the older woman's house, ensuring that all doors and windows were closed tight. Once she was sure that everything was secured, she looked around.

Ms. Tilly had photos on every wall and shelf around the house. She had been a widow for nearly ten years and had made the most of her life. She said that she and her husband had so many things they still wanted to do, and it was her goal to do them all for him. Emily could only hope that she had reached her goal and done everything on her list, though she was sure that this was not how the old lady wanted to go out of this world.

Emily went to the kitchen and saw that the

cabinets and refrigerator were still stuffed with food. Emily chose a few things she thought Marley would enjoy, but would be safe for a dog to eat. Emily spent the rest of the day peering out the window, watching the dead wander back and forth in the streets. Later that night, she made her and Marley eat and then made herself a little bed on the couch. She just could not bring herself to even think about sleeping in Ms. Tilly's bed. Once laid down, she felt Marley climb on top of her, obviously not asking permission to sleep with her tonight. The couch was small, so he was lying on top of her. Emily welcomed the comfort of knowing she was not alone while she slept.

Chapter 8

Emily woke the following day in the quiet house, shocked to find that she was still herself. When she began to stir, the mountain of a puppy lying on her jumped to the floor and began stretching. Emily peeled herself up from the couch and sat for a few moments, reminding herself that this was not a dream. Marley had finished his morning stretch and began prancing before her, signaling that he needed to go outside. Emily forced herself to stand and open the back door. She watched as the pup ran through the yard sniffing everything in the new environment. After a little bit, he was finally done and walked back up to her. Emily and Marley headed back inside, and Emily set to work to find them something to eat. She found bacon and eggs in the fridge and set to work cooking.

Emily didn't know if this particular meal was considered "healthy" for Marley or not, but it was what they had. She placed a bowl on the floor with his fresh breakfast and another with water. Marley did not hesitate and jumped right into the food. He probably felt like he was eating like a king. Emily ate her breakfast slowly, enjoying it as much as possible. The power would surely be going out soon, and meals like this would be a thing of the past. When they finished, Emily cleaned up the dishes and washed them in the sink. As she finished, she could hear that Marley was already napping in the living room.

Emily returned to the living room and pulled fresh clothes out of her duffel bag. After looking at them for a few minutes, she slid them back in. She decided to go wash up, but put back on the same clothes. Surely in the coming days, fresh clothes would become a thing of the past. She needed to stretch them out as long as she could. Emily went to the bathroom, leaving the door open if Marley came looking for her. Once inside, she found the first aid supplies under the sink and began to remove her bandage. Once the bandage was removed, she began to examine the bite. There was no doubt about it. She was healing and still showed no signs that she was infected. Emily wiped off the bite and put another bandage on it. She then brushed her hair and put it back up in a ponytail.

Once satisfied, she returned to the living room and peeked out the window. A few zombies were walking on the street, but none of them appeared to be aware that she was in there. She closed the blinds and walked back to the couch. She spent most of the day sitting there. She cooked her and Marley's lunch and dinner before lying down to try to sleep again. Emily had no clue what she was supposed to do next. Staying here seemed to be the best plan. However, as she lay in the dark, she heard true silence spread through the house. The sound of the central air was gone, and the refrigerator was no longer running. The power was finally gone, along with Emily's hope that things might return to normal. As Emily tried to force herself to sleep, she thought about the bite on her neck and the fact that she had not changed. Emily decided that if she was still herself in the morning, she would find her family. There was no point in staying here alone if nothing was wrong with her.

Emily did not rest much through the night and was still awake as the sun rose. Marley had moved to the floor during the night as it became sweltering in the house. Emily did not want to risk opening the windows, though. She did not know if the zombies could smell them or if just the sounds of them breathing would be enough to draw them in. Either way, she decided it was not worth the risk when they had already been so lucky. She let Marley in the backyard, and sensing the danger, he was swift this morning. Once he was back inside, Emily dug through the cabinets, found him a few spam cans to eat, and ate a bowl of dry cereal herself.

While she ate, she began to pull anything out that she thought would travel well. She found the reusable shopping bags and began to fill them with all of her finds. Once she was done, she carried all of the bags to the garage. She opened the back of the SUV and loaded all of the bags. She looked around the garage and found three cases of water she had also packed. She then returned, took the first aid supplies from the bathroom, and stuffed them into the duffel bag. She looked around the house to ensure nothing else could help her or that her family might need. Once she was sure there was nothing helpful left, she led Marley back to the garage. She opened the driver's side door and watched as Marley gladly hopped inside. She followed and was glad to see that the older woman had left the keys in the ignition. As usual, she reached the visor and clicked the garage door opener. She felt a wave of confusion wash over her as the door remained still.

After only a few moments, she finally

remembered and could not help but laugh at herself. "The door won't open like that with the power off, pup."

Marley began bouncing in the passenger seat, excited about the car ride. In his bouncing, he knocked over Emily's purse, which had been on the center console. Emily watched as the contents spilled out over the floorboard. She laughed and set to picking them up and putting them back in the purse. She had no idea why she felt the need to carry it still. It's not like she would need her credit cards anytime soon. She slid her wallet back in, along with a handful of mints and lipstick, and lastly, she reached for her cell phone. As she picked it up, she noticed that she had received a voicemail. Without thinking, she unlocked the phone and clicked to call her voicemail. The familiar robotic voice came on, and Emily entered her passkey. The robotic voice told her she had four new voicemails. As Emily listened, she felt her heart drop into her stomach.

"Hey Em, it's Joe. This is stupid, but part of me was hoping you would answer. Maybe your battery is dead or something. I just can't believe that you could die that way. I feel like a piece of shit for leaving you like that, but Dad screamed. We had to get the kids out of there. I wanted to let you know we did what you wanted. We were able to find Veronica, and she is with us. Chad is, well, being an asshole, but that's not any big change. Everyone else is fine, and we have made it to the cabin. It seems safe here, so if you manage to get this, come here as quickly as possible. I love you, Em."

"Next Message"

"I'm sorry, dear, I just wanted to hear your voice. Your brother and sister speak as if you are on your way, and your father will not talk about it. I can't believe these phones are still working. We are all set up here at the cabin, and I have even set up a place for you. If you get this, Emily, please be careful. If you are able, try to give us a call. I love you."

"Next Message"

"So, it's day two at the cabin, and things are already starting to get crazy. I said I would never say "I told you so" about your husband, but he is starting to push my buttons. I have kept my temper because he always has that woman near him. I never saw him dote on you half as much as he does on her. She seems a lot like him, so perhaps they are meant to be. You'd better be looking for a charger or something. I'll see you soon, sis."

"Next Message"

"Um, it's dad. I know you will never get this, but we are all choosing to believe that you are safe and we will see you again. I can't go on if I think otherwise. Your mom and brother have called, but your sister lacks strength. I just wanted you to know that I have not given up on you, just in case these get through somehow. We are all here for you, Em, and we love you."

"End of messages"

Emily clicked to end the call and sat staring at the phone. It never rang the whole time, and according to the timestamps, all the messages were received just a few minutes ago. Emily quickly clicked through her phone and tapped on her dad's number. She waited for what seemed like forever for it to ring, but the phone never connected, and she hung up. Emily threw the phone back into her purse and grabbed the steering wheel. After a few moments, she looked up, refusing to allow herself to cry, and then glanced in the rearview mirror. The closed garage door seemed to be laughing at her silently. Emily opened the truck door and walked to the back. She looked until she found the emergency string and pulled hard to unlock the door from the electronic opener. She then walked to the door, and using every bit of strength she could muster, she managed to open the door. Her arms were shaking from exhaustion by the time she was done.

Emily looked down the driveway and saw that she had drawn some unwanted attention. A few zombies had turned and were making their way up the driveway. Emily turned and ran back to the truck and jumped back in. She turned the key and smiled as the engine came to life. She turned to look behind her as she dropped the SUV into reverse and slammed the accelerator pedal. She watched as the zombies slammed into the back of the truck and disappeared. The sound of them hitting the back of the SUV sounded like magic. These fucking things would not keep her from her family any longer. Emily pressed the brake as she hit the street and turned back forward.

"Time for us to go," Emily said to Marley as she put the SUV in drive and heard the tires squeal as she took off.

The sound had drawn some more attention, but there was no way they could catch her. Emily was surprised to see that the roads were clear as she drove. It looked like most people had done what the television said and stayed home. Emily could not help but wonder if anyone was still left hiding inside, watching her as she drove away. Looking at the dead as she passed, she could not help but think that if there were any actual people left, it could not be many. There were too many dead on the street for there to be a whole lot of people left. Emily cranked up the AC and could tell that even Marley was grateful for the comfort. A quick look at the gas gauge, Emily saw they had a full tank. There would be no need to stop before they got to the cabin.

Emily pressed down the gas pedal and sped through the streets of her neighborhood. She reached the highway in ten short minutes. There were a few cars here and there, but nothing that slowed her down. Emily maneuvered through the abandoned vehicles and even the few zombies that shambled along the highway. Emily had the air conditioner turned up all the way, and she and Marley soon became comfortable with the temperature again. Marley was pawing at the window, though, and Emily felt herself laugh. She reached over to the window controls and rolled Marley's window down part of the way. The pup stuck his nose out of the window and began wagging his tail. Emily watched him from the corner of her eye and felt like the world was ordinary at that moment.

After about twenty minutes, Emily finally reached her exit. She exited the highway and began working her way down the roads towards the cabin.

Soon, the streets turned to dirt, and Emily knew she was getting close. Emily saw the cabin as she came over the hill. Out front, she saw her brother's car. She quickly pulled in next to it and parked the SUV. She had already opened the door before the engine had enough time to shut off. She ran towards the front door, eager to see her family. As she reached the door, she could not help but notice that everything was quiet. She understood them not wanting to draw attention to themselves, but she should hear something this close.

Emily reached out, turned the handle on the door, and pushed it open. As it slid open, she knew immediately that her family was no longer there. The living room was empty, and a glance to the left showed the same in the kitchen. Emily walked towards the kitchen table, where a few papers were strewn over it. Emily picked up the papers one at a time and saw that they were drawings, probably done by the children. Emily walked back towards the bedrooms and found each was empty. It looked much like it would in early winter when Dad would be shutting it down for the season. A look through the kitchen cabinets showed they would not be back from wherever they had gone, as nothing was left. Emily walked back to the living room and sat on the couch. She had remained calm through most of this and had not allowed her emotions to take over. However, sitting in an empty cabin, she felt her emotions taking over.

Emily let the tears fall and let her face fall into her hands. She sat as the sorrow and rage began to flow out of her. She could not see any end in sight and feared that she would probably live out the rest of her days crying on this old couch. Sitting, she felt something cold nudging at the back of her hands. Emily lifted her head slightly and found herself face-to-face with Marley. The look of concern in his eyes was undeniable, but Emily still could not find the strength to stop. Marley seemed to want her to feel better and believed that could not happen as long as her face was wet with tears. He began licking at the tears on her face, and Emily started to laugh while trying to stop him.

She petted Marley on the head and forced herself to stand up. Her family is not here, but they must be somewhere. Zombies would not pack up everything before leaving the house. Emily looked through the kitchen drawers for clues to where they may have gone next. She walked back outside without knowing where to begin looking for her family. Marley followed her out the door and began to go back to the SUV. Emily considered staying at the cabin, but knew there had to be a reason her family left, and she did not want to find out what it was.

She knew she could not stay here and decided to return to the SUV. She walked past Joe's car and saw his lucky bandanna hanging from the rearview mirror. Emily opened the car door and pulled out the bandanna. She then walked to the SUV and hung it in her rearview mirror. Marley was already sitting in the passenger seat, ready to continue his car ride. Emily grabbed her cell phone and planned to listen to the voicemails from her family once again. However, after unlocking the screen, she discovered that she had a new voicemail. It must have come in while she was in the cabin. Emily called her voicemail and listened to the automated voice once again.

"You Have One New Message"

"Hey Em, I know I'm probably just talking to myself at this point, but it helps. The cabin is no longer safe. Not going to get into it, but Chad decided to turn on the generator. Dad thinks the dead will clear out eventually, but we can't wait it out. We are heading out to find a place, but we have no idea where we are going. The only thing for sure is that we are staying in Missouri. We don't know anywhere else well enough to stand a chance. I miss you, Emily."

Emily clicked the phone off and hit the steering wheel. Why was she always missing these calls, her chance to find her family and not be alone? Emily felt the hot tears run down her face as she tried to call Joe back, but yet again, the phone would not connect. She could not help but feel like the universe was trying to ensure she would die and do so alone. Emily heard something moving outside the SUV and knew she had to go. She was soon back on the road without knowing where she was going. However, she had a sudden determination to keep going. Her family was going to stay in Missouri; it might take her forever, but she would search every square inch until she found them.

Chapter 9

Emily had been on the road for a few hours and realized that this would not be a short journey. She had no idea where her family was and only had the determination to find them. She would need to make the SUV more livable. She had decided not to drive at night. Her getting too tired and falling asleep at the wheel would be a ridiculous end after everything she had been through up to this point. Emily had seen a sign a few miles back for a visitor's center. She hoped that people would not have gone there, and maybe she could find a few supplies to help make things more comfortable.

It was only a few more minutes before Emily pulled into the visitor's center. The parking lot was empty. Emily decided that was a good sign, grabbed her crowbar, and slowly opened the car door. She carefully scanned the parking lot, looking for any signs of movement. There was nothing she could see, and she cautiously started to move forward. Behind her, she heard Marley jump out of the truck and walk beside her. Emily turned and shut the car door as quietly as possible behind Marley. She then started to make her way toward the visitor center. She reached the glass doors and could see that it was dark inside. She grabbed the cold metal handle of the door and pulled. The door slid silently open to Emily's delight, and they could walk inside. The lobby area was large, and a wooden desk stood in the center. Behind the desk were several racks of souvenirs and maps. Emily saw a sign behind the racks indicating that the restrooms were located back there; to the right was a sign indicating a restaurant was located there, and to the left was a sign for a general store.

Emily turned to the left and headed into the general store. The store was filled with many things targeted at people on a road trip; everything was travel-size. Emily looked through the shelves for something she thought would make things better for life in an SUV. She found dry shampoo, small bags of dog food, travel bowls, pillows and blankets, self-heating soups, and many different road snacks. Emily put all the finds in travel bags and stacked them at the door to the center. She then went through the clothing in the souvenirs. She wouldn't be winning any fashion contests, but at least she had a few more sets of clean clothes. Once she had gathered anything she thought could be helpful, she started carrying it all to the SUV. It took several trips, but she got it all packed away in the back. She decided it would have to do for now, but she knew that she would have to organize it later, not while she still had daylight left and could drive.

Emily started up the SUV and left the parking lot, heading east down the road. The hours continued to pass, and Emily's eyes searched along the road for any signs of her family. Deep down, she knew that the odds of finding them today were zero, but she didn't want to miss anything. Soon the sun was almost completely gone, and Emily could feel her eyes growing heavy. She spotted a clearing near the side of the road. Emily pulled the SUV into the clearing and put the SUV in park. Her eyes were drawn to the gas gauge. She saw that she was down to a quarter of a tank. She would have to find a gas station tomorrow, but she would worry about that later. Emily turned off the engine and locked the doors.

Emily turned and climbed into the back seat. She had to turn to stop Marley from following her. She needed some space to organize all of her loot in the back. If she had to live in the SUV, it might as well be comfortable. She took a few minutes and finally figured out how to lay the back seat down. Now she would have a bed, and the trunk area could be like a small, organized apartment. She began moving around the things and organizing them by what they were. She put the clothes on the floorboard, stacked according to what they were, and her self-cleaning supplies on the other floorboard.

She organized all the other items on one side of the trunk and made the folded seat into a bed with the blankets and pillows she had gathered. On the other side of the trunk, she set up bowls for Marley. She filled one with bottled water and the other with the dog food she had found. Marley was excitedly dancing in the front seat as the food clanged into the bowl. Looking around at her handiwork, she was proud of what she had accomplished. She made a mental note that the next time she stopped for supplies to try to find something that would work for curtains. She felt exposed just sitting here, and the curtains would help.

Emily patted the back seat, calling Marley, who jumped through the seats and began eating and drinking his food and water. Emily reached back to the front for her cell phone and was glad to have plugged it in while she drove. The battery was fully charged, and a glance showed no new messages. Emily unlocked the phone and set herself an alarm for six in the morning. She did not want to sit here long once the sun was up. She slid the phone inside the back of the seat after ensuring the ringer was turned up. Emily then reached back to the food stack and chose a self-heating soup. She pressed the button on the bottom and heard the "pop," signaling that she had activated the self-heating chemical in the cup. According to the instructions, it would take ten minutes for the soup to be ready.

She set the soup down on the makeshift bed just as Marley finished his food and lay down towards the bottom of her bed. He was full, but Emily knew he would only be able to get a few minutes of rest before he would need to get up. The poor puppy would need to go to the bathroom before they went to sleep for the night. Emily sat watching the pup for quite a while before checking her soup. She was sure it had been at least ten minutes. She turned the soup lid to sip it out of the can. To her surprise, the soup was very delicious and filling.

Once Emily finished her hot meal, she grabbed one of the bags she had taken from the visitor center and put her trash inside it. She would have to make sure to empty this as often as possible. She then slid down the bed towards Marley and reached to open the door behind him. As soon as the door opened behind him, Marley jumped out and began looking for his perfect spot. Emily sat on the bed in the open door, watching him to ensure he did not wander too far from her. Once he had finished, he walked back over to her, and Emily moved to allow him to jump back inside. Emily closed the door behind him and ensured that it was locked. She then moved back up towards her pillow and slid under the blanket. Once she was lying down, she felt Marley snuggle up next to her legs. This was much more comfortable than the couch they had been sleeping on.

Emily spent the early sleeping hours thinking about her plan to find her family and how she would explain to them that a bite from a zombie does not make you one. She tried to think of places her dad would think might be safe. As she thought, she heard the light snoring coming from Marley. Soon, she joined him in her dreams, where she happened across her family the next day, and everything was perfect.

Emily was awakened the following day by her cell phone alarm going off. Emily reached into the back seat and grabbed the phone to turn it off. Once the phone was silent, she slid it back into the seat pocket and sat up. The sun was just starting to creep across the world as Emily pulled herself into a sitting position. As she moved, so did Marley. He stretched into the space where her legs once were and let out a giant yawn. Emily reached into the back and put some more kibble into the bowl and some fresh water into the other. She then grabbed a box of dry cereal for herself. Soon, she and Marley had finished breakfast, and Emily opened the door to allow Marley to go to the bathroom. While Marley was outside, Emily took the opportunity to change her shirt and freshen up. Once changed, she joined Marley outside with a toilet paper roll. There was no way to make this more comfortable, but at this point, she and Marley had to share the same "bathroom." When she had finished, she found Marley waiting for her by the SUV. He seemed to understand that they would need to get back on the road.

They both climbed back inside the truck. Emily cleaned up the dog bowls, made her "bed," and climbed back into the front with a bottle of water and her cell phone. Marley was already in his spot in the passenger seat, looking ready to be her navigator for the day. Emily plugged her cell phone into the car charger and started the SUV. She started down the road, continuing east. She had decided to pick a different route when she reached the state line and turn around and drive west. This way, she could cover more ground. She hoped they would not cross the state line before she found them.

Emily remembered, after a glance, that she would need to stop for gas soon. She felt like she was in the middle of nowhere and hoped a gas station would be somewhere along the way. She drove for a few hours, watching the gas gauge slowly drop as she went. She had not seen anything all morning and feared that she never would. She thought it could be a mirage when she spotted what looked like a gas station ahead. As she pulled closer, she felt relieved to see that it was real. She pulled up to the pumps and sat for a few minutes with the engine off, watching for any dead that may wander out. She then opened the door and walked towards the gas pump, Marley following behind her on alert. It seemed he could sense that they needed to be careful and quick.

Emily opened the gas tank and put the gas nozzle in. The pump had power and was flashing instead of displaying the regular price and gallons pumped. She crossed her fingers and pulled the gas handle. If nothing came out, she had no idea how to make it work. She breathed a sigh of relief as the gas filling the tank filled her ears. She set the pump to keep filling until the tank was full. Emily walked back to the front door and reached in to grab her crowbar. She felt unsafe out here without it. She saw him as she turned to walk back to the gas pump. An older man, probably in his late sixties. He probably ran the gas station, that is, when he was alive. Marley began growling very low and positioned himself between Emily and the old man.

This was not the first zombie that Emily had seen, but it was the first she would need to take care of herself. She stepped forward next to Marley, who planted himself next to her. Once the old man was close enough, Emily swung her crowbar as hard as she could at his head. She heard the crack as it broke through his skull, and the body fell lifeless to the ground. Emily planted her feet and pulled the crowbar out of the man's skull. The gas pump clicked to the off position, and Emily turned, blood dripping from her crowbar as she returned the gas handle to the pump. She closed the gas tank and looked back at the body on the ground. She could not help but feel sorrow for the poor man. He did not ask for this. He did nothing wrong. He was doing his job when everything was taken away from him. Emily's attention was drawn back to the crowbar, still dripping with the ruby red blood. She turned, grabbed some paper towels from the windshield cleaning station, and wiped them clean.

"This is just something I have to get used to," Emily said to herself. She then turned and followed

Marley back into the SUV. She turned over the engine and began driving east once more.

This is how her life went for months—stopping every night to rest, looking for gas stations with fuel, and scavenging any supplies she could find. Things got scarcer and harder to find as time passed. She had picked up a couple of gas cans to keep in the SUV, just in case she needed to buy more time to find a gas station. The smell had caused her to constantly keep the back windows cracked, or the fumes made her a little loopy. Soon, she had forgotten the man at the gas station, her first zombie kill. As time went on, they all started to blur together. She had seen almost everything at this point, except for any living people. Her map was covered with marks on routes she had already tried and had not found her family. No more mysterious voicemails had come through. She feared that those were long since over. She kept the phone charged, though, just in case.

Four months of living in an SUV and living off of what little food she could find had become her life. She had tried so many roads that some of them were beginning to look the same. Every day, the SUV needed gas; she thought about finding a smaller car, but that would cause more problems. She didn't want to change to another vehicle to have the engine go out in the middle of nowhere. Gas was just as important as food or water at this point. That was what had led her here, another gas station on an old country road. Emily pulled up to the pump and shut off the engine. She had this down to a science at this point. She lay on the horn three times and waited. Sure enough, three zombies wandered into view. The cooler temperature of the November days did not seem to slow these things down. Emily hoped for a good snowfall this year, as the snow would undoubtedly have to slow them down at least a little.

Emily opened the door and took her position in front of the SUV. She swung, hitting them each in the head as they approached. As the last one fell to the ground, she heard Marley let out a guttering growl. She looked down to see that his attention was focused on something behind her. She turned to see another zombie working its way up the side of the SUV. She walked towards and struck the zombie with a crunch to the skull. She then walked around and opened the gas tank. She discovered that it was off after trying to turn on the pump. Not the first time she had had this happen to her. She found her way to the building and located the pump switch. Soon it was on, and the gas tank was filling.

Emily was sure that the gas would start to go bad eventually if it already wasn't. But for now, it made the engine run, and she planned to keep using it as long as it did that. The food supplies in the SUV were growing low, especially the water. Emily patted her leg, signaling Marley to follow, and headed inside. Opening the glass door, she heard the bell ring through the building. She entered, and she and Marley waited by the front door. Everything was quiet, and nothing dead or alive was moving in here. She reached behind the register and grabbed the plastic bags. She began filling them with all the food she could find and was thrilled to find four cases of water. Once she had everything she could find, she began to head towards the front door, stopping for only a moment to look at the t-shirts on a rack near the register. Looking down at her own, she saw it was starting to get tight. She had to be the first person to gain weight while practically starving.

She looked through until she found a couple in the next size up and decided to go ahead and change her shirt now. There was no point in hauling around one that didn't fit anymore. As she slid on the new, more comfortable shirt, her hand knocked something off the shelf behind her. Once her shirt was on, she looked to see what she had knocked over. She picked up the small pink box off the floor to see that it was a pregnancy test. She laughed to herself. Who would want to be pregnant with a world like this? She then looked at the supplies she had gathered. She knew she had grabbed some tampons before leaving home, but had never used them in four months. She looked back at the box and remembered the couple of nights that she and Chad were intimate when she thought he wanted to save their marriage.

"You have got to be kidding me!" she exclaimed.

Marley looked up at her with a face of confusion. "Let me know if you see someone." She hoped he understood as she ducked into the bathroom with the test. She went into the stall and did the very technical procedure of peeing on a stick. As she walked out, she set the test on the counter and waited. As she watched, she counted.

"One pink line... Shit! Two pink lines."

Emily stared at the test, unable to believe what she was seeing. Her last pregnancy had gone wrong, and she had not even made it this far. How could she not have lost the baby without all the medications her doctor had said she would need if she ever got pregnant again? It's not like she had been on a good diet or stress-free. Emily just could not understand, and that's when she heard the bark. She slid the test into her pocket and ran back to Marley. He was staring out the door, but Emily did not see anything. She waited a few minutes, and though Marley did not relax, Emily felt confident that whatever he had seen was gone. She reached down, grabbed two cases of water, and pushed the door open. She made three trips to bring everything to the SUV and put it away. She returned the gas handle to the pump and was soon back in the SUV.

Only a few hours of daylight left, and Emily was soon parked off the side of the road and snuggled into her bed. She had pulled the test out of her pocket and stared at it for quite some time, but it had not changed. Soon, there would be a baby joining them in this SUV. Where would she put a crib? How would they ever be able to stop a baby from crying? Who was going to help her deliver the baby? Marley would be no help in that area, though the thought of him in a doctor's coat made her smile. Emily knew that she would not be able to have the baby and raise it in the SUV. She would have to find somewhere stationary and safe to do this, even if it meant she had to stop looking for her family. This second pink line changed her mission. Instead of trying to find her family, she had to protect the one she was creating.

She couldn't think of anywhere she had driven through that seemed safe enough for a stationary home, but she had a little time left. She had been driving for four months, which meant she was about five months pregnant. The baby would be due around March sometime if it didn't come early. She could only assume that her limited food was what had contributed to her tiny bump. She decided she would give herself a month, and then she had to pick somewhere. She would need time to make it safe and suitable for a baby to be born, and she did not want to cut it too close if the baby came early. She felt the thoughts drift away as she drifted away to sleep. Usually, she would do this to the sound of Marley's soft snores, but not tonight. Tonight, Marley was still sitting up and staring out the windshield. Emily assumed that it had to be all the day's excitement. She was sure he could tell that something was on her mind. He would fall asleep and get his rest as soon as she did, so off to sleep she went.

Chapter 10

Emily was awoken in the morning by the sound of Marley growling. She sat up slowly in her bed and began looking out the windows. She didn't see anything moving outside and relaxed her shoulders a bit. Marley had been acting strange since the gas station yesterday. She hoped that he was not getting sick or something. She was not ready to lose him and go through this whole thing alone. She reached down and ran her hand down his back, trying to get him to calm down. While he acknowledged her attention, he stayed alert and stared out the window. Emily reached past him and opened the passenger door. Maybe it was that he was tired of being cooped up. It took some coaching, but Marley finally jumped out of the SUV and cautiously began doing his morning routine. Emily watched him for a few minutes and then stepped outside herself. She reached back, grabbed her bathroom supplies, walked just a few feet away, and took care of her business.

She was headed back to the SUV, where Marley was already waiting just inside the door. He looked on high alert, his head quickly turning in every direction. Emily would have to keep a close eye on him until he started to feel better. She was nearing the door, watching Marley, when suddenly the door on the SUV slammed shut, locking Marley inside. Marley instantly began barking and slamming into the window. A man stood looking in the window, laughing at the dog who wanted nothing more than to rip the man apart.

"Was beginning to think that damn mutt would never leave your side," the man said while slowly turning back towards Emily. "We've been following you since last night, but none of us were in a hurry to get bitten by a dog. It's a good thing we are patient men. Otherwise, we may have wasted a bullet and shot it to get it over."

Emily started looking around and saw several other men stepping out behind trees. She looked down at the roll of toilet paper she carried. Her crowbar was back in the SUV with Marley. She knew that they had planned it this way on purpose.

"No need to shoot him, but there are easier ways to say hello." Emily smiled and said to the man. "It's amazing to see living people. There was no need to hide from little old me."

The man let out a low laugh as she finished talking," We have been watching you for a while. If you want to play the cute, innocent little woman, that's fine with us. It would probably make this go smoother, but we know you are more than capable of defending yourself. You've killed more of the dead by yourself than some of my men combined."

"True, I can fight off the dead ones just fine. However, you all appear to be living. I have no reason to attack you." Emily felt her stomach drop as she tried to keep the smile on her face. The men moved in closer, and she felt they didn't want to say hello.

"Yes, we are alive. We are living men whose needs have been neglected since the world went to shit. Finding living people is rare enough, but finding a living woman is impossible. Especially one that is as good-looking as you."

"So, what is the plan here?" Emily had to keep him talking while her mind raced to find a way out of this. "Are we talking about dinner and a movie type of deal?"

"Nothing so complicated, love," the man laughed back at her. "It's straightforward. You belong to us to do whatever, whenever, we want."

"Well, can I at least know the name of the man seeking to be my owner?" Emily felt like the air was being sucked out of the world around her. The men closed in, and she could not think of any way out of this situation.

"It's simple, love. You call us all husband, and we will call you love if you're good or bitch if you need to be put in line, understand?"

"Well, that's a problem, you see. I am already married, so betraying those vows would not be right. I'm sure such fine gentlemen as you understand my predicament." Emily felt no need to share that her marriage was over because her husband got another woman pregnant.

"Those vows are gone. If he decides he wants you back, he can come to us, and we will tell him the purchase price. Now, if you are done talking your pretty words, it's time for us to go, love."

Emily looked at Marley, still barking and slamming against the window. There was no way he would get through it and be able to help her. Emily knew that her chances of getting out of this area on foot were slim, but she had to try for herself and her baby. She clutched the toilet paper in her hand like it was a grenade.

"Sorry, but I guess I'm a bitch."

Emily threw the toilet paper at the man as hard as possible and ran in the opposite direction. There were two other men directly behind her, whom she just barely managed to dodge away from and continue on her run. She was swerving in and out of the trees and could hear voices and footsteps following her. Emily continued to run as hard as she could. Whenever she thought she had lost them, another one would step out from behind a tree. She had dodged several, but could feel her stamina starting to slow. Emily ducked behind a rock formation and tried to be silent while catching her breath. She watched from her hiding place as several men ran past her. After a few minutes, everything fell quiet, and Emily had not seen anyone for some time.

Emily looked back in the direction she had come. It was a long shot, but maybe she could get back to Marley and get out of here. She looked around one more time and emerged from her hiding spot. She was prepared to take off at a run when she heard his voice from behind her.

"There you are, love."

Before she could react, Emily felt a pain in the back of her head, and the world around her went dark.

When Emily could finally see and think, she found that her hands were bound in front of her at the wrist. She was sitting in some vehicle, and the back of her head was throbbing. She opened her eyes and looked to her left. The sat the man who had closed the door on Marley and called her "love". He was driving what appeared to be an old, red pickup truck. The sun was very high in the sky, and it had to be around midday by now. Emily began to look out the passenger window. She hoped to get some idea of where she was. They were on a dirt road, but not one of the ones she had driven yet. It looked more like a small farm road that the farmers would have only used to get home.

"I was beginning to think I may have hit you too hard, love," the man spoke without looking at her.

"I'm not your love, you son of a bitch!" Emily was not up to playing the good girl anymore.

"Now, we can have none of that. I think you have a lot of potential, if only you would stop fighting so much. You are good-looking enough that I will make you my woman that no other man can touch. I can do that, you know? Now that doesn't sound so bad, does it, love?" The man spoke as if this were a common situation that Emily should accept, and she should be grateful.

"No man will touch me. Not you, not anyone!" Emily began to struggle with the rope around her wrist. If she could just get her hands free, she could kick this guy's ass, take his truck back to find Marley, and get out of this place.

"You are starting to wear my patience thin, love. Just sit still and do as you are told."

Emily had no intentions of listening to him as she felt one of the ropes begin to loosen. She continued to fight even harder with the ropes, determined that he would not win. Emily feared that he had noticed that she was getting free as he pulled the truck to the side of the road and put it in park. While still moving her wrists and trying to get free, Emily pushed herself as far as she could into the passenger door.

"You have a fighting spirit. I like that. I think you need a release just as much as I do." The man began to come across the seat toward Emily. He grabbed her legs and reached for the button on her pants. "Don't worry, love. I'll be gentle." Emily began kicking at him, but felt him getting closer and closer. "Unless you want me to get rough," the man sneered as he popped the button on her jeans and pulled down the zipper. He leaned slightly back and began pulling off her pants, giving Emily the needed opening. She used all her strength and caught him flat in the nose with her foot. The man shot back, holding his face. Emily could see the blood pouring from between his fingers, and he strung together curse words.

Emily tugged at her ropes and felt her hands finally free. She reached down and fastened back up her pants. She then turned and attempted to open the truck door, but was disconcerted by what she found. The door handle and window handle were missing. He had done this before and wanted to ensure his victim could not escape. Emily quickly turned to see if the back window opened when he grabbed her and slammed her back into her seat.

"What the fuck is wrong with you, bitch?" he hollered like a wounded animal.

"I'm sorry, love, I thought you liked it rough?" Emily sneered back at him.

"I will break you; you will be mine. You hear me, you crazy bitch?"

"If you think I'm ever going to let you touch me, you are out of your fucking mind!" Emily was surprised at the amount of confidence she had and the lack of fear. "The only way you will get to touch me like that is if I am dead!"

"Oh no, you'll be warm and alive." He was wiping the blood from his face with his shirt. "Not only that, but you will want it just as much as I."

"You are insane."

Not a strong statement, but the only thing Emily felt was worth saying at this point. He simply laughed, put the truck in drive, and continued up the road. While they drove, Emily glanced back at the back window and saw a solid piece of glass, no exit. She would have to stop and wait for him to let her out before she could try to escape again.

They drove for about ten more minutes when he finally said, "We're here."

Emily looked out the windshield to see a line of farm equipment and cattle fencing. They were obviously on a farm, which had been here for quite some time. As they drove up, a barricade section opened and allowed them to enter. Once inside, he put the truck into park and stepped out. He motioned for Emily to follow, and she slid across the seat and out the door. She realized that just running from here would not be an option. Standing where she was, she could see a farmhouse, a barn, and several tents set up throughout the grounds. The barricade, from what she could see, went around everything. She could see men walking around it, keeping a lookout.

She counted at least twenty men here and only three other women. The women looked like they were an inch from death. They had all been beaten and were so exhausted. Emily did not know how they were doing the chores they were doing. They were all skin and bones, while the men looked like none of them had missed a meal. Emily could not hide the horror or pain she felt for these women; her captor immediately noticed it.

"Don't worry, love, that won't be your life. You will be mine." Emily felt his hand running through the back of her hair. "But first, I have to make it so that all you know and want is me."

Emily pulled away, but not fast enough. Two men grabbed her and carried her kicking and screaming towards the farmhouse. They walked to the back and opened what appeared to be a cellar. The men tossed her down the stairs, and she landed on the dirt floor at the bottom. In the light that showed down from the doorway, she saw a shadow creep over her where she lay. She didn't even have to look up to know it was him.

"A little time down here, and when you see me again, I will be everything you want and need."

With that, she heard the doors close, and the darkness swallowed her and the room around her. Emily felt the laughter begin to trickle out of her. His plan to make her swoon for him was to leave her alone and starve her of human contact. The idiot does not know she has been without people for four months. Emily reached down and rubbed her stomach. She hoped that the fall down here didn't hurt the baby. She had to keep her pregnancy a secret from them. Who knows what they would do if they found out?

The thoughts of the baby ran through her mind as she rubbed her stomach. She was looking for a safe place to give birth and raise the baby. While the men here were crazy, there was no question about that, but they would be able to keep the baby safe from the dead. Sure, it would mean that she would have to be that man's "love" and be the obedient woman. Maybe he was even dumb enough that she could convince him that the baby was his, even though she was five months along already. That raised a whole different set of things to consider. If the baby were a girl, would they make her one of the communal women and want her raised to be their obedient slave? They would want it to be like her captors if it were a boy. Emily felt a cold chill run down her spine at the thought of either scenario. This was not the place for her or her baby. She would have to buy her time and get out of here as soon as possible.

Emily looked around and was pleased to see that her eyes were adjusting. While there were no windows, a bit of light did manage to find its way through the cracks. It looked like this was used as a basement before the world went to hell. There were shelves with jars lining them. Most of them were empty, but some had liquid in them. Emily could not determine what it was. Nothing down here would serve as a bed, so the dirt floor would have to do. Emily continued looking through the shelves and found a lot of useless junk, but found one thing that gave her hope. An old screwdriver was in a bin of scraps towards the back of the room. She took it back to the central area of the cellar and hid it under the dirt with her hands. Emily then curled up on the dirt floor next to her buried weapon. She bent her arm under her head to use as a pillow. She knew the sun was still up, but there was nothing else to do until those doors opened again. She might as well be as comfortable as possible while she waited. After a few hours, one of the doors opened, and before she could see who it was, the door was closed again.

Emily stood up from her spot and walked up the stairs. On the top step was a tray of what appeared to be food. She picked up the tray and sat down on the step. There was a bottle of water and a sandwich. It was better than nothing, and at least now she knew they would not let her starve. She ate the sandwich and set the tray back down on the step. She took the water bottle with her and lay back on the dirt floor. He was not going to break her, but maybe letting him think he could, would give her the opportunity she needed to get the hell out of here. She would just need to be patient and wait for the perfect moment.

Chapter 11

Emily did not know how long she had been in the cellar. She had tried to keep track of the meals as a measure of time, but she had lost count. No one had come down here since they had thrown her down. She kept a feel on her stomach, and it did not feel like she was showing any more than she was before, but she could not be sure. Her routine remained the same: she lay on the floor and waited for the food, ate on the stairs, and returned to the floor. Now and then, they would put a bucket on the stairs. Emily would use it to do her business, and at the following food delivery, they would take it away. It wasn't the most dignified existence, but they were not breaking her. She spent most of her time thinking of baby names, figuring out where she would look for a haven when she was free, and hoping that Marley had found his way out of the SUV and was alright.

She was in the middle of one of her thinking spells when the cellar doors opened. She started to stand when she realized that this was not another food delivery. Both doors were open this time. She looked up towards the door, shielding the sunlight with her hand. She had been down here long enough that the direct light hurt her eyes.

"Are you finally ready to behave, my love?" She knew the voice instantly; it was the man who wanted her to call him husband and serve only him. While her stomach churned just by the sound of his voice, she knew she had to make the most of this opportunity. She pulled herself up to her knees and bent towards the doorway.

"As you wish, husband." The words tasted like ash in her mouth, but she could deal with it if it got her closer to getting out of here. She kept her eyes on the ground but could hear him coming down the stairs. She was convincing enough to get him to come closer to her. She remained still as he drew closer and used her strength not to bolt towards the door.

"Well, either your treatment is working, or you are just trying to play me like a fool." She could hear the speculation in his voice.

"You are no fool, husband; I see that now." Emily kept her eyes toward the ground. He stopped before her and lifted her face to look at him. His nose was still bruised and swollen, so she could not have been down there more than two or three days. Maybe she was laying it on a little heavy. She had not been down here long enough to be completely brainwashed.

"If I could ask one thing of you, is there any way someone could bring my dog to me? He is the only family I have left, and I hate to think of him stuck in that SUV." Emily hoped that bringing up Marley would show him that while she was willing to give in to him, she still wanted what she had before. Not brainwashed but closer to being what he wanted her to be.

"That dog is loyal only to you, and I can only have things inside these walls that are loyal to me." Emily knew that this was going to be his response, but it still hurt her the same. She continued to look at his face as he was still holding his hand under her chin.

"I promise, if I am loyal to you, he will be too." She had to convince him to bring Marley to her or let her out where she could get to Marley.

"That's the thing, isn't it, love? How can I be sure you are loyal to me? You broke my nose just three days ago for trying to give you what we both need." He kept staring at her face as if hoping the answer to his question would be there.

"I am so sorry for that husband. I see now that you were just trying to take care of me." She swallowed hard, hoping that it was not visible. She knew what she needed to say, but the words did not come easily. "I am ready to allow you to..." He pulled her face up even more before she could finish.

"You do not allow me; I choose what I do and what you do. Once you understand that, you will be ready. You're almost there, but not yet." He let go of her face and headed up the stairs. She wanted to call after him, to try to find the words to convince him, but she knew that saying anything else would show that she had been faking everything she had said. She watched as he closed the doors, and the darkness crept back in. Emily lay back down in the dirt. Just in case he had some way to watch her, she wanted to look as broken as possible.

Emily lay in the dark and watched as the dim light faded between the cracks, and the room grew even darker. Usually, she would have received another

meal before the sun was down, but nothing came.
Perhaps he thought that if she were to eat less, she
would break faster. This was fine with her. She wasn't
even hungry and ate the food each time it came to
show that she trusted him. Emily allowed herself to
slip back into her thoughts. Before getting too
involved with her thoughts, she heard the doors open
again.

"Get up here."

It was him. Emily pushed herself up from the
floor, grabbing the hidden screwdriver as she stood
and tucking it into her pocket. She then walked very
slowly up the stairs and stepped outside. The sky was
dark and littered with bright stars. He led her into a
circle of people. It had to be everyone who lived here.
Once they were in the center, everyone closed around
them. Emily did not see the women, just a bunch of
men all cheering and laughing. Some were cheering on
the man holding her by the arm. Based on the cheers,
his name was Jeff, and he seemed to love the attention.

"What do you desire of me, husband?" she
asked in a timid voice that she wished she was faking.
She was afraid she might have to do something that
would make her feel dirtier than lying on that dirt
floor, but now she feared that he might want her to do
that in front of all of these men.

"Well, love, you looked so comfortable when I
saw you. You looked like you belonged on your knees,
trying to please me."

Emily knew where he was taking this, and she

had to resist the urge to vomit where she stood. He turned and let go of her arm,

"On your knees."

Emily looked around for a second, but dropped to her knees as she was told. All of the men cheered and clapped for the victory that Jeff was celebrating. She placed her hands on her knees and waited for further instruction from the pervert holding her captive.

"You know what to do, don't be shy."

Emily did not have to look at his face to know that he was grinning from ear to ear. She wiped her hands on her jeans and felt the screwdriver in her pocket. This was the dumbest idea, but it was the only one she had. She sat forward on her knees and looked like she would undo his pants, and the cheers grew even louder. She moved so fast that no one noticed her pull the screwdriver out of her pocket until she had buried it in the flesh below Jeff's zipper.

Jeff howled in pain and yelled, "KILL THE BITCH!!".

Emily had expected this and jumped to her feet as fast as she could. Emily turned to look at the men slowly moving towards her, some with weapons, and the same look in their eyes that Jeff had. Emily searched the circle looking for a weak spot in the ring that would allow her to make a run for it. She noticed that the men broke apart or ran away in one section. She didn't know what they were running from, but whatever it was, it had to be her friend. Emily took off at a run towards that section of men as fast and hard as she could. Just as she reached them, she saw what was causing all of the commotion. Marley was tearing his way through the men, and he was covered in blood. When he saw Emily running towards him, he did a bark that made more men take a step back. Marley then turned and proceeded to lead Emily back through the crowd.

Once they were on the other side of the crowd, Marley ran towards a barrier section, climbed up, and jumped over. Emily attempted to follow his path but could not get the footing that he had. She could hear him barking from the other side and searching for a way out of this place. She then saw Jeff's truck and ran for it. Once inside the cab, she said a quick prayer as she reached for the ignition. She felt hope once again as her hand met the keys. She roared the truck to life and turned it towards the barrier. Once she was facing the correct direction, Emily pressed the accelerator to the floor and watched as the wall broke down around her. Once on the other side, she stopped and waited while Marley jumped in the truck's bed. When he was safe inside the truck, she took off down the road. She saw a few men try to follow her on foot, but she did not see any vehicles following her once they were gone. Once she reached the main road, she pulled over, shut down the engine, and got out of the truck. She couldn't hear the sounds of anyone following her. They were probably too busy trying to help Jeff and what was left of his manhood.

Emily ran to the truck's bed and looked through the various tools. She found a hunting knife that still looked to be decently sharp. She took the knife and jammed it into the tires on the driver's side of the truck. This thing would not be going anywhere for a good while. This made Emily's heart happy. She then looked back and forth, deciding which way to go on this road. She was not awake during this part of the drive; it's what Jeff wanted, so she would not know how to get back to the SUV. It was probably part of his plan to make sure she had no choice but to stay with him.

Marley jumped out of the truck's bed and went down the road to the right. Emily opened her mouth to call him back and decided it was probably best to follow him. He had been right up to this point, and she needed to start trusting him. She turned and followed Marley down the road. The stars above provided just enough light to see where she was going. She clutched the hunting knife as she walked. She was breaking her rule of traveling in the dark; it would be impossible to see zombies coming at her until they were on top of her. After a few hours, the sun started to shine over the treetops. Emily was thankful for the warmth it would bring, and then she noticed something ahead on the road. Emily saw what looked to be an SUV pulled over on the side of the road ahead. She couldn't believe it and ran to close the distance between her and the SUV.

Sure enough, Marley had led her back to their home, the closest thing they had to home in this crazy world. Emily noticed that the back glass on the hatch was open. This must have been how Marley got out. She reached up and tried to close the window, but the latch was broken. The window remained open no matter how hard she tried to shut it. She felt herself becoming frustrated when she suddenly realized how the window was broken. She looked down at Marley, and all she could see was the poor dog slamming into the window until the latch broke and opened. He did all of this just to run to that farm to save her. Emily reached into the hatch and grabbed a water bottle and a worn shirt. She then sat on the bumper and cleaned the blood and dirt out of Marley's fur.

Once he was clean, she used a second bottle of water to clean herself up as best as possible. She then used the shirt to tie the window shut. Then she and Marley loaded up into the front seats and began driving further from the farm. Emily glanced at the gas gauge and was happy to see that she was not even down to three-quarters of a tank. She drove for a few hours until satisfied that she had put enough distance between herself and the farm. She then pulled over and grabbed the map out of the glove box.

It was time to pick a new route far away from this hell on earth. Emily folded the map and began looking at the roads she had not tried yet. She was running out of back roads to try and, maybe, after this, it was a good thing. She needed to start trying main roads, which were both good and bad. It would mean more places to try for supplies, but also more dead between her and those supplies. She was not ready to try a large city, so she picked a relatively populated route and much further to the north than this place. She refolded the map and placed it back in the glove box.

She sat back in her seat and looked over at Marley, sitting calmly in the passenger seat. She couldn't imagine having to go through all of this without him. She had spent months looking for her family because she was afraid and didn't want to do this alone. She couldn't defend herself if she ended up in a tight spot. It never occurred to her that she was never alone and had someone with her who would travel to the ends of the world to fight for her. It was hard to believe that he was almost a year old. She remembered that chubby little puppy she had brought home because her therapist told her she needed someone to help her with her emotional struggles. She reached over and ran her hand through his soft tan fur. She was never alone and never would be as long as he was with her.

Marley wagged his tail and tried to lick her hand while she petted him. She rubbed her hand through his fur several more times, trying to avoid his tongue. Then she turned and put the car back into drive and turned to head towards her new route. She wanted to get as far as possible from that farm just in case they decided to come looking for her. Jeff had said they had been watching her, which meant they probably knew her routine, meaning that she would need to break it for today at least. She would drive until the gas light came on and then stop to rest, even if it meant driving after dark. She would then put the gas cans in and look for gas the next day. She felt confident it would be easy to find on her new route.

The hours went by quickly, and soon the sun was setting. She still had a quarter of a tank of gas before the gas light would come on, so she continued. Marley seemed confused by this and wailed for a few minutes. However, he seemed to accept that she was doing this for a reason. He then went back to staring out of the passenger window. Emily felt her eyes growing heavy as she continued to drive, but she forced herself to keep going. Finally, the little orange gas indicator came on, and Emily found a spot to pull over for the night and shut off the SUV. This part of the routine was normal. She and Marley climbed into the back and then went outside to relieve themselves. Emily carried the hunting knife with her. She would not be caught unprepared again; she had learned the hard way that living people are still left and are more dangerous than the dead.

Soon they were back inside the SUV, and Emily reached into the seatback to find that her cell phone was still there with a fifty percent charge. She looked to ensure the alarm was still set for the morning and then slid it back for safekeeping. Marley curled up next to her legs and looked like he was falling asleep. Though Emily was exhausted, she could not bring herself to sleep. Marley had tried to warn her that something was wrong that night, and until he felt safe enough to sleep, neither could she. After a few minutes, she heard the light snoring and felt herself relax. She rubbed her stomach and, for the first time, talked to the life that was growing there.

"We will be alright, kid." She felt the tears welling up in her eyes. "Just remember that no matter what scary things are, your mom and Marley are unstoppable. We will find a place where you never have to worry about people like that, I promise." Emily finally closed her eyes and fell asleep with her hand still on her stomach.

Chapter 12

Emily continued to drive, marking sections off her map, looking for a safe place to have her child. She had certain areas she refused to go close to because there was no chance that there could be anywhere safe. The areas like St. Louis, Springfield, Rolla, and Kansas City were off the list. It was too dangerous to even go and see if her family was there. The number of people who lived in those cities meant that many corpses would be walking around. She had heard a radio broadcast at the beginning about safe areas being set up in the major cities. But if movies and television had taught her anything, those were long gone, if they ever existed. It would be best for her to try to find somewhere off the beaten path. Maybe a farm with a big fence around it or even an old military base.

She would have to keep looking, and time was not on her side. Her baby's belly seemed to appear out of nowhere, making life on the road harder and harder. She was getting slower and would have been zombie chow on more than one occasion if it wasn't for Marley. He seemed to understand what was happening to her and was even more protective these days. He refused to leave her side even for a moment. It amazed her how he seemed to know things before even she did. It was now late December, and the cold was setting in. The snow had come, but not enough to slow the dead. The only thing that showed was her new size and the cold. In a few months, everything would thaw, and the warmth would return just as her baby would arrive in this world.

Emily was running out of places to search, and the map provided fewer and fewer new roads to try. Ever since Jeff and the farm, she had avoided going south again, but the north led to nothing. Emily looked down at her growing baby bump and rubbed her hand over it. She had to try, and she had to try now. She just had to get past the pervert farm line she had drawn across the whole state, and she would have so many new options, new chances.

Emily weaved her way through the few cars on the highway, some she didn't remember being here when she drove it last. It was probably other living people trying to find what she was looking for. She didn't dare to slow down and look for them, not after the last ones. She would never trust a living soul in this shit storm. It would just be her, Marley, and the baby. It was the only way she could keep them all safe, and that was all she wanted at this point.

It was about noon when she crossed the "line" she had avoided. She was back in the southern half of Missouri, and dread filled her instantly. She remembered a gas station she had cleared a couple of months ago and planned to get to it before nightfall. She could then take care of any stragglers that may have wandered to it and fill up again before continuing to go south. Marley seemed to feel her tension as his head looked to be on a swivel. He was slowly looking around, keeping a watchful eye on everything. Emily reached over and patted him on the head while forcing herself to smile.

"Everything will be okay, boy," she only hoped he believed her. "We won't be here long, and no one will find us."

She could tell he would not be standing down anytime soon, while he appreciated the attention and the conversation. She had to keep going, though. She had left quite a bit of food that she could not fit in the SUV last time she was at this gas station, and she was trying hard to eat more to help the baby. It was probably the reason for the sudden appearance of the baby bump, but it also meant that her supplies went much faster.

The sun was setting as she made it to the gas station, but there was still plenty of time to get what they came for and find a place to park before dark. Emily went through the same routine as always. She honked the horn three times and waited. After about fifteen minutes, there was still nothing moving. Emily breathed a sigh of relief and checked to ensure she had her weapons. The hunting knife had become a staple and was attached to her waist. She grabbed the crowbar and sat for a moment, looking at it. It was the same one her brother gave her the day after the flash. For some reason, she felt like she was invincible with it. Marley nudged her shoulder, ending her trip down memory lane. Emily opened the door and stepped out into the cold air.

She made her way to the gas pump, praying they still worked and had gas. She opened the gas tank and inserted the nozzle. After selecting her grade, she squeezed the handle and heard the sound of the gas filling the tank. She then began to make her way

toward the store. She opened the door and allowed
Marley to walk in first. She followed and closed the
door behind her, locking it so no one could surprise
her. She then slammed her crowbar on a nearby metal
shelf a few times and waited. After a few minutes,
everything remained quiet, and Marley had sat down.
All was safe once again. She quickly set to work
grabbing food and water. She had this down to a
science at this point, though carrying it all back to the
SUV had become increasingly difficult. Instead, she
stacked everything by the door and walked back to the
SUV.

The gas pump was done, and she returned it to
its proper place. She then jumped back in the SUV and
backed it up to the door where Marley was waiting.
Soon they were resupplied and back on the road.

A few miles down the road was a car
dealership. The cars were all just as dirty as hers, and
there were many of them. It was the perfect place to
hide in plain sight. She found a parking spot with
vehicles on either side of her and backed in. It was
time for the nightly routine yet again. She and Marley
ate and drank, and then it was outside to take care of
personal business. Marly made sure that he could see
Emily at all times. Emily spotted an RV on the lot and
could not help herself. She waited until Marley had
finished and made her way to the RV. She carefully
opened the door and made her way inside. Being in
something with an actual bed felt strange, but here she
was. Despite the small kitchen, bedroom towards the
back, and even a living room set, Emily was interested
in only one thing. She opened a small door and saw
that the toilet was still there—the restrooms where she

stopped proved to be more dangerous than doing her business outside.

"Watch the door," she said to Marley as she stepped inside and sat on the toilet.

She felt like an average person for the first time in a while. People always say you don't know what you have until it's gone. For Emily, this included small comforts such as a toilet. She finished and stepped back out of the little door, and looked around. This place could have been a perfect home; it was like a mansion compared to the SUV, but it was not defensible, would do worse on gas, and would not be able to go on some of the roads she traveled looking for a home. Emily felt her eyes grow warm with tears and forced herself to shake them off.

She did not have time to cry over a loss of comfort. She had only a few months left to find a place to have her baby, which would not help. She patted her leg, signaling for Marley to follow, and headed out of the RV. Once outside, she shut the door behind her and began to walk back to their SUV. However, Marley suddenly stopped and began to let out a low growl. Emily froze and gripped her crowbar, ready to swing at anything that moved. The sun was completely down, and the shadows surrounded them. This would have allowed anything or anyone to hide. Emily's eyes still searched, and she watched Marley. If he ran, so would she. He had only done this once before, and she was going to follow his lead this time.

"Well, now, the pretty little bitch has gone and gotten fat."

Emily knew that voice and turned towards the front of the RV just as Jeff stepped out.

"Well, I guess someone got to my prize before me. No matter, a boy will mean another for our group and a girl, well, the boys will have something to look forward to, won't they?"

The smile that sneered across his face reminded Emily of the Grinch in the old Christmas cartoons. Marley lowered his head and positioned himself between Emily and Jeff. The growl he was releasing even scared Emily, but Jeff remained calm.

"You'll be happy to know that your aim was not perfect," Jeff patted his crotch," Everything is working as it should below."

"You son of a bitch," Emily growled, "I wish I had killed you! A mistake I will gladly fix if you don't leave me the fuck alone."

"Spirited, I love how spirited you are. I have not given up on you, love. I have been looking for you since you left."

His voice had become so calm it was unnerving. It sounded like he had just stepped out of a hippy van in a cloud of smoke in the sixties. Then it happened. It was all so fast that Emily didn't have time to think. Marley let out a bark and lunged at Jeff, who barely managed to get out of the way. Emily took off at a dead run towards the SUV, and soon Marley ran beside her. She reached the door and opened it just as Marley bounded inside. She then felt a hand grab her hair and pull sharply. She couldn't see who or what it was and didn't care. Emily swung the crowbar over her head and felt it connect with something solid behind her. A man cried out in pain, but he released her.

She jumped in the SUV, slamming the door shut and locking it. She turned the key in the engine and heard it roar to life. Emily turned on the headlights to see that a group of men had gathered in front of her. Not the best place to stand, considering she wanted them all dead at this point.

"There's nowhere for you to go, love. Come with me, take your punishment, and then you can do your duty and get rewarded."

Jeff seemed to believe he was saving her and giving her a gift. Emily smiled, put the SUV in drive, and gave them all the middle finger as she floored it towards them. They jumped out of the way as she sped out of the parking lot. Emily began to make her way toward the highway to get further south as quickly as possible. After only a few blocks, she hit a roadblock where vehicles blocked the road. She was sure this had not been here when she drove into the town. She quickly turned around but found that the streets were blocked no matter her direction. At some of the roadblocks were men who blew kisses and cat-called her.

Emily was out of roads to try, and every turn she made seemed to be another dead end. She was close to the car dealership when she allowed the SUV to slow to a crawl. Sitting on the hood of a car at the front was Jeff. The meaning of his words was now crystal clear. He had made sure she could not leave. Her hands gripped tight around the steering wheel, and she wanted nothing more than to ram him where he sat. She had to think. She had to find a way out. There was a forest line behind the dealership, but it was questionable if she could fit the SUV through the thick trees, and there was no way she could outrun all of them on foot.

Jeff had now gotten up and was walking towards the SUV. Emily was drawn back to the truck where he had tried to force himself on her. Then, he made her kneel in the dirt while the others cheered him on. She would not go back, and she was done with this shit. Emily drove the SUV back into the dealership and around the back of the building. There was a chain-link fence, but that was nothing for her. She hit the fence as fast as she could, and the metal tore around her. The trees were close together, just as she feared, and they banged against the sides of the SUV. The side mirrors were broken off in a matter of minutes, and she constantly had to turn and hope that she picked the suitable two trees to try to fit between. One mistake would cause her to be on foot, and she needed to be as far away from Jeff and his lackeys as possible.

Emily let off the gas pedal but only slightly. The loud bang of something putting a new dent in the SUV shook her to the core every few seconds. She kept moving on, though, and after what seemed like hours, she found herself on what looked to be an old logging road. Emily stopped and shut off the engine and headlights. She watched the woods line she had emerged from for signs of being followed. She

reached over to the passenger seat and patted Marley
on the head. A good boy would not be enough. He had
warned her again, and they managed to escape because
of him. The two of them sat for hours, long after the
sun had risen, watching, but no one came.

"I'm sorry, boy, but I can't wait anymore."

Emily opened the door and stepped just outside
the door. A pregnant woman getting bounced around
and then waiting for hours to pee was borderline
torture. She didn't wander away from the door but
instead squatted right outside, using the door handle to
steady herself. Once back inside, she rolled down the
passenger window. Seeming to need it just as much as
she, Marley leaped out the window and went onto a
tree. Emily watched him run back towards her and
jump back through the window. Emily rolled up the
window quickly and started the engine. She hadn't
noticed last night, but she had hurt the SUV with her
trek through the woods. She turned up the heat and
grabbed the map. She found the dealership and tried to
trace her way back to a road behind it, but there was
nothing but forest.

"Shit!" Emily yelled as she threw the map onto
the floorboard. "How can I find a place to hide from
assholes like that if I can't even find where I am?"

Emily looked over at Marley, who had a
confused puppy face. It was then that it hit her. She
was on an unmarked road in the middle of nowhere. It
was the perfect location geographically. If she could
find some building out here, everything would be
ideal. She was complaining because she had found

what she was looking for this entire time.

"You just think you're so smart," she said as she tussled Marley's ears. "I don't know how much further this rig will go, but we will take it as far as we can." With that, she put the SUV in drive and started down the road.

Chapter 13

Emily had been driving down the road for only a few minutes. The tree line remained thick on either side, and the sound from the engine was getting louder and louder. She kept pushing the poor SUV forward, though. If the dead were hiding in the trees, this sound would surely draw them out and show her an infestation in the area. She kept darting her eyes back and forth, searching the tree line for any signs of movement. Marley remained vigilant next to her, but he showed no signs of seeing anything either. The further Emily drove, the more apparent it became that this road had not been used in some time. The tracks engraved in the dirt were old and appeared from large machinery, not an ordinary car or truck. The tracks were easy to follow, but she hoped they would not just lead her to an empty field where the trees had been harvested.

Emily did not have long with these thoughts, and all of her attention was drawn back to the engine. It had just made a considerable banging noise, and the smoke poured out from under the hood. She felt it slow to a stop and listened to the hissing sound that had replaced the engine's hum. It was official, the vehicle she and Marley had lived in for months and set up as their home was dead. Not dead like people these days who still walked around, but dead who remained still. Emily leaned back against the seat, felt the tears again, and shook them off before they could start. She knew that it could not last forever. It was why she was looking for a new place to live.

Emily turned and looked at the stuff in the backseat. There was no way she could carry all of it. She would have to take just enough to go on a hike to see if she could find anything. She would return for the rest only if needed. She climbed into the backseat and grabbed the duffel bag. It was the same one she had left her house with months ago. The photo album was the only thing that remained in it at this point. Since she grabbed it, she hadn't been strong enough to look through the pictures. But it was probably the only way her child would ever know her family. She left the photo album at the bottom and put a change of clothes, several water bottles, a small sack of dog food, and food for herself into the bag. She then climbed back up to the front seat to check for anything she may need. Her crowbar and knife would be going, of course. She also grabbed the map from the floorboard. She then saw the cell phone sitting on the dashboard, plugged in.

Emily grabbed the phone and clicked on the screen. It was nine in the morning on December twenty-third. This was about all it was good for anymore. She had not received any new voicemails and had given up trying to make any calls herself. She unlocked the screen and looked through the pictures she had stored. She felt herself wanting to break down, and this was not the time. She turned off the screen and returned the phone to the dashboard. However, before her hand could let go of the phone, Marley made a whining sound. Emily looked over to see that he was staring at her and the phone. He had always seen her with it since they had been on the truck. Perhaps he had come to depend on it as much as she had as a source of comfort. It did have more pictures that she could share with the baby and a camera where she could even take the same. Emily unplugged the phone and slid it into the duffel bag. Emily then removed Joe's lucky bandana from the rearview mirror. She tied it around her head to hold her hair back. It felt like it would allow her to take him with her as she traveled into the unknown.

"Let's go, boy," Emily stated as she climbed out the door.

She waited as Marley jumped out before grabbing the duffel bag and her weapons. With one last look around the truck, she shut the door, confident that she would not be returning to it ever again. Marley was sitting on the dirt, watching her as she turned around. Nothing was nearby that he thought was a danger. Emily patted her leg and turned to continue down the dirt road. The cold air whipped around her, and she could not help but miss the warmth of the SUV. She had on a red puffer jacket she had found a few months back, along with a black cotton hat and scarf. The further she walked, though, it felt like the cold wind was tearing her warm clothing from her piece by piece. She knew she could not do this forever and had to find someplace at least to warm up. She reached into the duffel bag and pulled out the cell phone. She had been walking for nearly two hours, though it felt much longer. She put the cell phone back and forced herself to look up into the cold wind, something she had been avoiding to save the little feeling she had left on her face.

Marley had stopped just a few steps ahead and was staring at something in the distance. Emily knew that if there was a fight ahead, she did not have the strength, which would be the end of the line. She followed Marley's gaze, and a few hundred yards in front of her was something unexplainable. It appeared to be a large silver plate at the end of the road that went further than she could see in either direction. Emily followed the plate up and guessed it had to be at least four stories tall. This thing did not make any sense. Emily thought about turning around and getting away from it as fast as possible. But the wind ripped through her once more. There was no way she would make it back to the truck; even if she did, there was nowhere else for her to go.

Emily looked down to protect her face and began moving towards the giant structure. Marley followed, and they were standing close to the massive structure in a matter of minutes. Emily looked back up to see an opening in the metal plate. It looked as if part of it was swung open like a gate and was open enough to drive a semi through. Emily looked through the opening and saw that the plate was about five feet thick. On the other side, there was a gap, about twenty feet, and then a second plate that was also open. Emily looked down at Marley and hoped the dog genius was ready for what they might find inside. Emily was careful to watch all around her as she made her way through the opening. The area between the plates appeared empty, and she easily made her way to the second opening.

The giant plates seemed to block most of the harsh winter winds, and she moved slightly more easily. Emily peered through the second opening and was taken aback by what she saw inside. It appeared to be a large town. She could see several houses and business-type buildings from where she stood. A couple of buildings were started and not finished, and some looked like they had collapsed. She stood silent, watching for signs of movement or life inside the walls. All the windows were dark, and she saw no one after several minutes. Emily moved inside the plate and saw a staircase leading up to the top of the plate. Perhaps the view from up there would give a better idea of this place. Emily made her way slowly up the staircase, keeping a sideways eye on the town beside her.

She finally reached the top and saw that a platform was built out of the same material to attach the two metal plates. The plates continued up from the platform and were chest high on her. The wind was back to its tricks up here, but was easier to hide from if she stayed close to the plates. Emily pulled her head up over the side and looked into the town. She could not help but gasp at seeing what she saw below. It was much larger than she could have ever expected. She saw hundreds of buildings lining many streets, a two-story building with a red cross on the front that she could only assume was a hospital, and so many other things that just made no sense here. She pulled her gaze away, crossed the platform, and looked back into the world. No matter where she looked, she saw only more forest. Perhaps she would see more once the cold winds died, but today, she felt safe that no dangers were coming for her.

Emily slid back behind the plate and backed out of the wind. She saw that Marley was making his way down the platform, but was now frozen and growling at something. Emily gripped her crowbar and moved to follow him. The closer she got to Marley, a structure came into view in the distance with a light shining through a small window. Emily first thought of the structure's warmth, then glanced down at Marley, reminding her of the danger. There was probably someone in there, someone like Jeff, waiting to make her living hell even worse. Holding up here would make sense with the likely supplies below and a low chance of the dead finding their way up here. This was precisely what she and her child needed. She could not run because there might be someone here. She had to try. Emily tightened her grip on the crowbar and began to close the distance between her and the structure.

Emily moved as quietly and quickly toward the structure as she could and peered through the window. It appeared to be some kind of workstation. A metal desk lined a wall section with a computer and several file folders. There was also a microphone set up at the station and a control panel. There was a computer chair at the desk, but it was empty. Emily moved her eyes to the remaining half of the small structure and saw a table with two chairs and a sofa. In one of the chairs was a man. He was slumped over and appeared to have been this way for some time. He was no longer among the living, but the living dead was still a strong possibility.

Emily made her way towards the door and slowly opened it. The door opened without a sound, and Emily felt the warm air wash over her. She and Marley made their way into the room, working hard to hold down the little bit of food that remained in her stomach. Emily opened the door to allow the smell to escape the small space. The corpse remained in the same position, and Emily looked over him carefully from a distance. He was in a suit, nicer than one she had seen anywhere but in the movies. He was probably in his early fifties, from what she could tell. There were no signs that he was living here, only that this was the last place he was alive. Emily took a few steps closer, making as much noise as possible. The corpse remained still, and the closer she got, the more she felt confident that it would stay this way. The man had a wound on his head, probably inflicted by the handgun on the floor next to him. His brain was already damaged, and that's what the dead needed to be able to walk around.

Emily used her crowbar and poked the corpse a few times to be extra sure, but it remained still. Emily saw that under him was a journal of some sort. She thought of reaching under him for it, but did not quite have the stomach for that. Instead, she turned her attention toward the desk. The computer had a symbol flashing on the screen of an eagle holding a rolled-up scroll tied with an orange bow. Emily had never seen this symbol before, but was sure it was the symbol for whatever this place was. The folders contained documents about the wall itself. Emily did not have time to read them right now, so instead, she set them aside and resolved to read them later.

She then made her way to the control box. There was a standard keypad in its center and several buttons on either side that Emily had no idea what they were. Across the top was an LED screen that flashed "Input Command." Emily looked over the buttons for a few more minutes and gave up trying to figure out what they did by staring at them. She felt exhausted from her cold walk, and the warm air felt as if it were drawing her into a deep sleep. She turned back towards the small sofa and again saw the dead man in the chair. She was not going to rest in the same room as a corpse, and this awful smell. Emily placed her crowbar on the table and grabbed the corpse by the arms. Still not trusting that he was laid to rest, she observed him as she dragged him from his chair out the door. She pulled him a reasonable distance from the structure but could not escape the fear that he could still move at any moment.

Emily pulled her hunting knife from her belt and knelt beside the corpse. She slid the blade down to the hilt between the eyes. Now she felt confident that this thing would not move. Emily placed her hand on his chest to help steady herself as she stood up. Tucked in his jacket was something hard and rectangular. Emily paused to open his jacket and see what lay inside. Inside was a hardcover book, and a quick flip through the pages told her it was a handwritten journal. Emily stood and tucked the book under her arm while she returned the knife to her belt. She then carried the book back inside and was surprised to find that the smell was almost gone. Emily felt she could live with what remained and shut the door behind her. Once the door was closed, she decided to lock it to be safe. The man may look like he ended it himself, but she was not going to risk that there was a crazy person out there waiting for a fresh kill.

Emily then looked at the book once again. It was very thick, and filling every page was writing and a few drawings. However, Emily did not have the mental strength to comprehend any of it right now. She tossed the book on the table and picked her crowbar back up. She set the crowbar on the floor beside the couch and stretched herself. Marley seemed to know that there was not enough room for him to join her, especially in her pregnant state. Instead, he lay down on the floor in front of the door. Emily remembered him lying in the same position after she was bitten. He had kept her safe even though she should not have been able to be saved. Emily reached up and felt the scar on her shoulder, something she had not done in months. She still did not understand how she had survived, but looked down at her baby's belly. She didn't care and had a reason to live now.

The warm air wrapped her in an invisible blanket, and Emily could feel her eyes growing heavier. She tried to resolve that this would only be a short nap. She had so much to do after all. However, before she could even make the promise to herself, her eyes had fully closed, and she drifted off to a night of deep sleep. A sleep where the dead stayed still, her family was around and consistently trying to touch her belly. A life where she carried a picture of an ultrasound around in her purse. It was how she wanted her life to be if the flash had never happened. She even cut Chad out of her dream life. He may be the baby's father, but it was her child and her dream life. This sleep provided the peace Emily needed to rest.

Chapter 14

Emily woke on the small sofa and, for a moment, forgot where she was. The air around her was warm, and the sofa was much more comfortable than the back seat of the SUV. Emily stretched and pulled herself up into a sitting position. She looked around the room and saw that Marley was still sleeping in front of the door. Emily looked over at the table and saw the book she had found on the dead man, but the rumble in her stomach would not allow her to read right now. Emily looked outside to see that the sun was shining brightly. She must have been asleep for quite some time. Emily stood from the couch, and as she did, Marley stretched and stood to join her. Emily reached for the duffel bag she had dropped on the floor, pulled out Marley's food, and poured it onto the floor. Dishes were not a luxury she was able to manage quite yet. Emily pulled out a few granola bars for herself and sat while she and Marley crunched away on their breakfast.

As Emily finished, she grabbed a water bottle and took a few sips. She did not even have to look down to know that Marley was staring at her. He was waiting for his drink. She scanned the room and saw nothing that would work as a water bowl for him. She stood and walked towards the door, carrying the open water bottle. As she opened the door, Marley ran out onto the platform and relieved himself on the wall. When he returned, Emily made sure to have his attention and slowly poured the water from the bottle onto the ground. Marley lapped at the stream, and when the bottle was empty, he licked at the ground a few times. She hoped it was enough to tide him over for a little while. They headed back inside, and she sat at the table with the book she had found the day before.

Marley took his position by the door and watched as Emily picked up the book and looked at the heavy cover. The word "Sanctuary" was written in a fancy-looking script on the cover. She opened the cover and began reading:

Humanity has always been fascinated with the next big thing and immortality. However, this fascination could lead to their very destruction. I was part of a research team studying several different types of genetic projects. I can say that I had no idea how the information we uncovered would be used. When they showed their true intentions, I took as much of my research as I could and ran. I was a man of means, and science was my passion. Now I must use every resource available to me to help ensure that humanity will survive. When they release what we created, it will not do as they hope, and the few people who survive will need a place to be protected. That is what I will build here. The closest town is small, and it is grateful for the income my project will provide. I feel confident I can keep it off the radar of those trying to stop me. Perhaps the name Robert Devow will be known for something other than his part in the attempted extinction of all humanity."

Emily finished the words on the first page and could not hide the shock she felt. The corpse she had drug out of here the night before had played a part in the flash. Emily tightened her grip on the book, resisting the urge to go outside and kick the corpse just for good measure. She forced herself to turn the page and continue reading the journal. The entries seemed to have been made every day for the past two years before the flash. Robert documented everything he had done here, including the buildings he wanted to build, the number of houses, and his plan to run a society inside these walls. He referenced several times that the wall took a year alone to build. According to the journal, Emily was impressed by its height and thickness when she first saw it, but it was in the ground just as deep. As she continued through the end of the journal, she could feel the remorse Robert felt for his part in what happened. He discussed trying to find a vaccine several times against what he had helped to create, but had been unsuccessful so far.

Emily sat for hours, turning the pages and learning more about the man who wrote them. She had only a few pages left when she read.

"It happened early. I should have had one more year, but the damn fools did it early. The light filled the sky, and I watched as several members of my crew felt the effects immediately. I have closed the gates, but very few are still inside, and some of them may show the effects in the next few days. This was not the plan; I don't know what more I can do."

Emily turned the page and continued to read on:

It is over. I cannot make it work. Everyone has died, and I hide on the wall like a coward from their walking corpses. I can't live by myself; I can't send those below to their final rest. I just can't. I am opening the gates. Perhaps someone who can make something of this place will find it. Once the gates are open, I will join the permanently dead. If someone finds this, know that if you wish to continue to fight, Sanctuary is yours. The gate can be closed with the default code. The instructions on the gate and walls can be found under the couch. May God Have Mercy On Our Souls.

Robert Devow"

Emily closed the journal and ran her hands over the lettering on the cover, "Sanctuary." This seemed to be precisely what she was looking for, though, perhaps, Mr. Devow had grander plans for this place than just a single mother and her child living here with the family dog. He had wanted a community to live here. He wanted life to be as close as it was before the flash. However, Mr. Devow could not have known about the evil that would be awoken in the people who continued to live. She would stick to her vow never to let anyone near her child, and this would be their home. Emily made her way to the couch and reached under it. She pulled out several books and stacked them on the table. She looked through each quickly, attempting to figure out how to close the gates. This had to be done first. Those men could still be looking for her. That would be the end if they found this place with open gates.

"Got it!!" She yelled as she looked through a book with a diagram of the metal control panel.

The instructions said to enter the default code and press a button that looked like two rectangles next

166

to each other. In the margin, Emily saw "*1,2,3,4,5,6*"
scribbled in Robert's handwriting. Emily ran to the
panel and located the button in just a few moments.
Emily punched in the code and then pressed what she
assumed to signify the closed gate button and jumped
as the metal grinding sound echoed around her. Emily
ran outside the building and to the edge of the outer
wall. She watched as the door closed, and the sound of
it closing echoed around her.

"Thank you, Robert," she whispered to herself.

She then went to look over the other side of the
wall that looked into the town below. She watched as a
few dead walked into the street and headed towards
the door. Two men were dressed in jeans, white shirts,
and work boots. Emily felt they must have been part of
the crew that helped build this place. The woman was
wearing a pink business outfit and heels. One of the
heels was broken, making her zombie walk even more
awkward.

Emily moved back inside to gather up her knife
and crowbar. She would need to put them to rest and
search the town for others who may be roaming.
Robert had said that very few were inside, but she felt
these three were not the only ones left. Once armed,
she made her way outside and down the metal steps.
The zombies had stopped their movement and were
standing almost still in the street. The woman was at a
reasonable distance from the men, but the men were
reasonably close together. Emily would have to be
smart about this, or they could quickly overtake her.
They may both be dead, but they were larger than she
was, and from experience, she knew they were strong.

She slowly made her way up the main street close to the buildings and was as quiet as possible.

Soon, she was close enough to act. She snuck up behind the first one and buried the knife in his disheveled sandy blonde hair. As the body fell limp on the ground, she took her crowbar in both hands and swung at the second. The first blow made him stagger, but he was still up and was now angry. Emily acted quickly and swung again. The large man fell to the ground but was already trying to get back up. Emily could see the woman further up the street, now beginning to make her way towards her. Emily swung hard and fast at the head on the ground, breathing a sigh of relief at the crunch that signaled that the skull had broken and the body no longer moved.

The woman was still a reasonable distance away as Emily turned and pulled her knife from the first man's skull and placed it back on her belt. She then walked confidently toward the woman, struck her hard with the crowbar, and once the woman was on the ground, she buried her knife in her long brown hair. Emily did not take time to celebrate her victory. She quickly removed the knife and began to scan the area around her. Marley stood quietly by her side, appearing to be doing the same thing. No movement came after several minutes, but Emily did not relax. She needed to get an idea of what she was dealing with here. She and Marley headed back to the metal steps and up to the top of the wall.

The morning was bright and clear, and this would give her the best idea of what she was dealing with. Once at the top, she stood close to the inner edge

and began to walk the wall. She looked as she moved,
noting buildings and landmarks and looking for more
signs of the dead. It took her hours to reach the front
again at her slow pace. This place was much larger
than she had expected and looked designed to grow.
Outside the wall on the west side were shipping
containers and stacks of materials. The materials
seemed to be the same that made the wall. The only
houses that appeared to be complete were those on the
few streets around the main street. The further away
she went, the more there were half-built houses,
frames, or empty spaces. The east side provided
something Emily found most interesting. There was a
farmhouse and several plowed fields with crops
growing. Emily had stood and stared at this for a long
time and could have sworn she heard cows in the barn.
She did not know if barnyard animals could be
affected by the disease, but she would want to check
that out as soon as possible.

Her walk had not allowed her to see any more
dead, but she could only see close to the wall. There
may be some towards the center that would have
escaped her view, but she could certainly say that there
were no big groups. She stood looking down at what
she was calling the main street, to look at the different
buildings. Everything on this street served a purpose.
There were several store-type buildings, and Emily
could see they were fully set up and stocked. There
was a building that looked like a government building
from the outside. A two-story building simply said
"School" in stone above the door. At the end of the
street was a large house. It looked to be modeled after
a colonial-style type of home. It was the only house
directly on the main street. Emily thought it was

probably meant for Robert, the planned leader of this place. If he had stayed there, it might have held more of his notes and information about what was happening.

"Well, boy, I think I picked out our new house. What do you think?"

Emily looked down to see the dog wagging its tail.

"Glad you like it! We should probably head down there. I don't know about you, but I am getting hungry."

With that, Marley let out a little bark and started down the stairs. Emily walked back inside the small control building, just a moment to grab her duffel bag and place the books inside. They walked up the main street slowly, checking for any signs of movement. As Emily looked in the storefronts and restaurant windows, she could see that everything was stocked on the shelves. The town looked like everyone had just disappeared.

Everything was clean and tidy, and there were no signs of any fights or people being eaten. She was sure that if she went inside, everything probably had a nice layer of dust, but from the outside, it looked perfect. Emily heard a dragging noise from the side yard as they approached the house. She snapped her fingers, signaling for Marley to stop, and they waited. After a few minutes, a medium build man wearing jeans and a plaid shirt walked into the front yard. Emily would have thought he was still alive if not for his slow walk and milky white eyes. His clothes were clean, and he looked to have just been working in the yard when she walked up. Emily knew that no matter how nice he looked, he still wanted to eat them. She motioned for Marley, who ran towards the man, staying just out of his reach, and got him to turn around. Emily then used her knife to put him to his final rest. She pulled the knife back out and turned back towards the front door.

She knew she would have to clear the house before they would be safe. The big wooden door made Emily feel small as she stood in front of it. She grabbed the handle and clicked it, and pushed it open slowly. Once inside, she closed the door with a loud thud and turned to face the large entryway. This was possibly the most beautiful house she had ever seen. However, she did not have time to admire all the details until she was sure she was alone.

"Hello! Anyone living or dead in here!"

Emily smiled to herself. She felt confident that she had covered everything. After several minutes, she heard and saw nothing. It made sense. If this were Robert's house, he would have been locked up in it until he went to the wall. To be sure, she called out one more time,

"Hello! If you're living, I don't want to hurt you, and if you're dead, well, I do."

She waited several minutes and then began making her way into the house. A cherry wood floor spreads through the entryway and into the living room.

Emily could not help but feel she was in a place way above her means. She started to think of how much the property taxes alone would be and then laughed at herself. If the tax collector could make it through the zombies, find her, and fly over the wall, she would just let them have the house.

Emily looked around the living room. A cream-colored sofa and armchairs were positioned around a large television. Even Robert could not imagine life without television, not that there would be many new shows now that the world had ended. Emily noticed that the walls next to the TV had small brass handles. She gripped the handle on the right side and slid the door open. Movies and television series lined the shelves. Emily moved to the other door and found the same there as well. There must have been thousands. Robert had planned on how to fill his television addiction. Emily closed the doors and turned back to the room. How had he planned to watch them after the flash? He must have known that the power would shut off. Emily walked over to a lamp that sat on a small table and turned the power knob. She nearly jumped out of her skin as the bulb came to life, and the glow of the light filled the room.

Emily thought electricity was something she would have to tell her child about, like an old fairy tale, but it was real. How she did not know, but that was just something she would have to discover about this place as she went. Emily headed to the left side of the room and opened a set of French doors. She saw what looked like shelves lining the walls through the glass. Once the doors were open and the light turned on, Emily felt a gasp escape her lips. The walls were lined with shelves, floor to ceiling filled with books. In the center of the room was a tidy desk, and to the right was a rack of rolled-up papers that looked like maps of some kind. Emily turned off the light and closed the doors. There was a lot more house to search before she began researching things. The next door opened up into a large bathroom. As soon as she looked at the toilet, Emily felt a familiar pressure.

"Well, better now than later. You coming in, or do you think I can handle this on my own?" Emily turned to see Marley lying on the floor behind her. "Alone it is then," she laughed as she walked in and closed the door behind her.

Why she closed it, she did not know. It's not like anyone else was here or would see her. It just seemed like the thing to do. Emily resolved that this was something she would have to work on, her need to close doors when it wasn't necessary. Closing the door was what had gotten her bitten on day one, and she was closing the door when those perverts found her again. She unbuttoned her overly tight jeans and fought to get them low enough so she could pee. Soon, that struggle was over, and Emily could use the toilet. Once she finished, the joy she felt at seeing a fresh roll of toilet paper waiting to be used was more than could be described. After struggling for a few minutes to get back into her pants, she turned back to the toilet.

"The power works, but I wonder does the..."

Emily pressed down the lever and watched as the water swirled and emptied, and the toilet began to refill. She turned back, walked to the sink, and turned on the hot water. After just a few moments, she watched as the water began to steam as it exited the faucet.

Marley would surely bark if there was any trouble outside, and she needed this. Emily turned on the cold water just a little, and once the temperature was just right, she washed her hands and arms. Once she rinsed off the soap, she splashed the warm water on her face several times. She had tried to remain clean these past several months, but it was not easy. She also washed her face with hand soap, and when she finished, she used the hand towel to dry herself. Emily avoided looking at herself in the mirror just yet. She wasn't ready to see what this world had done to her, and she had work to do still. She opened the door, and Marley stood and stretched.

Emily made her way to the next door and found a large dining room. The table was cherry wood, just like the floor, and was large enough to seat twenty people. Emily stood looking and imagined a fancy dinner party happening during colonial times. Maybe she and the baby would make that a game and have a fancy dinner party monthly. They could invite eighteen high-class teddy bears to join them. Emily turned and saw a door on the right side of the room and walked to open it. Much as she expected, the kitchen was on the other side. Emily made her way through the large room, finding that the cabinets were fully stocked, the refrigerator was bare of food, but the freezer was fully stocked with snack foods. She felt her stomach protest as she closed the door and promised she would return later.

There were two more doors in this room. One led back to the backyard, but the other was tucked away in the corner of the room. Emily slowly opened the door and discovered a staircase on the other side.

"It must be a basement or a cellar of some kind," Emily muttered as she flipped on the light and made her way down the stairs.

Once down there, Emily found herself in a large open room with a concrete floor. There were two coffin-style deep freezers and shelves with more boxes of canned food. Emily opened the deep freezers to see that they were filled with various types of meat. Her mouth began to water at the thought of all the meals she could make in that large kitchen. As she shut the door, it took all her mental will to push away the thought of food. She turned and saw a washer and dryer on the wall next to the staircase. The smell of fresh laundry flooded her senses. It was another thing that she thought was gone forever.

Emily made her way up the staircase and closed the door after shutting off the light. Once back in the main house, she looked up the stairs on the far side of the living room. The only place left to go is up. She had seen the back door in the kitchen but had decided against going out. Emily slowly climbed the staircase with Marley behind her. Each step hurt as Emily became aware of how tired and sore her body was. She had never had time to realize it before, but inside these walls, this house, she felt safe enough to let herself feel again. Emily found the master bedroom with a king-sized bed. There was a dresser in the room and, to the left, a master bathroom. Emily moved more quickly as she cleared the room and moved on to the next. There were three more bedrooms up here. All but one had a full-sized bed, a dresser, and a nightstand. The beds were not made, and the mattresses were bare on each. The room that was not furnished was directly next to the master bedroom. Emily resolved that it was always meant to be her house, and that room was meant to be the nursery.

She and Marley were alone in the house and probably in the town. Emily doubted that they still required oxygen if there was anyone else here. She felt her stomach rumble again and began to descend the stairs. Once in the kitchen, she opened the freezer in the refrigerator and grabbed a bag of pizza rolls. Hopefully, these were safe for Marley to eat. She would have to check the stores in town for dog food, and all of the meat was frozen downstairs. She heated fifteen on a plate in the microwave and then put them into a bowl. She put fifteen more on a plate and began to heat them for herself. While she waited, she filled a second bowl with water and placed both on the floor for Marley. She then filled herself a cup of water, which she set on the kitchen island just as the microwave beeped, signaling her lunch was ready. For several minutes, all that could be heard in the kitchen was the sound of eating. This was the best either of them had been able to eat in months, and they were enjoying it. Once they finished, Emily washed their dishes in the sink and placed them in the strainer to dry. She was going to live here, so she needed to keep it clean.

As Emily turned off the hot water, she realized how much she wanted to go upstairs and take a hot shower. However, she had no clothes to change into, still needed dog food, and doubted Robert had any soaps for women. If she was going to do this, she would do it right. She also needed to check out that barn she had seen earlier. If there were live farm animals there, she would need to take care of them moving forward to ensure that the food never ran out. She also didn't know much about growing crops, but she needed to see what was down there to learn about it. Emily returned to the entryway and grabbed her duffel bag from the floor where she had dropped it. She walked back to the living room and emptied it onto the table. She had a change of clothes, but they were just as ill-fitting as what she was wearing and were slightly less dirty. She put everything back in the bag and zipped it closed.

"Well, boy, it's time to go shopping." With that, she headed back towards the entryway, armed with her knife and crowbar, and stepped back out into the ghost town.

Chapter 15

Emily made her way to the east of the town first. She had decided to check out the farm before shopping because she did not want to carry all the stuff back and forth. She had only made it a few blocks when she saw something moving to her left. She and Marley must have seen it simultaneously because they both stopped. Emily watched as another man dressed in construction clothes walked toward them. Much like the one in the yard, she would not have known he was dead without his eyes and walking. He was very clean and looked like he had just died, maybe a day or two ago. The zombie movies always seem to have a certain amount of rot and decay, but these folks did not, just the eyes. Emily dropped the empty bag on the ground and moved quickly to handle their unwanted friend. She had just raised her knife to strike when Marley began to bark. He did it so rarely that it scared her, but she still managed to hit the brain. She removed the knife quickly and watched as out of a building, three more men wandered out onto the street.

"No big deal," Emily thought to herself, "Just move around, and with Marley's help, we can split them up, and it will be easy pickings."

Emily began to move and distance herself from Marley when a fourth figure emerged from the building. It was not a construction worker, and Emily felt her heartbreak as she looked at her. The girl could not be more than five or six years old. She was wearing a blue dress, and her red hair was pulled back in a ponytail. As the dead moved, the girl seemed to stick close to the one wearing a St. Louis Cardinals baseball cap. Emily could not help but suspect that if she removed that hat, she would find the man had a head full of red hair. Is it possible that he would still protect her even though they were dead, and she knew he would? Emily watched the little girl so closely that she did not realize how close the other two men had gotten to her until one reached out to grab her. Due to her size, she was not as agile as she used to be and narrowly managed to escape his grasp. When she moved, he fell forward, and she scrambled to sink the knife into his skull. Without time to breathe, she jumped back to her feet and removed the blade. The next one was already right on top of her. She could hear Marley barking and only prayed that father and daughter were following him.

Emily could not move quickly this time, and the second man grabbed her shoulders, and they both fell to the ground. Emily felt the knife fall from her hand as she hit. The man fell on top of her. Though their flesh looked to be well preserved, the smell was overpowering. He bit at her, and she was using all of her strength just to keep him from getting the meal he so badly wanted. Emily feared that if she moved one of her hands to look for the knife, he would overpower her, and it would be over. Emily could still hear Marley barking and dared not call to him. He may have been able to knock this thing off of her, but that would lead the other two straight towards her before she was ready. Emily's mind scrambled for what to do. The last time she had been this close to a zombie, it had taken a nice bite into her shoulder. That's when she remembered the bite. She had not turned. It had only knocked her out for a few hours. She would have to move fast and not let him take a big bite.

Emily craned her neck and saw the knife right next to her. If she were fast enough, she might even be able to stab him before he got a taste. Emily looked up into the man's milky white eyes and counted three.

"One…Two…. Three!"

Emily dropped her right hand and felt the handle of the blade. She felt her left arm giving, and the man's mouth dropped towards her chest. She raised her hand, and just as she felt the man's teeth on her flesh, she stabbed him in the skull. The man's body fell limp on top of her, and Emily struggled to get him off. Soon she was back on her feet and saw Marley a short way up the road. The father and daughter had their backs turned toward her, and she had to act fast. She ran up the road, killed the father first, and then ran a short way back as the daughter turned towards her.

Emily did not have time to feel the emotions she had let paralyze her before, as she couldn't have much time left before she passed out. She ran towards the child and, in one motion, put her body to rest. Emily collapsed on the pavement next to the girl's body and took several deep breaths. Marley came and sat next to her, looking exhausted. Emily ran her hand over the dog's head,

"Good boy," she breathed.

Emily then looked down at her shirt. She could see where the zombie had bitten through the cloth. It was so thin and worn that it wouldn't have taken much, but her soft pink flesh was under the teares in the fabric. Emily reached up and touched where he had bitten her. There were teeth impressions on her skin, but no blood. She had managed to avoid him breaking the skin and testing the fact that she was immune.

"That was close," Emily told Marley, and she lowered her hands. "We'd better get moving to the farm. I want to be back at the house before it gets dark."

Marley seemed to agree and stood up, looking ready to go. Emily couldn't help but groan as she stood up from the ground. The farm still had to be checked out, and they were losing time. They continued to make their way up the road and soon found themselves at the farm. There was a fence around, and some of the fields were bare. Emily made her way towards the barn, noticing only a few things that appeared alive. One was carrots, and the other she thought was maybe cabbage. She hoped some books on crops back in the library could help her determine what was growing and whether it was harvestable. As she approached the barn, she paused outside the door and listened. The barn was huge. She had seen that from the wall, but the sounds inside were terrific. She knew she could hear a horse, maybe two, cows, and sheep. There were other noises, but she was unsure what they might be; they did not sound like zombies.

Emily opened the door, stepped inside, and felt like a small child seeing animals for the first time. A few horses were in the barn, a couple of sheep, and three cows. They all looked pretty healthy to her, and she noticed that the back of the barn was open. These guys must have been going out and grazing since everyone here died and kept themselves healthy enough. There may be more out in the fields that have not wandered here yet. Emily knew it had been months since any of them had seen a live person and was surprised as she slowly approached one of the still horses and allowed her to pet it. Emily then looked around and saw that the barn was a mess. The animals did not clean up after themselves.

"Alone in a manger on Christmas Eve, this has to be a good sign, right? A sign that something good will happen and change the world forever." Emily ran her hand over her stomach. "No pressure though, little one, just saying."

Emily looked around at her new animal friends and could not help but wonder if she would ever see an actual person again. Emily pushed the thought from her mind and headed back outside. Once outside, she began to explore a little bit more. She found a storage building overflowing with bags of grain and oats, and another filled to the ceiling with canning materials. Emily had visited a petting zoo or two when she was younger and tried to have a few vegetable gardens. However, she had no idea how to run a farm or care for the animals. Emily shrugged and decided she would just have to learn as she went. Perhaps there were some notes in the journal or some books in the library on farm life that would help her.

Emily headed for the farmhouse next. It was a typical farmhouse, as if the owners had just stepped out. Emily thought for a moment that it might be best for her to take this house instead of the one on the main street. However, after several moments, she decided it would not be the best for her. She would have to journey here every day to take care of things, but the house on the main street gave her a clear view of the gate and was close to all the supplies. At least for now, this was not the best place for her to live. Emily closed the door behind her and started to make her way back to her new home.

Emily saw the bodies of the zombies she had killed on her way back. The men did not bother her; it was just another body, but the little girl brought tears to her eyes. It was the first child she had seen all this time, and it made her sick to her stomach to see that little girl lying there with a knife wound to the head. Emily forced herself to move on without stopping and turned her mind to more practical things. She would need to figure out what to do with these bodies. She did not have the strength to dig a grave for each of them, but she could not leave them where they were. The smell would become overwhelming, and she didn't want her baby growing up in a place where dead bodies were left to rot on the streets. The more she thought about it, a fire would be her only option. She could move the bodies back to one of the undeveloped places and burn them there.

Emily had finalized her decision to burn the bodies just as she reached the main street. It was pretty late in the afternoon, and she had only a few hours before the sun would begin to set. She didn't need food for herself. There was

plenty back in the house. She did need dog
food, though, and she felt she could not wait.
She opened the door to what looked like a
market and held the door open as Marley
followed. She scanned the area around her and
waited a few moments. When she saw nothing
move, she cried out, "Hello!" and waited a few
more minutes. Silence other than the hum of the
refrigerated units. Emily saw that there were
shopping carts just inside and pulled one out of
the row. This would make things much easier
on her already exhausted body. Emily began to
make her way through the aisles, in awe of the
amount of dry packaged food she saw. The
refrigerated units were all empty except for the
freezers, full of different kinds of meat. Emily
remembered that everything back at the house
was frozen, and it would take a while to thaw.
She opened a freezer and pulled out a small
package labeled *GROUND BEEF*, and placed it
in the cart so it could thaw while she did all of
her shopping.

Emily made her way through the aisles and
picked up everything she would need to make herself a
pasta dinner. She had not taken the time at the house to
take inventory of the food to know what she could and
could not make. Once she had her meal in the cart,
Emily located the pet section and was thrilled to see
bags of dog food lining the shelf. She grabbed a
yellow bag that said it was steak flavored and put it
into the cart. She also grabbed a couple of dog bowls,

a new collar for Marley, and dog shampoo. Emily continued to wander the store until she found shampoo, conditioner, body wash, deodorant, and a hairbrush for herself. She grabbed a package of razors but knew she did not have the strength to tackle that mess tonight. Once she was done, she made her way to the front of the store. For the first time, Emily felt terrible pushing the cart outside without paying. She had been scavenging for months with no feeling and could not explain why she felt it now.

There was no time for this now. Emily pushed her cart up the main street to a clothing store she had seen on her way in. She opened the door, pushed her cart inside, and repeated her tried and true process.

"Hello!" she yelled into the store.

After several minutes, there was nothing. Emily left her cart by the door and started to make her way through the racks. She knew what size she was before the flash, but the bump she was now sporting changed all that. This was not a maternity store, and after trying on several pairs of jeans, Emily was beginning to lose hope. She would need something to hold up to the work she had to do on the farm and in the town. The skirts and stretch pants here were just not going to cut it. Emily continued to make her way through the store when she spotted overalls. She had not worn them since she was a kid, but right now, they were the most beautiful piece of clothing she had ever seen.

Emily walked over to the rack and tried on a couple of pairs until she found her size, and then grabbed all four pairs they had in that size. As she walked her find back to the cart, she could not help but laugh that she would learn how to work on the farm, and the first piece of clothing she got was overalls. Emily worked her way through the store and found several shirts that fit and would work nicely with her new pants, along with bras, underwear, and socks. She was disappointed that this store did not have shoes, but she was sure she had time to find a store that did before dark. Emily grabbed her filling cart and headed back outside. It didn't take her long to find a shoe store where she got a pair of tennis shoes and work boots.

As she returned to the house, she felt proud of herself for everything she had found that day. Tomorrow was Christmas, and she had received all of her gifts tonight. Emily looked in the store windows as she walked and noticed a store called "Baby." The sun would be setting soon, and she did not have time to explore, but she surely had time to look through the window. Inside was every baby thing a child could need and more. There were cribs, dressers, mobiles, clothes, toys, and many other things. Emily felt overwhelmed. She would find everything she needed for the nursery in this store. It was hard for Emily to pull herself away from the baby things, but she did and pushed her cart the rest of the way home.

She didn't want to mess up the floor inside the house, so she left the cart outside the door and set everything in the entryway. The meat was still partially frozen, so once everything was inside, Emily took it straight to the kitchen and put it in warm water to finish defrosting. She then brought the rest of the groceries to the kitchen, set them on the counter, set up the dog bowls, and put the dog food in the pantry. She took the new collar and dog shampoo into the downstairs bathroom and set them in the tub. Marley was going to look like a different dog when she was done. She then took her clothes and personal supplies up to the master bedroom. She set the private supplies in the bathroom and then opened the closet. Robert's clothes were still hung here, catching her a little off guard. She quickly recovered, removed them from the hangers, and set them in one of the spare bedrooms. She opened the dresser drawers and did the same. She then put away the few clothes she now had.

She went into the bathroom and found the towels in the linen cabinet. Later, she set a couple on the sink for herself and took one back to the downstairs bathroom. The house was becoming darker as the sun began to set, and the light that the one lamp provided proved insufficient. Emily did not want to draw attention, though, if any dead were still roaming the town. She set to work on closing the heavy curtains throughout the house. Once they were all closed, she set to work, turning on the living room lights. She then went into the bathroom and called for Marley. He came without hesitation, bounding into the room.

He had always hated baths, but even he was excited for one at this point. Once he was in the tub, she began to scrub. It took half an hour to get him clean, but soon he was. She dried him down, placed his new collar on him, and watched as he ran out of the bathroom. She quickly cleaned the tub and floor and took the towel to the kitchen. She opened the basement door and looked down. She resolved to get a basket to put down at the base of the steps. For now, she tossed the towel down and allowed it to land on the floor.

She then looked at the clock in the kitchen, which showed it was six-thirty. There was no time for her to shower yet. They needed to eat. She checked the meat and was relieved to see that it was thawed. She set to work on dinner and could hear Marley snoring in the living room. Once it was done, she served it on the kitchen island and filled Marley's bowls with food and water. At the sound of the food, he was awake and running into the room. They both ate their meals, and everything felt completely normal for the first time since the flash. Once they had finished eating, Emily put away the dishes from lunch and washed the dinner dishes, leaving them in the strainer once again to dry. She then headed out of the kitchen, turning off the light. She considered maybe watching a movie, but decided to head upstairs instead. She turned off all the lights except the two table lamps in case she needed to come back down.

Once upstairs, Marley jumped right up on the bed and got comfortable. Emily headed into the bathroom and began to peel off her clothing, hanging Joe's lucky bandana on the hook in the bathroom. When trying on pants at the store, she noticed how tight her jeans were, but pulling them off again provided a fantastic sense of relief. Emily continued to remove her clothes and then turned on the shower.

While she waited for the shower to get hot, she looked down at her stomach. The indent marks from the tight jeans shone brightly on her waistline. She could not help but feel guilty about putting that much pressure on the baby. She stepped under the warm water and stood there as it washed over her. She did not dare look down at her feet because she knew the water would be disgusting. She wanted to stand here for a few minutes and enjoy this feeling. She decided to start with her hair. She lathered up the rich shampoo, set it for a few minutes, and then rinsed. She knew she needed to rinse and repeat for as long as it had been since she washed her hair. She lathered her hair once more and rinsed. She then grabbed the conditioner and, despite the warm water, could not help but feel a shiver down her spine, thinking of how much her hair was going to have to soak this up. Emily allowed the conditioner to stay in her hair while she began scrubbing her body. Halfway through the scrubbing process, she felt her body relaxing and energy-draining. The razors would have to wait for another day. Soon she was clean and rinsed, wrapping herself in a towel.

She looked up at the fogged mirror in front of her, feeling the fuzzy bathmat under her feet. She had avoided looking at herself for months out of fear. She remembered that woman in the bathroom mirror at her house, and she knew that woman would not be in this one. She reached up and wiped away the fog with her hand. When she finished, she stood staring at the stranger who stared back at her for a long time. Her face was deathly thin, and her cheekbones looked as if they could tear through her skin at any moment. Her shoulders looked like the skin was draped over the bones, with nothing between them. Her belly was more prominent, but everything else looked like she should have been among the dead. She leaned forward and ran her hand over the scar on her shoulder. Even

now, she could tell it was a bite mark. She forced
herself to keep moving. She unwrapped her hair from
the towel and brushed it. Once done, she put the
clothes in an empty hamper by the door and walked
into the bedroom. She put on a fresh pair of underwear
and a T-shirt.

She looked back at Marley, who was still
awake, waiting for her. She closed the bedroom door
and locked it. Though she was sure there was no one
alive here and that the dead could not open doors, she
was not going to risk it just yet. She turned off the
lights and crawled into the bed next to Marley. She
had forgotten how comfortable beds were. It was
amazing how this mattress seemed to absorb her;
before she knew it, she was asleep.

Chapter 16

Emily woke the following day, forgetting everything that had happened and thinking she was back in her bed. As she opened her eyes and looked around, the truth flooded back. Marley was still asleep; if his snore had not drawn the dead in, nothing would. Emily reached over and petted him on the head, causing him to wake. He jumped down, stretched, and walked towards the door. Emily suddenly remembered that she had not let him out the night before.

"I'm so sorry. You probably feel like you're about to burst."

Emily threw back the blankets and stepped out onto the cool floor.

"Just give me thirty seconds."

Emily made her way to the bathroom and barely made it herself. Once she finished, she considered getting dressed for the day, but Marley's dance by the door told her he could not wait any longer. She unlocked the door and followed Marley as he ran down the stairs. He ran for the front door, and she followed, but instead of opening the door, she grabbed her crowbar and began to walk to the kitchen. Marley didn't hesitate and followed her to the back door. Emily unlocked and opened the door, allowing the sunlight to pour through it, blinding her for a moment until her eyes adjusted. Marley seemed to have no problems as he bounded out the door immediately. Emily waited for her eyes to adjust and then scanned the backyard. It had a privacy fence, and the only gate was still closed. The yard was almost as big as the house and had several what looked to be fruit trees growing in it.

Emily left the door open and turned back to the kitchen. The clock on the wall said it was seven-thirty. The day had just begun. Emily filled Marley's food and water bowls and then made herself some toast. As she waited for the toast to cook, she remembered the girl she had seen in the mirror. That girl needed more than just toast for breakfast. She needed food. Emily looked through the cabinets and found a box of flavored oatmeal packets. She had just chosen a strawberry packet when Marley came back through the door. Emily set the packet on the counter and closed the door. The toast popped out of the toaster, and Emily set it on a plate. She then grabbed a bowl, mixed the oatmeal and water according to the instructions, and put it in the microwave. She grabbed a piece of toast and began to eat while she waited for the time to run in the microwave. Behind her, she could hear that Marley was already enjoying his breakfast.

Emily had just finished her second piece of toast as the microwave timer went off. She opened the door and carefully grabbed the hot bowl. She set it down at the table and then turned to grab a spoon and close the microwave. Sitting back down, she could still hear Marley chomping down on his breakfast. Emily poked the oatmeal for a few minutes. She already felt so full from the toast. The image of herself in the mirror came back to her mind. Emily forced herself to take a bite and was surprised that she felt the hunger come over her. Perhaps she had just trained her body not to hunger after a small meal, but one bite of that oatmeal made her feel ravenous. She repeatedly reminded herself to slow down as she devoured the oatmeal.

The bowl was soon empty, and Emily could not help but feel happy about the feeling of a warm meal filling her belly again. She had enjoyed dinner the night before but had not allowed herself to overindulge. Most of it was stored in the refrigerator for dinner tonight. Just the thought of it made her mouth start to water again. Emily feared that overeating too soon, though, would make her sick. Instead, she washed her bowl and spoon and put them in the strainer to dry. Marley had also finished his breakfast and stood watching her while she did the dishes.

It was now eight, and Emily had to think about how she would spend her day. Her routine had been the same for months, but things would need to change now that she was here. She had reached her goal and found a place where her child could be safe. But now, she had to find a way to ensure that they were the only ones here, dead or alive, find out what supplies they had or didn't have, and ensure that the food here would not run out. Emily could not help but feel overwhelmed by the changes, but that feeling quickly changed to excitement and determination. If only Chad could see her now, the mayor of a town. An empty town, sure, but still the mayor. Emily laughed to herself as the thought went through her mind.

Emily looked down to remember she was still dressed in only the shirt she had slept in the night before. She returned upstairs and put on one of her new outfits. She did not have to wince in pain to get the pants on. This was enough to make her life complete. Once dressed, Emily made her way to the study and was happy to find notebooks in one of the drawers and pens in another. She had kept track of everything at work with lists and felt this was a list-worthy situation. Emily started by writing everything she needed to get done in the long term. Some of these things included setting up a nursery, while others covered the town and learning how to farm. Emily turned the pages as things kept coming to mind. By the time she was done, she had three pages of things she had needed to do before the baby got here. Emily sat back and reviewed the list again, and felt herself trying to become overwhelmed again. She glanced at the clock on the wall to see that she had been there for two hours.

Emily forced herself to push back the negative feelings and rip her list out of the notebook. She had only a few months to get this done, and feeling sorry for herself wasn't going to help. She would not get anything outside done today. She was going to take her Christmas and make a plan. Emily then set to work making herself a daily schedule for the next week. She would follow it as much as possible and make adjustments the next week as needed. She knew she would need to check on the farm every day, and she wanted to get the nursery set up before she couldn't move the big items up the stairs. It would already be a challenge. She decided she would try to research hunting and farming, making looking after the farm productive. Emily decided it would be after lunch that she would walk the town and look for any death that may be wandering.

Once she had finished her schedule for the next week, she looked at the clock to see that it was noon on Christmas. She felt excited like a kid as she went to the kitchen to reheat the pasta from the previous night. The microwave seemed to be moving extra slowly as she watched the seconds tick off one at a time. She quickly opened the door to retrieve her meal and began eating it as soon as possible. She again tried to remind herself to slow down, but it was hard to slow down after breaking the mental block of not feeling hungry when she was starving. Soon the leftovers were gone, and Emily sat enjoying the warm, full feeling in her belly.

She finally forced herself to stand, wash her dishes, and add them to the strainer next to the oatmeal bowl and spoon. Emily then looked through the cabinets to see what she would like to have for dinner that night. She should have picked something that morning, as all the meat was frozen downstairs, but she would need to be careful with her decision now. She had forgotten how many meals there were when you did not have to eat out of a can and could cook. The kitchen was fully stocked; she decided on sloppy joes after several minutes. Not a gourmet meal, but to her it sounded like a five-star dish. She headed to the basement, being sure to pick up the towel she had thrown down the night before and add it to the washer, and found a package of ground meat. She also grabbed a package labeled chicken and a loaf of frozen bread. Emily carried her finds upstairs and could not help but feel excited.

The chicken would be for tomorrow, so she slid it into the refrigerator. She then placed the ground meat into the sink to thaw and the bread on the counter. She hoped that both would be ready in time for dinner. There were several bags of chips in the cabinets that she would eat with her sandwiches. She was already following the list. Meal planning for the next day was one of the things on her schedule. Emily then made her way upstairs and opened the door to the room next to hers. The room was empty except for a twin-sized bed that was not made and a small dresser. This would be the one she would use for the nursery. She was sure the baby would share her room for a while, but she still wanted this space to be set up. Emily decided that she would leave the bed; her child would need it eventually, and she would push it against the far wall. The room was reasonably clean, and only a thin layer of dust could be seen on the dresser. It would not take her long to have it ready for the baby stuff to be moved in. Emily headed back downstairs and went to the study. Marley lay on the floor here, sure that she would be returning.

Emily looked through the bookshelves to see if maybe anything she needed was in there. Robert had collected many books here, both fiction and non-fiction. As she looked through the spines, she noticed a few that she would like to read, but forced herself to move on. As she made her way through the shelves, Emily saw that Robert had wanted to educate himself on everything he might need to run the town. In addition to a fantastic collection of fictional works, he also had books on physiology, medicine, construction, agriculture, and many other subjects. Emily found that one of the bookcases was filled with journals and books. The books all appeared to be written by Robert. She would need to add these to her reading list as they may have more information to help her run the town or perhaps protect her child.

Emily felt confident that she had enough reference material to start learning to take care of the farm and that she would not need to look for more in the town just yet. Emily looked out the study window and could see the fruit trees in the backyard, and Emily felt her mouth water at the thought of an apple. It was, of course, too late in the season for there to be any fruit on the trees, but Emily remembered seeing apple sauce in the kitchen. She turned to the shelves and grabbed one of the books on agriculture. This one seemed to cover farmyard animals. Emily walked to the living room, placed the book on the table, and retrieved her snack from the kitchen. When she returned, she found that Marley had changed positions and was lying on the couch. Emily giggled as she sat down on the spot he had left open for her.

Emily ate her applesauce in silence, and soon the tiny cup was empty. She set it on the end table and began to read her book. She slowly turned the pages, trying to absorb every detail of the words. There were many things to remember about milking cows, but the one fact that caught her eye was that cows could go dry if not milked regularly. The text said that there is a chance that if the cow gives birth, the milk can return, or even stimulating the udder can help. However, sometimes there is just no getting it back. She had been looking forward to fresh milk for her and her child, but she would just have to see what happened. Emily sat for hours reading up on different farm animals. Some sections she chose to skip as they pertained to animals that she did not see that day. If she saw some later, she would surely return to it.

As Emily finished the book, she felt that her brain was heavy with all the new information and that she could at least do primary care for the animals. She had seen a wagon at the farm and hoped to learn how to attach the horses to pull it, but it was not covered in this book. For now, at least, she would be walking and carrying everything on her own. She considered going to see if she could find a book that may have the information, but a glance at the clock showed that it was already after five. Emily stood from the couch, carried her book back to the study, and placed it on the shelf. She then grabbed her cup and spoon from the side table and headed into the kitchen. Sensing dinner time, Marley jumped down from the couch and followed her. Emily grabbed the meat from the sink and was excited to find it defrosted enough to cook.

Emily cooked her meal and refilled Marley's food and water bowls before eating. She couldn't help but laugh that the two of them might get fat now that they could eat. Emily ate her sloppy joes and chips more slowly than she had her breakfast or lunch. The starvation phase of her eating seemed to be over, and now she could enjoy her meals. Once she could not eat another bite, Emily cleaned up her dinner dishes and added them to the strainer. She resolved to return here later and put them away so she could have a fresh start tomorrow. It was now seven, but Emily did not feel nearly ready for bed just yet. Instead, she made her way back to the living room and began to look at the DVD collection. The amount Robert had collected was overwhelming. Much like his books, there were many fiction and non-fiction choices to choose from in the collection.

Emily looked at each title carefully and considered watching documentaries about farm life, but decided that she needed to relax if she could remember how. She stopped when she came across "It's a Wonderful Life." Her mother had made the family watch this every Christmas when she was growing up, and it was something that Emily had done even when she left home. Emily pulled the DVD from the shelf, deciding that this would not be the year she broke the tradition. She carefully put in the DVD and pressed the button on the TV. Emily sat on the couch as the TV sprang to life and its glow spread across the room. Emily found the remote and pressed play on the title screen. The opening credits started as Marley jumped back on the couch and placed his head in her lap.

Emily ran her hand over his soft fur as the familiar story played out on TV. As she watched, she was not alone in an empty town with the dead walking around, but instead back on her mother's couch on Christmas. Emily allowed herself to become immersed and only came back to reality when the end credits started. She looked around the living room and realized how truly alone she felt. She ran her hand over her stomach.

"Next year, you can watch it with me, too," Emily whispered to the baby.

With that, she stood and returned the movie to its place on the shelf. She then pushed the button to shut off the TV. Emily looked up at the clock and saw that it was well after nine, and she could not help but want to crawl back into that soft bed. She headed to the kitchen and opened the back door for Marley. She watched for a few minutes to ensure nothing had gotten into the backyard. Once she was sure everything was safe, she went to the sink and washed her dishes. When she had finished, she sat at the table while waiting for Marley to come back in. Once he did, she closed and locked the door behind him.

"Time to get ready for bed. Did you have a good Christmas?"

Marley wagged his tail, and Emily decided to take this as a yes. She climbed the stairs back up to her room. Once they were both inside, she closed and locked the door. She considered removing her overalls and climbing into the bed, but scolded herself for the thought. She had put down in her daily routine that she would take care of herself daily. She went to the bathroom and added her clothes to the hamper. She then climbed into the shower and began to wash. She decided that this was the night she would tackle her legs. She set to work with the razor and found the task a bit more challenging than it used to be. Not only had it been five months since she last shaved, but her baby bump forced her to come up with some new ways to be able to reach everything. After some time, she was satisfied with what she had accomplished. She finished washing and wrapped a towel around herself. She wiped the fog off the mirror and saw the same skinny girl looking back at her. However, there was a slight difference. There was some color back in her cheeks, a sign of life. Emily brushed her teeth and hair, proud that she looked like there was life in her once again. Once she had added her towel to the hamper, she turned off the light and joined Marley in bed.

Emily slowly lay her head on the pillow and reflected on the day. She still had so much to do, but somehow, she felt unstoppable. Within minutes, the sound of Marley softly snoring was beside her. He had slept so much since they arrived here. He had to be exhausted from looking out for her every second over the past five months. Emily rolled to her side to face her sleeping protector. She ran her hand through his fur and listened to the rhythm of his breath. There was no way she could have made it this far without him, and she knew it.

Emily closed her eyes and attempted to let sleep come to her as well. However, though she was tired, her brain refused to stop. She kept making plans in her mind and felt the time slip by. She grew frustrated with herself for not being able to sleep, but her mind continued to race. Emily was about to give up on sleep and get up to find something to do when it happened. She thought she had imagined it. First, it was so faint that she barely felt it. She lay still and waited to see if it would happen again. She nearly jumped out of bed as the baby softly kicked once more. It was her first confirmation that there was a baby in her belly. The test had said there was, and she had watched her belly slowly grow, but no actual proof.

"Okay, little one, it's time for bed," Emily cooed

as she rubbed her stomach.

Suddenly, all the thoughts that had kept her from sleeping were gone. She began to hum lullabies and drifted off to sleep. Her dreams were filled with memories of her family and their reaction to the baby. She enjoyed the moments she should have had in her dreams, and her mind was even kind enough to erase Chad from the picture. She had a reason to calm herself and believed she could make it work. She would meet that reason in March, and there was no time to lose her strength. Many people would say that what she tried to do was impossible, but she had already proven that the impossible meant nothing to her. It should have been impossible for her to survive this long in an SUV with only her dog. It should have been impossible for her to escape those men. It should have been impossible for her to not only be pregnant but not lose the baby with everything she had been through up to this point. It should have been impossible for her to find this sanctuary and everything in it. Impossible was just an opportunity for Emily, and the next day would hold even more.

Chapter 17

Emily woke the following day feeling excited about the day. She knew Missouri's snow and freezing temperatures did not set in hard until January. That was only in a few days, so she had a lot to do before then. She quickly dressed and made her way through her morning routine. After breakfast, she gathered all her dirty laundry and decided to try the washer. Once it was started, she headed back upstairs and made herself a lunch to take with her. There was a lot to get done in the town, and she did not want to waste time coming back home to have lunch every day. She was happy that Marley seemed to have gotten plenty of rest and was back to his usual energetic self.

With her lunch and crowbar, Emily opened the front door to head to work. She had decided that her first stop would be the farm. She would work here every morning to take care of the animals and crops once the growing season started. As she made her way down the road, she kept an eye out for movement. She had no delays except when she passed the bodies she had left the day before. It was on her list to find a way to move them and a place to burn them, but she had discovered neither. The smell was worse than she remembered, or perhaps it was because she had gotten used to the smell of cleanness in the house. Emily looked down at the little girl and forced herself to move along. She could not let herself get pulled into those emotions now. She had work to do.

Emily went to the barn and began inventorying

what needed to be done there. The only animal in here this morning was one of the horses she met on her first day here. The horse seemed to recognize her and walked towards her, nudging her face.

"Good morning to you, too," Emily laughed.

Emily then looked at the barn floor and decided it would be the best place to start. She would need a wheelbarrow and a shovel to get the muck out of the floor. She found both just outside the back of the barn and cleaned the floor. The process took long hours, but Emily finally carted the last mess out of the barn. Her horse friend had stayed the whole time, watching her while she worked. A few troughs looked to have once held hay and water, but they were all empty now. Emily found a hose, dragged it inside, and rinsed each out as best she could. She then filled a few with water, a process she would need to do every day, as whatever water source the animals had would soon be freezing over.

In cleaning the barn, she had found no hay or straw. There may have been some here before, but the animals probably helped themselves. Emily headed out to explore more behind the barn and was delighted to see that her new horse friend and Marley had decided to join her. A little way behind the barn, she found a tall metal fence. Inside was an animal that Emily was sure wouldn't warm up to her. The bull looked to have kept his strength up in solitude, but he was not happy to see her. Emily could see that he had water and looked to survive by grazing like the other animals. She would have to find a way to give him food once the grass was killed by frost. While it was another challenge, Emily could not help but feel excited at the possibility that the cows would be able to get pregnant. She had no idea how to let the bull out to get them that way, but it was still a new possibility.

Emily continued to explore and was excited to find a supply of hay, straw, and oats. This would give her everything to keep the animals fed through the winter. It had remained untouched as it was stored in a smaller barn further back. It would be a lot for her to carry into the barn, and she would need to find a way to load and move the food. Emily walked through the fields and tried to take count of the animals she saw. She counted four horses, five cows, six sheep, and three goats. While this was probably a tiny amount to a seasoned farmer, Emily felt like she hit the jackpot. She returned to the barn and headed back out front after saying goodbye to her horse friend.

Emily took her time and began to look more closely around. All of the crops were dead; this was to be expected, but it was not the time to figure out how to plant new ones. She would research to see if she should be doing anything during the winter to prepare, but the fields were on their own for now. On her exploration, she also found a chicken coop that she had not seen before. The chickens and a rooster were all around it and seemed healthy. Emily had skipped the section on chickens but would make sure to read up on them tonight. For now, she would leave them to their own devices. Emily had hoped to find a truck on the farm, but there was nothing.

As the morning drew to a close, Emily sat on the porch swing and ate her lunch. She was not in the mood for her bread crust, but Marley enjoyed the treat as she tossed it to him. Once she had finished, she gathered herself and headed back towards the main street. This was when she decided to ensure that the town was empty, but she had not thought out this part. Robert surely had some maps back in the study, but she had not thought to look for one or bring it with her. A lesson learned for tomorrow. Instead, Emily made her way back to the main street and decided to check the few streets closest to it. The first two she checked were empty. She went into each of the houses and checked them room by room. The places looked to have had people, but now stood empty.

Emily was finishing the last house on her goal for the day and was allowing her mind to wander. She began to think about what things she should try to find for the nursery when she was done, or other things she would like to try for her home. She entered the last house and didn't notice Marley's pause as she broke her routine. She did not call out and waited to see if anything moved. She just walked in and started walking through the rooms. Her mind was on a bassinet when Marley barked and pulled her back to what she was doing. She had walked past the damn thing without noticing, and now it was coming at her. The woman was dressed in jeans and a t-shirt; if not for the white eyes, Emily would have thought she was alive.

Emily raised her crowbar and swung it hard at the woman's head. She heard the crack of the skull and watched as the corpse fell to the ground. Emily moved quickly and stabbed the thing in the head to ensure it stayed down. She stood and looked around the room, just in case there were more. Marley seemed to be relaxing, and Emily moved to put her back against a wall. While it was late, she decided it was time to get back to the plan. She called out several times and waited to see if anything responded. After several minutes, she allowed herself to breathe.

"What the fuck was I thinking?!" Emily yelled at herself. "I can't let my guard down like that!" Emily could not have been more upset with herself. She knew better than to let her mind wander while clearing a place, but she had allowed herself to do it anyway. She then looked at Marley. He looked upset that she was mad.

"Good thing the brains of our team were still on duty. Good boy." Marley began to wag his tail and seemed to understand that she was not mad at him.

They then went through the rest of the house and back outside. Emily turned to start her way back to the main street when she noticed something under a piece of tarp behind the house. She carefully made her way to the backyard and pulled down the tarp. She felt like she had found a unicorn at the sight of the old flatbed truck. It was nothing pretty to look at, but precisely what she needed. She opened the passenger door and climbed inside. The keys were nowhere to be found in the truck. Emily then thought of the corpse inside. She had not looked through the belongings but had just checked for any more dead. She climbed out of the truck and headed back inside the house. It took her a while, but she found the keys hanging on a nail by the back door. Once back inside the truck, she prayed as she turned the key. The engine roared to life, and the gas gauge showed half a gas tank. That was enough to do what she needed for now.

Emily shut the door as Marley jumped up on the flatbed. She drove the truck to the front of the house and shut off the engine. This was the most noise she had made outside since coming here, and Emily decided it was best to sit in the truck for a few minutes to ensure she had not drawn any attention. She was sure there were more dead and did not want to be caught by surprise again. After some time, she decided it was safe and headed inside. She found a blanket and wrapped the woman's body in it, and used the blanket to drag her outside. Emily then tried to lift the body onto the truck, but this turned out more difficult than she had realized. She looked around the house and found a piece of plywood just big enough to make a ramp on the back of the truck, which she dragged the body up. She was exhausted when she was done and then remembered the men on the other road. They would be even heavier and harder to get up here, but at least she had a way to move the bodies now. She and Marley climbed into the truck's cab and drove back to the main street.

Emily parked the truck on the street in front of her house and headed inside. One thing she would need to do tonight is find a map and decide on a place to get rid of the bodies. She would not load more onto the truck until she had that information. Once inside, she set to the chores she had designated for herself that night. She put the laundry in the dryer, took care of Marley, and cooked herself supper. Once supper was done, she headed back downstairs to get the laundry from the dryer and grabbed some meat for the next night. She took everything back upstairs and put it away. She had resolved to be as clean as she could every day so that she would only need to clean maybe once a week. Once everything was done, she headed to the study and began looking for a town map. She found that Robert had many maps of the surrounding area and was delighted to see one of the town.

She spread the map over the desk and began to study it. It looked like Robert had updated it as the town was being built. Everything between the main street and the farm seemed to be completed, and it was all public housing. All of the shops and such were located on the main street. Behind her home were several more streets, all with completed housing except for the last two, which looked to be partially done. On the other side of town, there were only four streets of constructed housing, four more partials, and a largely undeveloped area. Emily turned from the map and went to the bookshelf containing the things that Robert had written himself. His journal that she found had a lot of information in it, but she knew that he had to have something with all the records for the town.

She finally found what she was looking for and headed back to the desk. Based on what he had written, the undeveloped part of town was supposed to have more housing. However, they used part of it as a construction hub where they stored supplies. The book also contained a list of every house built, whether occupied or not, and whether the partially done homes were marked as available. Emily returned to the bookshelf and returned to the desk with two more books. One was a ledger of the town's supplies, broken down by where they were. She found the section on the construction site and looked through the materials. Everything needed to build houses was listed, but what excited Emily was gasoline. Several pieces of large equipment were also listed, including a front loader. Even though she had no idea how to work one, she felt confident that this might help her on the farm and with the bodies on the street.

Emily returned to the front of the book to look closely at what other locations were listed. She saw the names of all the stores on the main street. However, there was a location called "Security" on the map. Emily turned to the security section of the log and gasped at what she saw. She knew what guns were, as far as rifles, shotguns, and handguns, but the list of specific weapons here was astonishing.

As she turned the pages, she saw that even more ammo was listed to go with the guns, along with vests, riot gear, grenades, and many other things. She quickly looked back at the map and looked over the buildings; one was marked with an "S" that she had not paid much attention to. She made a note to check this building out as soon as possible.

Emily then turned her attention to the other book labeled "Census." She turned through the pages, reading the names. Each name also told how old the person was, if they had arrived, and where they lived. Emily began to count those who were marked as arrived. She tried to ignore the ages as she went, but she could not stop counting how many adults and children were there. Some of the names had been marked with a single line. Emily assumed that these were the ones who had died before Robert had lost control. Emily finished the last page and collapsed in the chair. There were fifty-seven adults marked as arrived and seventeen children. She had not bothered to count the ones that were crossed out. The ledger had been numbered for each name that was entered. According to it, five hundred people were expected to live here when it was finished.

Robert had tried to save as many as he could, but not one of them made it. Emily closed the ledger and returned both of the books to the shelf. She folded the map and left it on the corner of the desk for the next day. She glanced at the clock to see that it was seven-thirty and decided it was time for some lighter material. She returned to the agriculture books and grabbed the same one from yesterday. She then headed to the living room and turned to the sections she had skipped the night before. It only took her about an hour to read it, and she felt her eyes growing heavy as she closed the book. She was tempted to set it on the table and head to bed, but forced herself to return it to the shelf.

Emily then made her way to the kitchen, where she opened Marley's back door and set to putting the dishes away. Once Marley was back inside and the house locked down, Emily climbed the staircase and forced herself into the shower. This day was beginning to wear on her, and she knew that sleep would not be hard to find tonight. Once clean and dressed for bed, she locked the bedroom door and lay down next to Marley. Tonight, she was asleep before he began to snore.

Emily woke the following day, again feeling the pain in her muscles from the work she had done the day before. She forced herself out of bed and got dressed for the day. She knew that her body would adjust, and the farm would require her daily attention. Farmers don't get a day off. She and Marley made their way through their morning routine much like the day before, but with no laundry load today. Emily gathered the map, and soon they were out the door. Emily considered leaving the truck because of the noise and saving gas, but her muscles warned her that they were not up to the walk and the work they had to do. She climbed into the cab with Marley and soon arrived at the farm.

Emily started with the chickens, checked the eggs laid as the book had told her, and loaded the ones that were not fertilized into the truck's cab. She then made her way to the barn, where her horse friend and another were waiting.

"Good morning, you two," Emily said as she and Marley entered.

The horses watched as Emily cleaned the muck added to the floor the day before and refilled the water. She knew she needed to try to milk the cows and maybe the goats; the book had made it seem like it was pretty tricky to milk the goats. Based on the pictures in the book, the sheep were not ready to be sheared yet, and it may be spring before they are. Emily decided to fill the hay troughs in the barn to see if that might draw the animals inside. She grabbed the wheelbarrow and headed to the other barn. It took her a while to figure out how to load the hay.

The process of going back and forth was taxing. Emily had considered using the truck, but did not want to pack the animal's food next to a rotting corpse. It just seemed wrong and twisted to her. She would be dropping the corpse off in the undeveloped part of the town later today so that she would not have to do this again.

As Emily made the trips, she noticed that more and more animals were in the barn each time. They seemed to have seen what she was doing and were coming for the food. Emily had put hay in each of the troughs in the barn, and though they were not full, her body would not allow her to do any more. She headed over, grabbed the stool and bucket she had found the day before while cleaning, and walked toward one of the cows. She may have read about this, but that didn't mean she knew what she was doing. The cow didn't seem upset by her presence and continued to enjoy her meal. Emily had read that she was supposed to wash the udders first to keep bacteria out of the milk. She headed to the house and got a bucket of soapy water, a washcloth, and a towel. She was grateful to see, when she returned, that the cow was still eating. She sat next to the cow and talked to her while working. The cow paid no attention as she washed and dried it.

Emily placed the bucket under the cow, just as she had seen in movies, and attempted to milk it as the book had said. Emily tried for several minutes and was about to give up, believing the cow had gone dry. Emily nearly squealed with glee as milk shot into the bucket. When she had finished milking the cow, she moved on to repeat the process with the others. By the time she had finished, the pail was nearly full. She was sure this wasn't an average amount considering how many there were, but she would take it. Emily carried the bucket to the front of the barn and set it on the ground. She wasn't sure if cow's milk could sour due to non-milking, and the book had not said anything. But she had decided not to try to keep the first few milkings to be safe. However, pouring the milk in front of the cows felt wrong, so she would do it where they could not see.

Emily headed inside and put away the stool and the bucket she had used to wash the cows. She would take the clothes home to clean and would return them later. She could not help but feel proud as she turned to leave the barn. As she walked towards the door, her horse friend came close and began to nuzzle her again. Emily stopped and ran her hand down the horse's neck.

"You just want attention, don't you?" Emily spoke to the horse. "I think I'm going to call you Buttercup." Emily continued to pet the horse as she talked. "I have to go, for now, Buttercup, but I will be back tomorrow." Buttercup stomped her hoof as if she didn't accept this response.

"I know, you probably want to go for a ride, but look at me. Even if I knew how to put a saddle on you, I couldn't ride you if I wanted to. But soon, I will be able to. I promise I'll read and learn how to." Emily patted Buttercup and walked towards the door, and the horse did not stop her this time.

"I'll see you in the morning," Emily called back as she shut the door.

Marley sat outside watching Emily and seemed less chipper than usual.

"Now, don't you go getting jealous. I make Buttercup sleep in a barn and take you home with me every night." Marley stood from his spot and ran towards the truck. "I guess you're over it then," Emily laughed as she followed him.

It wasn't lunchtime yet, and Emily decided to drive the truck to the other side of town. She needed to try to find a spot to put the bodies. It would probably be better to take them outside to burn them, but she did not want to risk opening the gates. Emily watched the sides of the road as she drove. She saw a few dead in the streets, but they did not seem to move. But neither did the one in the back of the truck until Emily had walked past it. Maybe they went dormant if there was nothing to eat and woke up when something alive crossed their path. She didn't know if there might be something in Robert's journal about this or not, but would keep an eye out for it.

It wasn't hard for her to find the construction area, and she drove until she found a bit of space with nothing around it. Here she shut off the truck and climbed onto the bed. She pushed the corpse off the back of the truck onto the ground. She knew she should probably dig a hole to put the bodies in for burning, but that would have to wait until she figured out how to use the equipment. Until then, this was far enough away from town that she would not have to smell it. She then climbed down and back into the cab. She drove the truck back to the main street to park and enjoy her lunch. She did not have an aversion to the bread crust today, but Marley patiently waited for her to share. She gave it and watched as he enjoyed his treat.

When they had finished, she pulled out the map and decided to start on the farm side of town. She started with the streets she had done the day before and was careful not to let her mind wander. She and Marley made quick work of it and found five dead. Emily did not know if they were in hibernation or just dead, but they moved quickly on each other and damaged the brain before they had the chance to move. None of them had responded to her calling out in each house. Perhaps sound did not wake them if they were hibernating, or maybe they were just dead. As she killed each, she wrapped it in a blanket and dragged it outside. Once she had finished the streets and returned to the farm, she returned to the truck and drove it up and down to collect the dead. It was hard work to drag each of them onto the truck, but she powered her way through it. She then returned to where she had dumped the other and added these five. The dead she had passed earlier had not moved an inch and were still in the same spot.

Emily then returned to the farm road, gathered blankets from a nearby house, and wrapped the two men and child in the street. The men were hefty, but she got them up and forced herself not to cry as she loaded the child. She then returned to the main street and gathered the two men and the woman. She was about to leave again when she remembered that she had left Robert's body up top. Emily drove close to the wall and climbed the stairs with a blanket. She did not know why, but felt sorry for him as she wrapped his body.

"Sorry about this, Robert," she heard herself say, "But there is no other way for me to get you down."

Emily pulled the blanket and winced as the body struck each of the stairs. She pulled Robert's body onto the truck and drove back to the spot. She checked again as she went, and the dead had still not moved. At first, they had made her feel uneasy, but it bothered her less and less each time she passed.

She pushed each of the bodies off to join the others. She lifted the girl and placed her on the ground. When she reached Robert, she couldn't just add him to the others. Instead, she put down her makeshift ramp and pulled him off the truck to a different spot. She then loaded up and headed back home.

Once inside, it was through her nightly routine again. Marley was picking it up very quickly, and soon they had both had supper, and the dishes were done. Emily then headed to the study and began to look through the books to decide which one she would study tonight. She had promised Buttercup that she would learn to saddle a horse, but she was months away from needing that skill. Instead, she found herself standing in front of the books that Robert had written and thought about him. When she first saw his body, it was just another corpse. But the longer she was here, the more she learned about him and felt like she knew him. It was the closest she had been to a human being since the flash, and she couldn't help but mourn him.

He had been a part of whatever the flash was, but did not know what he was being used for until it was too late. He had built this place and tried to save hundreds of people. He didn't have enough time because it happened sooner than he thought, but what he created and the information he left behind gave her and her child a chance to survive. The numbers ran through her head again: fifty-seven adults and seventeen children. Today, she had driven seven adults and one child to the construction zone. That left forty-nine adults and sixteen children unaccounted for at this point. Emily hoped that some of them had made it out, but she knew they had not. She had worked towards the bottom of the bookcase and, for the first time, realized that the journals here were blank. Robert had probably planned to use them in the future, a chance he would never get.

Emily grabbed one of them and walked over to the desk. She opened the journal to the first page and wrote "The Journal of Emily." She then turned the page and wrote December 27th on the top. She then watched as she started from the night of the flash and all the events she had witnessed. She wrote about the town and all she had learned and done so far. She watched herself write about Robert and the good he tried to do with this place. She didn't stop to think and instead just turned the pages and allowed the pen to continue to move. She wrote that she knew nothing about the other dead, and to give them a proper burial just seemed pointless. However, she knew about Robert and what he tried to do here, and it felt wrong to let him become another faceless corpse. She decided to go between the walls and find an area to designate as a cemetery. Here she will bury him.

It wasn't until she stopped writing that she realized she was crying. As much as she wanted to blame it on her hormones, she knew she couldn't. Though he was dead, Robert was the closest thing she had to a friend, well, a human friend, in a long time. Emily closed the journal and returned it to the shelf. She had no idea how long she had been writing, but was tired. She went to let Marley out and put away the dishes. Soon she is showered and crawled into bed. She allowed her thoughts to drift to Robert and the type of man he must have been, and thanked Robert just before drifting off to sleep.

Chapter 18

Emily woke the next day and went about her usual routine. She and Marley were out the door without incident and found Buttercup waiting for them inside the barn. Emily made her way through cleaning the floor and used the truck to haul the hay back to fill the troughs. The other animals seemed to be picking up on the new routine and slowly started to get inside. The weather was quite cool, but not cold enough that it could cause any of them harm. Emily worked her way through the cows and was pleased that they seemed to produce more milk as she came up with two buckets. The book had said that when they were regularly producing, they would need to be milked twice a day, something that Emily decided she would need to build into her schedule soon.

Emily quickly made it through her chores and still had time left before she headed back into town. Today, she was going to work her way through the section of town behind her house, and tomorrow would be the main street and the far side. She planned to repeat this pattern until she found everyone who was supposed to be there. As Emily headed for the door, Buttercup came to get her attention once more. Emily ran her hand over the horse and felt the coarse hair under her hand. She then walked over and grabbed a horse brush.

"You would probably appreciate this," she stated as she walked back to Buttercup and started running the brush over the hair.

Emily brushed until her arm started to hurt. She knew that she would have to haul some bodies onto the truck's bed today, so she could not use all of her strength. With one last pass, she stepped back and looked at Buttercup. The horse seemed utterly different from the little Emily had been able to do. The other horses stood watching and appeared to be waiting for their turn.

"I will get to all of you, and we will even tackle those tangled tails one day," Emily mused as she returned the brush to the shelf. "But for now, I have to go. I will see all of you in the morning."

With that, Emily left her animal friends and headed to the truck. It was still pretty early, but she had not yet explored the back half of the town. She pulled out her map and looked at the layout of the streets. She decided to start close to the farm and work her way over. Emily drove the truck to the first section and worked her way through the houses one by one with Marley. She found the corpses did not move when she entered, and did not give them a chance to wake up. She ensured each was dead, wrapped it in a blanket, and dragged it out to the street. She would bring the truck later to collect all of them.

Emily worked her way through the streets one by one and found only adults, which she found comforting for now. She had ten bodies to collect, and then she would stop for lunch. Emily walked back to the truck and began hauling them up. Once they were all loaded, she drove through these unfamiliar streets to the dumping area to see if anything stood out. Emily had almost worked her way back to the main street on this section and saw a building not far from her house that she had not noticed before. She stopped the truck and checked the map. The building was marked as "SL," and now that she sat in front of it, she knew what it meant: school. Emily stared at the building and tried hard not to cry. She had only found one of the children supposed to be here. What if the others hid in the school when things went crazy?

Emily knew that she would have to go there, especially with it being so close to where she lived. However, she feared putting down all those children more than she could bear at once. Emily put the truck in drive and drove back onto the main road. That was something to deal with when she made it that far. Emily stopped near the pile of corpses and added the new ones she had collected. She drove over to the buildings that seemed to hold all of the supplies and did a check to ensure she was alone. It didn't take her long to find the gasoline, and she took one of the cans out to the truck and poured it in. The truck had not dropped much in gas level, but she wanted to stall her work so she wouldn't make it to the school that day.

Once the can was empty, Emily placed it back inside and shut the door. She climbed back into the truck's cab and shared her lunch with Marley. She ate as slowly as she could, but soon, she had no more excuses, and it was back on the road. The school would be one of her last sections of the day if she made it that far. She pushed it from her mind and tried not to look at it as she drove past, but something moving on the playground caught her eye. One of the swings with a small boy was moving back and forth as if the boy was playing. Emily had not seen anyone before and immediately stopped the truck to watch. The boy's back was turned to her, but he was playing on the swing. Could it be possible that he had been hiding here all along? Were there others here with him?

Emily tried to steady herself enough to open the door to the truck, but her hand kept missing the handle. Finally, she felt the cool metal in her grasp, and the door flung open. Emily ran towards the chain-link fence around the school and searched for a way through.

Despite the noise, she was sure she made with the truck, the boy had not moved. He just continued to swing back and forth. Emily watched the boy and heard Marley let out a low growl next to her. She knew what he was trying to say, but did not want to believe it.

"Little boy! Little boy, are you okay?" Emily called out despite Marley's warning.

The boy stopped swinging and slowly stood up. As he turned, Emily saw that this boy was no longer alive. His eyes were the milky white of the dead. He slowly started to walk towards her with his arms outstretched. Emily just stood watching the child and allowed the tears to run down her face. She did not notice anything else until Marley started to bark beside her. Emily looked towards the school to see several other children and a couple of adults. A few dead had come outside in the houses just across the street. They were making their way towards where she stood. If they had been sleeping before, she had found a way to wake them up. She could not handle this many just standing out in the open. Emily ran back to the truck and watched Marley jump on the bed. It took only a few moments to get the truck back in front of the house, and she and Marley ran inside, locking the door behind them. Emily looked out the window and could see that the dead were following. She was sure the door was enough to keep them out, but she would have to wait for them to wander on or go back into hibernation.

"So much for them being asleep!" Emily exclaimed to Marley as she leaned against the wall, watching them walk down the road towards the truck.

She could not help but feel frustrated that she could not take care of the ones walking and be closer to being done with them. Instead, she counted as they each walked by. They were not moving fast, but slow in their typical zombie shuffle. After an hour, they all seemed to be gathered around the truck, and a few were moving towards the porch. Emily held her finger up to her lips, signaling Marley to stay quiet, and headed for the study. Marley followed her, and she shut the door behind him. She had wanted more time to read through Robert's journals to see if he might have known anything about the hibernation of the dead. Maybe he would know how she woke them up or how to put them back to sleep.

She could not take on everyone out there at once, so she would need to wait. She had counted twenty adults and thirteen children, but she could have missed some or double-counted. Especially the children, as they were so small and easy to lose track of in the crowd. Emily quickly picked up each book and glanced at the information inside. Each she grabbed contained information on the town and how Robert had planned to run it. She found an entire book on the currency and work system he planned to use, another regarding laws and regulations, and many others that may have been useful if she weren't the only one alive here.

Emily felt her frustration growing as she slammed the last of the books closed, with nowhere else to turn. Robert had been part of how the flash happened. He had to have more information on it. Emily looked back at the bookshelf and remembered the journal she had found in the control room, where Robert had taken his life. He had left many books under the couch that he said would help whoever found this town. She had quickly looked through a few of them to find the code to close the gate, but had not taken the time to return to them since she arrived.

She had stuffed the books in her duffel bag upstairs in her bedroom. It was then that she realized she had never unpacked her emergency bag. She turned to signal for Marley to follow her, but he was already standing by her side. She walked to the office door and opened it slowly, looking out into the living room. She was sure they could not get in, but didn't want to take anything for granted. Slowly, she moved across the living room and slipped up the staircase. Once inside her room, she shut and locked the door behind her. She then grabbed the duffel bag from the closet. It was heavier than she remembered, but she plopped it onto the bed and sat down. Marley did not jump on the bed to join her but instead lay in front of the door. He could sense that things were not right and had returned to his protective stance.

Emily unzipped the bag and began to pull out the stuff inside. First were the six books, including Robert's journal.

Emily was about to toss the bag on the floor when she saw the photo album sitting inside. It had been forever since she had looked at the pictures and seen the faces of her family. Part of her wanted to pull it out and let herself escape her memories. The slight kick to the belly reminded her that she had to force herself to move forward. There would be time for the pictures later. Emily tossed the bag onto the floor and began to look through the books. She knew the first one she grabbed; it was the journal that Robert had been holding. Emily set it aside and moved on to the next. It was the instructions for the electronics of the town. She had remembered flipping through it to find the control panel code, but now took her time to see what other information it had. The book had information on many different devices in the town, but the ones that caught her attention the most were the ones in the armory. It looked like the guns were locked up, and a code was needed to access the central supply room. There were also lockers for individuals with their own set of biometric locks.

While Emily wanted to read more about the high-tech equipment Robert had built into the town, she knew this book did not have the needed information. She set it with Robert's journal and moved on to the next. This book had a map of the town, specifically how it was supposed to look when it was done. In the pages, Robert talked about how the living quarters were designed to put people close to their jobs and family size. There was a lot of structural information about the buildings, and it looked like everything was designed with a purpose. However, Emily did not allow herself to read it in-depth and set it with the others. The next one was larger than even the journal. The cover appeared very worn, and the edges of the pages were torn from being turned. Emily opened the book and read the first page, "Research Journal of DR. Robert Devrow – Project Light." Emily knew instantly that this was what she had been looking for. She turned the pages and began to read slowly, trying to comprehend everything Robert was saying.

In the first bit of the journal, Robert seemed hopeful and glad about his work. He stated that he had been recruited with five other scientists to work on a project that would bring extinct animals back to life through the miracle of science. From what Emily understood, Robert listed experiments he performed that attempted to put the DNA of extinct animals into an undeveloped embryo to see if he could get it to change. Instead of growing into the type of animal that created it, it would take on the genetic properties of the extinct animal. The journal went on for about a year, and Robert's experiments were unsuccessful, but he remained hopeful. It was after a year that the tone of his writing began to change. He began to talk about how he was no longer allowed to speak to the other scientists. He also says he was only allowed in his lab or living quarters. He was being escorted to both by armed guards, and his meals were served to him as a prisoner. He wrote several times that he wished to quit the project, but was informed that it was not an option.

After months of doing the same thing and being treated like a prisoner, things changed for Robert, but not for the better. He was taken to his lab as usual, but was surprised to see the other scientists there. They were all surrounded by their escorts and looked just as afraid as he felt. Then a man they were told to call General addressed them all. He told them that the research goals they had been given were not entirely true. The project's purpose was to have them each work on a piece of the puzzle to be put together into what was truly needed. However, that was proving impossible, and the process took too long. Moving forward, they would all work together and provide a solution to save humankind. Robert wrote that he was confused and tried to ask precisely what they were trying to save humanity from, but the General grew angry with him. He yelled at him that they did not want to bring dead animals back to life, but people. No one gave a shit about animals or plants or any other bullshit they thought they were trying to save; it was people.

Robert wrote that after the General was done yelling, he told them to compare their experiments and develop something that would keep the human race coming back, even if they died. The General then left the room with guards and left the scientists to create a death cure. Robert was the only one to speak when he left. He immediately explained what he had been doing and asked the others. When they remained quiet, he told them that they had to start working or that none of them would make it out. It didn't mean they had to finish it, but they had to appear to be trying. Robert wrote that it was a woman named Sylvia who spoke first. She was trying hard not to cry, but could not help herself. She explained that she had been working on a device that could send sunlight for miles. It was supposed to help plants grow in areas where the smog was so thick that the sun could not reach the plant life. She thought that by saving the plant life, the animals in that area would have a higher survival rate because their food sources would no longer be dying.

Emily stopped reading and looked towards the bedroom window. She could still see that flash of light as it spread across the sky. She knew that it had to have been part of what Sylvia designed, though not used as she thought it would be. Emily returned to the book and saw that the other scientists' tasks were listed. There was one working on a chemical that could spread for miles if released into the air to inoculate the animal life against diseases the humans were introducing to them. The third was working on behavior modification that would allow the animals to be modified to populate different areas and survive the human condition. The last was an engineer, and he had been designing a delivery system that would allow a chemical reagent to be released into the air. Emily could see how these contributions played a role in the light and the dead now walking, except for Robert's experiments. Even in reading his words, Robert didn't seem to understand either.

During the next few days' worth of entries, Robert seemed puzzled and worked hard to figure out his role. It was evident from the others' work that the General did not want to grow more humans but wanted them brought back to life. She could tell by his words that he did not understand, and the others, according to Robert, did not either. It was nearly a week before Robert learned his role in all of this, and it seemed to be the most crucial of all. Robert wrote that he felt like a fool for not seeing it in the first place. Since the DNA he was working with was technically dead, he had to devise a way to bring it back to life. He had discovered this after his first several trials failed. He had worked for months to find the chemical solution that, if added to the DNA, would make it responsive once more. He had overlooked this because all his trials had continued to fail, or so he thought. The General had grown tired of trying to figure it out on their own and, in another rant, told them exactly what was wanted.

Robert's last few experiments were successful. However, his team had switched out the embryos during the night so that Robert would remain unaware. They believed that if his solution could be made into a gas, it would allow humans to cheat death without even knowing they had been made immune. However, the chemical makeup required heat to be activated and a catalyst to travel to make it great distances. The next few months' worth of entries were hard to read as Emily's heart broke for Robert. He talked of how he tried to refuse to cooperate, but the General savagely beat Sylvia until Robert agreed. He worked with the scientist who had developed the gas that could travel great distances and the man who had created the chemical for behavior modification. It was obvious to Robert that the General did not just want people to cheat death but also to do as he wanted.

Once the chemical was done, they handed it off to Sylvia and the engineer, who crafted a small release device that could not have released the chemical more than a few blocks. The small device had upset the general, but Sylvia was quick on her feet and told him they thought he would want to test it before they made one big enough for the entire population.

According to Robert, this seemed to buy them time, and the General said he would gather test subjects as quickly as possible. They were all taken into a new lab section a few days later, which none of them had been in before. Ten cells were lining the walls, and a man was in each. It was apparent from their clothes that the General had gathered his test subjects from the prison system. The General then instructed them to deliver the chemical to each subject. Robert knew they had to buy time. Side effects could take days, weeks, or even years to show. He wasn't sure what these men had done, but he was sure they didn't deserve this. However, it was either these ten lives or the lives of everyone in the world. He moved and began putting a device into each containment unit and apologized to everyone as he did. When he finished, the engineer told everyone to look down as the light would be extremely bright and activated the devices.

Robert wrote that at first, nothing seemed to happen. The prisoners complained about the light hurting their eyes, but everything else seemed fine. The General assigned them all shifts in pairs of two to monitor the prisoners around the clock. Robert's only relief seemed to be that he was paired with Sylvia, though part of him seemed to know that the General only did this so he could keep Robert in line.

Robert's notes contained many blood pressure

and heart rate readings that started several hours after
the prisoners were given the miracle cure. Emily
assumed that he was on the first shift. After each set of
readings, Robert had written "Normal." However, the
prisoners' symptoms started to change twelve hours
after the event. Three of them had begun to convulse
and died within minutes, six had vitals that were
dropping and had developed a fever, and one of them
remained healthy. When the effects started, Robert
worked to save the sick six, but within hours, they
were dead. Only one prisoner remained alive and
seemed to be just as healthy as he was before.

When everything started to go wrong, Robert
asked one of the guards to retrieve the General, but it
took him hours to arrive. While explaining the
situation to him, Robert wrote that the General
suddenly called him a liar and said that the prisoners
all looked alive to him. Robert said when he looked
back that all the prisoners were standing, though the
vitals on nine of them showed no heart rate. Robert
wrote that only their eyes showed the truth of their
condition as they had gone milky white. He noted that
the chemical had worked and brought them back from
the dead, but the person they were was long gone.
Robert wrote that what stood in the cells no longer had
a soul. The General was pleased with the work and
remained in the lab from that point on.

Robert wrote that they all tried to get the
prisoners to respond to basic commands or words.
However, the only actual response they received was
aggression if one of them walked toward the cells. The
one remained alive and responsive, though Robert
feared he would still die before leaving this place. The

General was already calling him a failed experiment, but was pleased it worked on nine out of ten. Robert's notes continued for several months. He said that while the prisoners were dead, their bodies continued to show no signs of decay, and only their eyes showed the truth. They regularly served meals to them per their orders, but the food was always left untouched. He did note that they decided to test one of them differently. They placed a blanket over his cell so he could not see and turned off the intercom so he could not hear. They continued to watch him on the monitor, and after two months of no contact, he sat down on the floor and did not move.

Robert wrote that he had hoped it meant the body was dead for good, and it stayed stationary for weeks. The General then ordered them to remove the blanket and treat him like the others again. It took a few days, but the sights and sounds of them moving around caused him to stand again and behave like the others. Robert noted that the lack of stimulation had led to a temporary suspension of activity but not actual death. Once stimuli were reintroduced, it took time, but the body was awoken. Robert wrote that he did not know how to put the bodies to their final rest and feared that the General did not want to learn that information. He seemed pleased that the prisoners no longer required food and enjoyed that the behavior modification kept them silent.

Robert wrote that he decided to point out flaws in the delivery system and why it would be impossible to spread globally. There was an obvious flaw with the chemical, as one of the prisoners was still not affected, and there was no way to ensure that those in remote areas could all be infected. Robert wrote that he hoped it would buy them time, but it only cost another man his life. The General ordered that the walls between the cells be lifted as soon as Robert finished. He wanted the prisoners to be allowed to interact with each other. Robert wrote that the only surviving prisoner was cornered by the others as soon as the walls were removed. The man tried to fight, but the dead did not feel pain, and nothing seemed to stop them. The man did manage to crack one of the dead's skulls against the wall; they all heard the crack, and the body fell to the ground, never moving again. Robert wrote that it must have been the damage to the brain that finally kept it down. They were all forced to watch as the other eight-bit apart from the last survivor.

Once they were done with their feast, they wandered through the cells again. Robert watched the body on the floor, praying it would stay that way. However, after only an hour, the body began to twitch and stood to join the others. The General seemed pleased and said that the ones who did get the cure would spread it to the others. It did not matter if the way of spreading it was a little less than perfect. They were all ordered to make larger batches of the chemical and a larger delivery system. According to what he wrote, Robert never intended to complete the order. He started to write as if he planned to take his life and hoped this mess would die with him. However, an accident in the lab kept him going. Sylvia was attempting to unload one of the small canisters they had made and accidentally set it off. Robert had seen the flash and ran to her as quickly as he could. He wrote that all she kept saying was that at least it only got her.

Robert monitored her closely, and she was still
herself the next day. Robert wrote that despite trying
to hide what happened, the General found out and
wanted more tests run on Sylvia to determine what
made her immune.

Robert ran the testing himself, comparing it to
the prisoners roaming in their cells. He noted a genetic
marker in Sylvia and the prisoner that the other nine
did not have. Sylvia's marker was extremely rare,
while the marker the prisoner had was probably held
by at least thirty percent of the population. He reported
his findings to the General, who seemed displeased
that there was nothing exactly in common with either.
Robert wrote that he was cuffed and forced to watch as
Sylvia's arm was thrust into the cells through the
feeding door. One of the dead clamped down on her
arm, and he wrote that her scream would haunt him
forever. It was different than when they fed on the
prisoner, though. After one bite, the dead backed away
and left her arm alone. The General pulled her arm out
and ordered her to be put into containment to be
monitored.

Robert again volunteered and watched over
Sylvia as best he could. He believed it wouldn't be
long until her soul left this world, and he did not want
her to be alone. However, as days passed, Sylvia's bite
began to heal, and she showed no signs of the
infection. Robert thought it a miracle and wrote that he
could not wait to help her escape this place. The
General was not nearly as pleased by her recovery.
Robert noted that if the bite was not enough to help
her move to the next stage, the General would help
her. Robert watched as the General shot Sylvia in the

heart. Robert wrote that he stayed with his friend and intended to put her to rest even if her body rose again, no matter what it cost him. However, after days, her body lay still in her cell. The General ordered Robert to find out what made her immune to the disease despite the gas and the bite. Robert wrote that he said it might be that they worked so closely with the chemical that they had developed an immunity, though he doubted it. Then, the General took him to the other lab and showed him the other scientists. All of them were in cells, all with milky white eyes.

Robert wrote that their part was done, and the General had turned them. He must have done it while Robert was trying to take care of Sylvia. The date on the last journal entry was months after all these events. Before starting it, Emily looked around the room, knowing that whatever Robert said would explain why she was immune. She braced herself and began to read the words, taking her time to let them all sink in. Robert wrote that two different genetic markers allowed the subjects to remain immune to the gas. The marker is subject one, the prisoner, who only made him resistant to the initial gas release, but the chemical was spread through the saliva of an infected subject. If bitten, the subject with this genetic marker would not be immune and would suffer the full effect. Subject two, Sylvia, was resistant to the chemical makeup regardless of the delivery form. Robert estimated that less than one percent of the population would possess this marker.

Robert began to speak informally, and his words no longer read like a report. He told of his plan to escape his prison before he was forced to join the others. He planned to take his own life behind him, and now he planned to save the human race. He believed that he could find a way to share the immunity of those who possessed the same marker as Sylvia with others. He just needed more time to do it. He knew there was no way he could save everyone, but perhaps he could save enough to set the world back on course. He planned to slow things down by setting off one of the canisters as he left. He intended that none of them would make it out alive, and whoever was funding them would have difficulty putting the pieces together. Robert hoped this would give him enough time to make the immunity work and find a safe place for those who were immune before the light hit the sky.

Emily finished the book, and the stiffness in her back told her she had been sitting there for hours. Her head felt like it could explode with all the information she had. She was immune because of a rare genetic thing, and it was likely that her family did not share it. Emily reached down and rubbed her stomach, realizing that her child was not likely to have it either. While this news was heavy on her mind and heart, she had to push it aside for facts. Robert had said that it took weeks of no stimulation for the dead to go dormant, and stimulation is what woke them up. Her moving through the town as she had the last few days had gotten them moving again, and she could not wait weeks for them to go back to sleep. Emily walked to the bedroom window and looked down. A few of the dead were beginning to wander, but they would not be going still anytime soon. The days of having it easy, working her way through this town, were over, and she knew it.

Her best chance was to stay up here and be quiet for the night. If they didn't see signs of movement or hear her, they would begin to roam, giving her an opening to put them down. She was sure there were more walking around now as she thought back to the dead she had seen just sitting and lying on her way to the dump site. She had not realized until now that when she went down that same road today, none of them were where she had last seen them. They were all awake now and looking for a meal; she was the only one in town. Emily reached down and picked up the duffel bag from the floor. She found a few of the provisions she packed back at the truck. At the sound of the wrapper, Marley stood and walked over to the bed. Emily shared the food with him and felt sorry that she would not let him outside tonight."

While it was not ideal, she put up the toilet seat and knew that if he were thirsty, he would not care. She could only hope he would do his business on the bathroom floor if he could not hold it. She had no idea how she would get the carpet clean if he did it in here. She didn't bother showering or dressing for bed because she feared the sound would somehow travel down to the dead now marching in front of her house. She crawled under the blankets and pulled the photo album out of the duffel bag. There was still enough light coming through the window to see them, and she didn't want to waste a moment of it. She turned through the pages, looking at her family's faces one at a time. She tried hard to remember everything about them and imagine that they were right there with her.

After some time, the sun was gone, and she could no longer see the pictures. Emily closed the photo album and reached to return it to the duffel bag. As she slid it in, she touched something in the bag. She reached in and grabbed her cell phone. She had nearly forgotten about it since coming here. She had always made sure it was charged in the SUV, and it felt like her last chance to find her family. She pressed the button on the side, and the screen stayed dark. The battery was dead. Emily considered putting them back in the bag, but then placed them both on the nightstand and the bag back on the floor. Packing them up again felt like she was saying she was ready to run. Emily had no intentions of giving up this place. She was now unpacking and would be taking it back. Emily slid under the covers and felt Marley climb up to join her on the bed. These dead bastards had no idea who they were messing with, but they would in the morning.

Chapter 19

Emily woke the following day with a clear mind and was pleased to find that Marley was still lying beside her. She climbed out of bed, checked the bedroom and bathroom for any accidents, and found none. She quickly used the bathroom herself, but did not risk the noise of flushing the toilet. When she walked back into the bedroom, Marley was awake, and his eyes were pleading for help. The poor pup could not break the no potty in the house rule and looked like he would rather explode than go on the floor. Emily motioned for him to be quiet and opened the bedroom door. Together they slipped through the house, checking if the dead had found a way in while they slept. The doors were still secure, and it was just her and Marley. Emily unlocked the back door and scanned the yard. The gate was still closed, and the yard was empty. Emily stepped aside and allowed Marley to run out the door. She watched, scanning the fence for signs that anything was moving. Marley was quick, but the look on his face when he returned was pure relief.

Emily opened a water bottle in the cabinet, filled his water bowl, and gave him a small serving of food as quietly as she could. She grabbed herself a cup of applesauce for her breakfast and ate quickly. Once they had eaten, she moved around the house, looking out each window to get an idea of where the dead had gone. Most had wandered away from the house, but there were still four in the front yard, all children. Emily did not get her normal feelings of sorrow or regret this time; it was either the dead or her baby, and the dead had to go. She decided she would start with the ones closest to her, and after she put them down, she would return here to regroup. This was going to be a long day, but if she pulled it off, most of the dead would be gone, and she would be very close to being free of this crap.

Emily checked to ensure she still had the knife on her waist and grabbed the crowbar. She unlocked the door and opened it as slowly as possible, stepping out into the morning air. The first one was a little brown-haired boy just in front of the front steps. Emily moved across the porch as quickly as possible and caught the boy on the head. He went limp and fell to the ground. A glance at the other two, and Emily saw they did not realize what was happening yet. She moved to the closest one. Next, a blond girl was taken down with no fuss. When she turned to the last, it was clear that he had figured out what was going on. Emily rushed the boy, and her crowbar found its mark. Emily knew Marley's silence meant those on the street were not moving in. She returned to the front door and closed it behind Marley. She took a few deep breaths and looked back outside.

A few adults had started to make their way back to the house. Emily wasn't sure if it was her dropping the three in the front yard or if they were just wandering. She waited and watched as they started to pass the yard, but the bodies on the ground seemed to catch their attention. They must have thought there was a chance they were live people as the four wandered into the yard. But as they drew closer to the children, they lost interest and began to roam the yard.

Emily waited until they were far enough apart that she thought she could time it right. She opened the door once more and started hitting them with the crowbar. The first two were easy, but the third was a bit tougher than she expected. The man was a good bit taller than her, and Emily could not get the crowbar to hit the skull with enough power. She thought quickly on her feet, though, and instead smashed the man in the knees, causing him to fall over. Once he was on the ground, she stabbed him with the hunting knife. Knowing that this kill took too long, Emily rushed to her feet and looked for the fourth. It was then that she saw Marley had pinned the thing to the ground and was trying to avoid letting it bite him without making a sound. Emily ran towards him and stabbed the man in the head.

As she pulled out the knife, Marley let out a low growl. Emily didn't need to look to know that they were drawing attention. She ran back towards the door and shut it behind Marley. Emily leaned the crowbar against the wall and immediately started to check Marley for a bite mark. She was sure dogs would not share the genetic marker that made her immune. She finished checking and found nothing. She wrapped her arms around his neck and buried her face in his fur. Emily could not lose him now; he was all she had. After she gathered herself, she stood back up and grabbed the crowbar; it was time to get back to work. Emily looked back out the window to see that she was right. They had drawn quite a bit of attention, and the front yard was beginning to fill. Two of them were on the porch and within arm's reach of the door.

Emily knew that the plan was not the smartest,

but it was the only one she had. After several deep breaths, she signaled for Marley to sit and opened the door. She had planned to stab at least one of the men in the head before closing the door, but she had not seen the child through the window. She could have been no more than four and was right in front of the door. Emily hesitated for less than a second and stabbed the child's brain. She moved fast and got one of the men before retreating inside. Emily locked the door and looked down at Marley, who had remained seated but was unhappy about it. While it did not go exactly as she had wanted, her plan had worked. Emily watched out the window for a few minutes while the dead wandered around and settled down. Emily considered trying to keep reusing her door trick, but it would take a while, and she had learned that she could not see everything in front of the door.

By her count, there were still twenty-eight adults and eleven children out there, and the last thing she needed was for them to get in. She would need to wait a while for them to settle down and kill those she could before they got riled up again. After a few hours, they had begun to spread out once again. Emily started with those in the yard first. None wandered into the yard after her first outing, so she was forced to go out into the street for the next group. Instead of rushing back inside, she waited and watched. Only a few had noticed her, so she moved quickly to take them out before running back inside. Her second trip was successful as five more adults and two more children were put to rest. While this was not plan A, it was a much faster way of dealing with the deadly problem. Emily watched out the window and waited for a few hours as the dead began settling down again.

Emily continued this process until the sun began to set. She was careful not to go too far from the house and not to try to rush the kills. Marley followed her every time she went out and did his best to get the dead's attention if she caught the attention of too many. Emily no longer noticed details about the dead, such as whether they were men or women or their hair color. She simply kept her count of adults and children. As the sun began to set, she knew there was no more she could do today. Trying to hunt them in the dark would be a suicide mission. As she closed the door for the last time that night, she glanced back at the few further up the main street. She knew that she would have to find them, but for tonight, they would get away. Emily walked to the downstairs bathroom and began to wash the blood and muck from herself. She quickly did the math in her head, and once she dried off, she headed to the study. She grabbed her journal and opened it to the next blank page. She marked the date and began to write down all of the information she had learned about how the flash came to be, her immunity, and how she had woken the dead. She wrote about her day fighting them and trying to reclaim the city. The final line read, "10 adults and seven children remain."

Once she finished, she returned the book to the shelf and headed to the kitchen. She quickly filled Marley's bowls and set to making herself supper. She was going to enjoy the comforts she had earned here and wasn't going to let the few remaining dead stop her. The image of the bodies that now covered the yard and road by her house flashed into her mind. She did not feel pity for them, though. She was beyond that point. She knew it would take her hours to haul them all over to the dump site. She could not feel the fear of making noise inside anymore. She had put so many to rest that the remaining ones seemed very few and not scary. If she could handle that many, she could take the last few if they knocked. Once dinner was finished and the dishes washed, she opened the back door for Marley. The warm winter snap seemed to end, something she had noticed while working. The air was growing colder by the minute, and it was official that January was nearly here.

Marley was quick and seemed not to enjoy the cold wrapping around him. They had already seen a few days of freezing temperatures, but always bounced back to being decent. Emily knew from living in this area her whole life what the signs were that the cold was here to stay, and this was it. They would not see another nice day until February. She could only hope that this winter would be kind and that snow would be okay, but she did not know how she would even begin to handle an ice storm if it happened. Emily closed and locked the back door and headed up to her room. She went straight to the bathroom and peeled off the clothes she had been wearing for two days. Looking at the blood and muck she had splattered on them, she knew they would need to be washed tonight, or she would be looking at those stains forever. She cleaned herself in the shower and dressed in a t-shirt to take the laundry back downstairs. She felt fine until she started going down the basement stairs. She suddenly felt dizzy, and her vision began to blur. She immediately let go of the basket and heard it land at the bottom of the stairs. Emily grabbed desperately for the handrail to steady herself. Holding the wood, she immediately lowered herself to sit on the step.

Emily sat there for what seemed like forever, waiting for the world to stop spinning around her. When it finally stopped, she remained still, afraid it would start again. Marley was lying at the top of the stairs, watching her with concern. Emily knew that she could not stay here forever. She forced herself back onto her feet and down the last stairs. Anyone else would have gone to lie on the couch, but she was determined to do what she had set out to do in the first place. She put the clothes in the washer and, once it was started, slowly walked back up the stairs. As she made her way through the living room, she decided to head into the study. She went straight to the shelf with the medical information and began looking through the spines. Emily pulled out the one that brought her in and headed upstairs with Marley again. She closed and locked the bedroom door and climbed into bed. She then turned on the lamp on the nightstand and opened the book.

She began to read through the information, all regarding pregnancy. She had no doctor to call for help, and she needed to figure out what was going on to keep from passing out with a zombie in her face. This particular book was about pregnancy, and it contained examples of women who had given birth alone. Emily had known when she saw it that it was one that she needed to read, but didn't plan to do it just yet. However, that dizzy spell prompted her to speed up her plan. She turned through the pages, reading about the baby at different developmental stages and things to keep an eye out for, which you may want to seek medical advice if that is an option. Emily paid close attention to the section about dizzy and fainting spells. According to the book, several different things could cause it. If a mother's diet didn't contain enough iron or folic acid, she could become anemic. It states that a mother may need to take supplements to ensure the levels stay where they are required.

Emily knew her diet had been awful, mainly due to the lack of food before coming here, so this was a strong possibility. The book also said dehydration could cause a mother to be dizzy or faint. A mother's body requires more water later in pregnancy. Emily knew that she had not drunk much today. She was a little busy. She also knew that she had gotten used to rationing her water. She probably had not been drinking enough for quite a while. The book also said that standing for too long or over-exertion can lead to dizzy spells. Emily knew she could look for the supplements in the stores and force herself to start drinking more water. However, she could not slow down now with so much to do. She didn't have anyone to lean on. No one could pick up the slack, which was all up to her. She reached down and rubbed her stomach.

"How about I take more breaks and get off my feet for at least a few minutes? Do you think you could work with that?"

Emily closed the book and added it to the nightstand. She would read about delivering by yourself tomorrow. She needed to rest tonight, or else this baby would knock her on her ass. She tucked herself below the blankets and, within minutes, was fast asleep.

Emily woke later than she had hoped the following day and found it difficult to climb out of bed. She moved slowly as she got dressed, and Marley grew impatient with her pace as she headed downstairs. He ran to the kitchen and eagerly waited by the back door. Emily opened the door for him, and the sight gave both of them pause. A blanket of snow was covering the ground. Marley had never seen snow before and seemed to be afraid of it. Emily had forgotten how magical it was to wake up and find fresh snow had covered the ground. She stepped out the door to admire the scene, and Marley followed behind her with caution. When the cold snow touched his feet, he backed into the house. But after watching Emily stand in it, he found his bravery and stomped out. It didn't take long before he was jumping and playing through the white fluff. Emily watched until she could no longer take the cold and headed back inside. Marley was not far behind her, and they were soon inside the warm house.

The two of them enjoyed their breakfast. Once everything was cleaned up, Emily carefully walked back downstairs to put the laundry in the dryer. She breathed a sigh of relief that the blood had come out of her overalls. She grabbed some meat from the freezer and headed back upstairs for dinner. She put it into the fridge and promised to check on it later if it needed to sit on the counter to finish defrosting. Emily strolled through the house and made her way to the front door. The snow was just deep enough that, through the window, she could no longer see the bodies from the day before. Everything looked fresh and clean as if the previous day had never happened. Emily wanted to stay home today, but knew she had to go out. She had not made it to the farm the day before, and with the cold snap, she should probably try to get the animals in the barn and close the door to the pasture. This would help provide them with some warmth, and they were sure to need food and water by now. She could only hope that the truck could handle the drive through the snow because there was no way she was walking there.

Emily headed back upstairs to find the coat and hat she had brought from the truck. She then entered the room where she had put on Robert's clothes and was happy to find a pair of gloves. Ready to head out into the winter wonderland, Emily headed back downstairs. She was prepared to head out to the truck when she remembered what had happened the night before. She went to the kitchen, grabbed a few water bottles, and then returned to the living room. She forced herself to sit on the couch for fifteen minutes to give her body a break. While sitting, she decided she would try to find those supplements after the trip to the farm. She would not be hunting the dead today, at least not intentionally. If they crossed her path or got in her way, she would take care of them, but she would not go looking for trouble. Once her fifteen minutes were up, she was back on her feet and headed for the truck.

The world always seemed quieter after significant snowfall, and Emily enjoyed this silence. She climbed into the cab and smiled as the truck roared to life. The gas gauge showed it was nearly full. Her stalling a few days ago had turned out to be a good thing. She would not have to worry about gas now with the snow on the ground. It took a few times backing up and then going forward, but Emily did get the truck to start moving. She knew better than to stop or find herself stuck again. The drive took a little longer than usual, but she could make it to the farm. Pulling up to the barn, she saw that a few dead had found their way there. It looked like they may have been following a path they had taken in life, as, based on their clothes, they were supposed to be the farmers here.

Emily pulled as close as she could before stopping the truck. She moved quickly out of the cab and grinned as the snow slowed them down. She was able to make her way between them as they struggled to take a step. There were three more adults and a teenager, but Emily was sure he would have been listed as a child. Once done, she opened the barn door and waited as Marley ran inside. She joined him and shut the door behind herself. As always, Buttercup was the first to greet her as she came in.

"Sorry, I didn't make it yesterday, Buttercup. Things got a little crazy, and I had to handle it. Don't you worry now? I'm back, and I'll get everything taken care of." Emily stated as she entered.

Emily set to work cleaning out the muck on the floor, no easy task, as a headcount told her that all the animals had found shelter in the barn. Emily then refilled the water and moved the truck to haul fresh hay and straw. She spread the straw on the ground as best she could to provide some bedding and hoped it would help the animals stay warm. It was quite a task to close the big barn doors to the pasture, but Emily finally got it done after some time. With the doors closed, she could already feel it getting warmer in the barn. Emily grabbed the stool and the milking bucket and headed for the cows. She considered milking a rest as she was technically off her feet. Milking took a while as each cow gave a full bucket. This was within the normal range that the book had stated per milking. Emily would need to start doing this twice daily and storing it instead of pouring it out. This would be another research project for tonight when she gets home.

Emily put away the stool and bucket and headed towards the door with Marley. Buttercup seemed to be comfortable and sleeping. Emily opened the door quietly and stepped back out into the snow. She returned to the truck and followed Marley into the cab. It took several tries, but soon the truck was moving once again. Emily followed her tracks back home and parked the truck in front of the house. She decided to walk to the stores as it wasn't far and not worth the hassle of getting the truck stuck again. The pharmacy was only a few stores down, and Emily could easily make it there. As she had not been in this particular store yet, she followed her process of yelling out and waiting. She knew the things were awake now, so they would come out if they were here. Nothing moved, and Emily worked her way through the aisles. The prescription drug area was locked with a keypad. Emily was sure the code was in Robert's books, and she made a note to look for it later. She was able to find the supplements she needed and get back home without incident.

Once inside, Emily made herself a warm drink and opened the heavy curtains in the living room.

Snow was her favorite thing to see, but it never lasted long here. She decided to take the day and enjoy the view. She would go back to winning back the town tomorrow, but she just wanted to sit and enjoy the snow for today.

Chapter 20

Emily continued through the next month, much as she had done since she arrived. The cows produced a bucket of milk every time she milked them, and she had started the twice-a-day schedule. She was keeping the milk now. She had learned the process of straining it and found a supply of glass bottles in one of the stores. She was bringing home more than she could store in her refrigerator, so she dated the bottles and kept them at the grocery store. She managed to get all the horses brushed out and added that to her routine. Marley seemed to be adapting to life inside the wall, and as the days passed, he relaxed more and more.

Emily had continued her search pattern through the town and had found the last of the dead. She had to put down all seven adults, but the children were already done when she saw them. It looked like someone had tried to spare the kids from becoming zombies and had killed them all. Emily's heart was heavy when she thought about the kids, each watching as someone shot them in the head. She had taken all the bodies to the dump site, which was still piled there. While the snow had long since melted, the cold in the air had not let go. She knew she needed to dig a pit of some kind to put them in before burning, but she could not sit in the wind to figure out how to operate the equipment. The smell was strong as soon as she came within a few blocks, but there was nothing she could do for now. She had opened the inner gate and picked a spot to bury Robert. The frozen ground made it hard, and she spent days digging his grave. When she finished, she placed a makeshift cross as a marker and thanked him for giving her a chance.

It was the beginning of February, and the baby was due in about six weeks. Emily watched as her new diet, which included eating regularly, began to show. Her face no longer looked like a skeleton, and her stomach had nearly doubled in size. The baby was kicking much more these days, and Emily cherished every kick. She took it as a sign that the baby was healthy, which motivated her to work much harder. She had gathered all the furniture and baby supplies she could have ever wanted, and the nursery was ready to go. She had even hung Joe's lucky bandana above the crib. The baby could use all the luck it could get in this world. Emily had even read the information about giving birth alone. From what she understood, while it can be challenging, it was perfectly doable as long as the baby was not breached. At this point, she could only hope that the baby was in the proper position.

Emily had looked through Robert's journals and found all the default codes around town. She had gained access to the back of the pharmacy and the armory. She had also learned that all systems were wired to work through a computer. It was hidden behind a wall panel in the office. Once she found it, she could change all the codes, so they were no longer default. She also brought one of the handguns from the armory to the house. She stored it at the top of her closet, just in case. The lockers in the armory each had handprint scanners on them. Emily programmed herself to locker number one and filled it with a few of the guns and ammo, just in case.

She felt like she was as prepared as she could be. Lately, she had taken to dusting each store and keeping them clean. When she took stuff from the stores, she pulled the next thing forward so that the shelves always looked full. She found pallets of extra supplies in the backrooms that she could use if anything ran low. There was a small doctor's office that she also took the time to keep dust-free. There were only two small patient rooms and one operating room. Emily had also changed the codes here so that she had access to everything. While she was the only one here, she feared someone would try to take it from her. With the codes no longer set to the default, they would get nothing from it if they did. She felt this information would help protect her and her child if that were to happen.

The days began to blur, and Emily continued, her condition making her slower each day. The cold finally began to give way to warm days in February, and Emily enjoyed every minute of it. On one of these warm days, she found herself walking the wall and looking out into a world where the dead roamed. Emily had not opened the inner gate since burying Robert; at this point, she saw no reason why she ever would again. She looked up the old logging road, humming lullabies and enjoying the sun. That's when she saw them. They were too far away to make out their faces or fine details, but a group of people ran across the road. A couple was quite a bit smaller than the others. Emily knew they had to be children. A few adults were firing weapons in the direction they had come from, and everyone seemed terrified.

Emily continued to watch as a truck burst out of

the woods was a truck she would never forget. It was Jeff's truck, and from the sounds of it, that rapist piece of shit was still alive. Emily felt herself fall below the railing as the truck came into view. Even here, she still felt like he could get to her. Her eyes searched to find the people that he was chasing. She caught movement in the tree line on the opposite side of the road. The woods were thick over there, and he would never be able to chase them in the truck that way. Emily's mind began to race. She could open it if they could go to the gate without Jeff following. She thought back to her vow never to let anyone in the town. The sight of the children running from the same man who terrorized her made her question that choice. Jeff turned his truck and began to drive back up the logging road in the direction of where she had left the SUV. He would soon find it, and she only hoped it would not put him back on the hunt for her.

Emily watched in the woods as best she could for the people. Half of her was hoping they would find the gate so she could let them in, and the other half prayed they didn't so she wouldn't have to turn them away. Emily looked around and tried to think of a way to signal them without signaling the rapist gang with them, but she had nothing. This place was not designed to bring people in but to keep the dead out. She looked back into the woods and could no longer find them. She knew Jeff had gone the other way, so they were safe.

Emily felt her head getting a little light and realized it was time for her to rest and have lunch. She headed into the small control room and sat at the desk. She had figured out how to turn on the monitors, but

until now had never really used them. She flicked on
the monitors for the gate and watched the small
screens while she ate. Marley, who wandered around
town on his own, seemed to realize that it was
lunchtime and came trotting into the room.

"Were you chasing the chickens again?" Emily
asked without looking back at him. Marley let out a
happy bark and came running towards her. "You know,
one day, they will have enough and start chasing you.
And don't you come asking me for help then."

Marley let out a low whine that she learned was
his way of trying to get out of trouble. Emily finally
broke being stern with him and laughed as she tossed
her bread crust on the floor. Marley ate it quickly and
lay next to the couch to nap. When Emily finished her
lunch, she looked away from the monitors. The sight
of Marley sleeping made her realize just how tired she
was. Just in case, she turned on the audio for the gate
and went to lie on the couch beside him. Emily tried to
keep her eyes on the monitors, but they were heavy,
and within a few minutes, she was asleep.

Emily was woken by a sharp pain in her
stomach and around her back. The pain caused her to
sit straight up and let out a cry. Marley immediately
jumped up, prepared to defend her, but when he found
no one else in the room, he sat next to her with
concern. Emily tried to control her feelings and not let
the pain consume her, but at the moment, she was
losing. She had been positive that the baby was not
due until March at the soonest. This should not be
happening yet. Of all the things to worry about, this
may have seemed ridiculous to an outsider, but to

Emily, it was exactly what she needed. She went to the control panel and pulled up the calendar. She had not looked at one in a while. She felt a shock of surprise that helped her control her reaction to the pain. It was March 5th, and the baby was right on time. She had read in the book that the beginning stages can take a while, and it was not even close until the contractions were at least regular.

Emily stood from the console and began to walk; walking was supposed to help with the pain and get things moving. She planned to walk to the couch and see how she felt, but Emily was forced to stop halfway. She had been prepared for her water to break, which it just did, and even some blood as things started progressing. However, as her water broke, the floor below her was covered in thick, dark blood within seconds. This was one of the book's warning signs that a woman could not deliver by herself. Marley knew something wasn't right and began pacing like an expectant father. Emily worked hard to get herself under control and not start to panic. As she tried to convince herself that maybe she remembered wrong, maybe everything was fine, Marley rushed past her and began to bark at the monitors. Emily turned to beg him to be quiet, but looked at a group of people staring right into the camera.

"There has to be someone in there. I heard a woman scream, and now I hear a dog barking." A tall, thin man stepped back and looked up at the top of the wall. They had been there for a while, but Emily had not noticed.

"Is anyone in there? We are not here to cause

trouble. We just need a place to lay low for a while. These men are hunting us, and we can't seem to lose them." A blonde woman with pale skin was now talking to the camera.

"If they are in there, they aren't going to open up. Shit, I wouldn't open that gate for nothing."

It was a man's voice, but Emily could not see the face that went with it. There were quite a few out there, and Emily knew these were the people she had seen earlier. Another contraction wrapped her entire body in pain, and Emily watched as more blood fell to the floor. She didn't have time to think about this anymore. Emily reached out for the intercom button and spoke.

"Are any of you a doctor?"

The people she could see began to smile and rush towards the camera.

"We know a little medicine, and we have a guy who was an intern."

The woman seemed desperate, and Emily understood, but she had to ensure the risk was worth it.

"Does he have experience with delivering babies with complications?" Emily felt like she was cruel, but she had to know.

"Yes, yes, I do." A man rushed forward. He looked to be in his late twenties. "I am sure I can help, but we need you to…."

The man stopped speaking and looked behind him. Emily could hear the sounds and knew Jeff and his gang had found them and were driving up fast. She reached the keypad, punched the code, and opened the outer gate. As soon as the gate started to move, the people were out of view of the camera. Emily knew they were running inside.

"Shut it!" yelled a chorus of voices below, and Emily pressed the button to do just that. Within moments, the sound of the gate shutting echoed through the town. Emily walked out and looked down over the wall. All of her pain seemed to disappear as she looked down at Jeff as he stared at the gate.

"Well, this is some fun new shit right here," he laughed as he stared at the gate. "Once we get in, I think we have a new home, boys!"

Emily listened as the group began to cheer and felt her blood begin to boil. She marched back to the control room and grabbed her stored rifle. She walked back to the ledge and carefully aimed at the top of Jeff's head. Suddenly, the pain was back, and she pulled the rifle just as she fired. Based on his reaction, the shot was not a total waste as she did catch Jeff in the foot. She moved further down the wall, let off another shot, and kept repeating the process. Jeff and his group didn't realize it was one person and quickly left. Emily turned the rifle back and looked down into the area she called the in-between. Most of the group was huddled together, and a few men looked at the inner door.

"How many of you are there?" she called,

trying to hide the pain in her voice.

"Ten and two children," the skinny man said. "You were talking like you needed a doctor. Is someone here hurt?"

"Not exactly, are any of you bitten?"

"No, we are all fine," she could tell that her question had scared the man, and she understood why. To be immune like her was rare, and they had probably never seen it.

"Look, if you are, all I ask is that you stay in between the walls for twenty-four hours. You would be free to come in if you are fine after that." The man seemed taken aback but again insisted they were fine.

Emily felt the pain come on even stronger this time, and she could not hide the pain.

"Ma'am, are you alright?" the man shouted up at her.

"I don't think so. Stairs are on the right."

Emily forced herself to walk back into the control building, enter the code, and open the inner gate. She knew she should shut it once they were in, but her eyes were going dark. Her face struck the metal ground, but the pain did not even register. Her vision continued to darken as she tried to watch the door. Within moments, she heard Marley barking and realized he would not let them in here.

"Marley, no!" she cried with everything she could muster.

Marley went quiet, walked through the door, and lay beside her on the ground. Emily tried to make out the faces of the people who ran in, but could not. She was able to hear them clearly, though.

"Oh my god, why is there so much blood?" said a woman's voice.

"The baby may be a breach, or she may be hemorrhaging. I can't be sure until I examine her." She recognized the voice from the monitor.

"So, you will examine her and deliver a baby here?" This voice belonged to a much younger woman.

"I don't have much choice, do I?! It's not like we can take her to the hospital! Why don't you be useful and go try to find me some medical supplies!" the man shouted back at her.

"Clinic," Emily breathed no louder than a whisper. She wanted to yell it, but she did not have the strength. She felt someone lean down beside her while the doctor and the woman continued to argue. "Clinic," she managed one more time.

"Will, all of you, shut up, there's a clinic down there, and that's where we need to go. Doc, is it safe to move her?" She recognized the voice of the man who said no one would open the gate.

Doc mumbled something that Emily did not

understand. She felt lifted off the cool floor, and the heat began to burn through her body again. She was going to protest, but found some relief as her face rested against cool leather. Emily listened as they descended the stairs and started up the main road.

"Well, genius, where is this clinic, because everything here looks like it belongs in an old Western movie."

That young girl was starting to get on Emily's last nerve. She could tell that the man carrying was listening or looking at her to give them a clue about which door it was. Emily tried, but she could not, knowing they were only a few doors down from it. The man was turning. She could tell he was searching when a bark rang out.

"There!" he yelled at the others. Yet again, Emily owed her life to Marley, the pup who always seemed to know what she needed.

"Let's get her in a room!" the doctor said as they ran through the doors.

Emily knew the operating room would probably be best suited, and it was the third door. She tried and barely managed to tap her finger on the leather vest three times, but the man seemed to pick up on it. He ran down the hall, and Emily heard the door open.

"This will work," she heard the shock in the doctor's voice as they entered. He was not expecting this. Emily felt herself being laid down on the table, but then felt someone take her hand as the doctor walked around the room, inventorying everything.

"I'm just trying to help." She heard the older woman say. Then Emily listened to the snaps on the overalls come undone, and the woman removed them as carefully as possible.

"I have everything I need to do an emergency C-section except for the anesthetic," the doctor stated as he walked back into the room. The medication room is sealed with some kind of pin key."

"Then break the damn thing down!" the man holding her hand yelled. Emily could swear that he genuinely sounded concerned for her and the baby.

"It's a steel door. Not even you could put a dent in it. I can get the baby out, but the woman may..." The doctor trailed off, and Emily knew that without the medication, she would not survive. The grip on her hand tightened, and she could feel that the man holding it was getting angry. Emily struggled and began to tap on the man's hand lightly.

"Wait!" he yelled to the room, and Emily knew that he noticed. She tapped three times, counted to five, tapped eight times, counted to five, tapped one time, counted to five, and tapped five more times. She was sure she got it right and waited. "The code to the door is three, eight, one, five," the man announced. She could feel everyone in the room was staring at her, but was glad she could not see it. She was lying on a table, half-naked, pregnant, and dependent on a room full of strangers. She heard the doctor leave the room and return a few minutes later.

"I'm going to give you some medication now. The first will help with the pain, but it will cause you to fall asleep. The second will help fight any infection that may happen. Your baby is turned the wrong way, and we need to do a C-section to get it out. Do you understand?" The doctor seemed to be waiting for a response, like she had another choice. She tapped the man's hand one time.

"I think she's got it, doc," the man said. "Don't worry now. I'm going to stay here until you wake up and make sure that baby of yours is okay," he whispered to Emily. She wanted to thank him or at least learn his name, but the first needle was already leaving her skin, and she felt herself fall to sleep.

Chapter 21

Emily knew immediately she was not in her bed. The day's events rushed back into her mind, and she realized she did not feel the baby anymore. Her eyes shot open, and she tried to sit up as quickly as possible. Her entire body was sore, and as she pulled back the blanket, she saw a bandage on her lower stomach. They had gotten the baby out, but she did not see it as she scanned the room. She had been moved to one of the exam rooms, and a strange man was sleeping in a chair beside the bed.

He had blonde hair, and it was pretty long for a man. Most of the men she knew kept their hair business short. He looked to be rather large, not fat but muscular and tall. He wore a pair of black boots, old blue jeans, and a dark shirt. Over the shirt, he had on a leather vest, the kind that bikers wear on television. Emily had not known any bikers in real life, so this was her only frame of reference. She remembered the cool leather against her cheek as she was carried and realized that this was the man who had promised to stay with her until she woke up.

Emily pulled the blanket back over her bandage and tried to straighten herself in the bed. The man began to stir as she did, and when he saw that she was awake, he began to smile.

"I thought we had a real-life sleeping beauty on our hands. Doc said it would take you a while to wake up, but I've never seen him do surgery before, so I was a little worried."

Emily stared at the man, unsure how he could be so casual. She had so many questions to ask before she could be the same, but, at the moment, only one came to her mind.

"The baby…" she reached for her stomach as she had all those months.

"Oh shit, of course. She's fine, they found some formula nearby, and she was crying up a storm, so they just took her out to get her to eat. She is a stubborn one, though. She was refusing them and giving them all hell. Let me get her." He said as he stood up and walked out of the room. Emily only focused on one thing, though: her baby was a girl and was alive. Emily watched as a woman only slightly older than her walked in, holding a large yellow blanket. Emily could hear the cries of the baby hiding inside it.

"Here you go, little one, here's your mama," the woman cooed as she handed Emily the blanket.

As soon as Emily had her in her arms, the tears stopped. The two sat silently for a long time, staring at each other. Emily could not believe that after everything, she got to experience this moment. She was pulled back as the woman handed her the bottle.

"Babies normally eat within a few hours of being born, but it has been nearly six, and she hasn't eaten anything. Maybe she was waiting for you?"

Emily took the bottle and offered it to her daughter, who immediately took it and started eating. Emily heard everyone in the room breathe a sigh of relief. The bottle was nearly empty before Emily looked up at the sound of someone coming into the room. She was surprised to see that everyone had left, and the young man they had called Doc was now coming in.

"I'm happy to see that she is eating. That was a close one, too much longer, and we would have lost you both." Emily searched for strong enough words, but all she could manage was "Thank you." Doc seemed to understand and nodded.

"You will need to stay in bed for a while longer, and the bandage on your stitches must be changed regularly. I have put together some painkillers and antibiotics to help you," he said as he placed two bottles on the table next to her. Emily finished feeding the baby and noticed that the doctor looked awkward as he stood next to the door.

"Is there something else, Doc?" Emily asked, knowing that he had to have questions but did not want to bother her.

"We are all just trying to figure it out, and I told them that you needed to rest, but…." Doc was now staring at his shoes.

"But they still want to know. It's fine; I do owe you all an explanation." Emily looked around the small room. "I don't think all of you will fit here, though. Would it be okay with you if, using a wheelchair, of course, we moved this to my house?"

"Oh, of course, you would both rest better there anyway. I saw one in the supply closet. Give me just a moment."

Doc rushed out of the room, and Emily could hear him fighting to get the wheelchair into the room. Emily offered him the baby to hold while she climbed carefully out of bed and into the chair. When she stood, she could fix the gown to cover most of herself, but she still grabbed a blanket from the bed to put over her lap. Once she was covered, Doc handed the baby back and carefully pushed her out of the room. Emily tried not to look at the faces they passed as they made their way out of the clinic. The biker man had opened the door and smiled as she passed. Once outside, Emily watched as Marley ran from the front porch to her chair. As he neared, she held up a hand to signal him to be slow and watched as he carefully sniffed the baby in her arms. She knew he would be fine and protect the baby just as he had protected her.

Once the doggy introductions were over, Emily looked around to see that everyone had gathered around her. The evening was setting in, and everything would be dark soon. Emily wanted to stall outside in the fresh air as long as she could before going inside.

"So, I'm sure you all have questions," Emily spoke to the group.

"Where is everyone else? What happened to them?" It was the younger voice, and Emily now saw that it belonged to a girl who was maybe nineteen years old.

"I am the only person who lives here. I found this place a little over three months ago. The gate was open, and I needed a place to hide from the same men chasing you."

"That doesn't tell us what happened to the people here, does it?" Emily turned to look at an older man, probably in his late fifties.

"I can only tell you what I was able to figure out by reading journals. This place was built by a doctor named Robert. He was part of the team deceived into creating the device and the toxin released in the sky the night the world went to shit. He was able to escape, though the rest of his team was killed. He discovered that part of the population would be immune to the airborne toxin and wouldn't become walking corpses from it. He also discovered that an even smaller part of the population would remain immune even if bitten. He built this place to make the antidote and keep those he loves safe. According to his notes, he thought he had bought himself enough time, but the flash happened sooner than he expected. The crew he had working on this place was not done; he had not gathered everyone he needed to, and there was no antidote. He tried to contain it, but the dead took over the town. He climbed up on the wall in the control room where you found me and opened the gate. He made his final notes and took his own life."

Emily continued, "I learned from his notes what all the codes were and changed them to something I only knew. I thought it would help protect my family if someone ever got in. I worked the past few months to clear the dead still here, and they have all been accounted for. I have them all piled on the city's outskirts to be burned, but have been unable to. All of them except for Robert, I buried him in the in-between. It was a thank you for giving me a chance to survive."

Emily looked around at the faces. Half of them were in shock, and some thought she was full of shit.

"In the market, glass milk bottles are dated as early as today. How do you have fresh milk?" the older woman asked.

"There is a farm on the side of town. There are cows, sheep, horses, chickens, and goats. I haven't been able to figure out how to milk the goats. There are also a lot of supplies for growing crops, but as I arrived at the end of December, I have not tried to figure that out yet."

"If you were alone, then how did you..." It was the younger girl, and she seemed to be confused about how Emily had gotten pregnant.

"I had a husband before the world went to shit. After I was separated from my family, I had a little surprise on the way."

"When you let us in, you said if we were bitten, you only asked that we stay in the middle section for twenty-four hours, and if we were fine, we could come in. It's pretty well known that if you get bitten, you are dead. Why would you say that?" It was the skinny

271

man this time.

Emily looked over at Doc and the biker. They had to have seen the scar when she was in surgery. Their faces told her that they had kept it a secret. Emily reached up with one hand, pushed her hair back, and then pulled down the shoulder of her gown so everyone could see the scar. A few gasped, and a couple tightened their grasp on their weapons.

"Everyone, calm down. She's fine!" it was the biker yelling as he moved between her and the others.

"Look at it. It's healed and has been there for a while." Doc stepped up to join him.

"I was bitten the day after the flash. I had seen enough horror movies to know I would die, so I waited in my house to do just that. But I kept waking up every morning, and it started to heal. I never understood why until I read Robert's journals. Some people, like me, have a rare genetic marker that somehow makes them immune."

"Does that mean the baby is immune too?" It was a little boy who stepped forward this time. He could not be more than six years old.

"I don't know," was the only answer Emily could give as she stared at the sleeping baby in her arms.

"So, your plan was just to stay in here, alone, and let the rest of us stay out there to die!" A woman stepped forward with crazy blonde hair.

"It wasn't a plan. The only living people I had seen before you lot were Jeff's rapist gang. He grabbed me and told me I would be his. Then he tried to rape me, and when I fought back, he locked me in a cellar with very little food or sunlight until he thought I had broken and would give in to his will. I played along and allowed him to lead me into the center of his boys as he told me to drop to my knees. I played my part very well, and then I drove a screwdriver into his penis. I swore never to trust people again and protect my baby that day. But today, I broke that vow. Tell me, if that was the only living people you saw, would you be putting out open house signs and baking cookies?"

Emily could feel herself shaking, telling this part of her story. She had not been able to tell anyone except Marley what had happened to her, and she regretted it even as the words came out. The woman with the crazy hair looked down at her feet and stepped back. Emily felt the tears running down her face, and she looked down, trying to hide them from everyone staring at her.

"I probably would have shot us on sight if I had been in your shoes," the biker kneeled next to her chair. "You have nothing to be ashamed of. You opening that gate at all takes more courage than should ever be asked of anyone." Emily nodded and could not help but find comfort in his words.

"If you all are hungry, you're free to come up to my place. I pulled out enough ground meat for a small army last night, and I guess now I know why. According to the books, I also have a few beds that I've made up part of nesting. There's hot water, and you all are free to get washed up." Emily was surprised to hear herself saying the words. She listened as mumbles of "hot water" and "food" rippled through the group.

"We would greatly appreciate it," the skinny man replied. He then grabbed Emily's chair and began pushing her towards the house. "I assume this one is yours by the dog on the front porch. May I ask, how did it become yours?"

"Well, there was a bidding war, but in the end, I was the last person standing." Emily laughed and heard him join her in the laughter.

Chapter 22

Once inside the house, Emily felt herself taking them through the grand tour. She explained that other than the few clothes she had for herself, she didn't have much in the way of clothing. But they were all welcome to go to the clothing store and get anything they wanted. She told them about the washer and dryer downstairs and whether they needed to do laundry and the bathrooms. She told the children about the movie collection and made sure to have their parents' permission before watching anything.

"So, these journals you spoke of," it was the older man once again. Emily would have to find a way to figure out what their names were.

"They are in the study. Robert had an entire bookshelf of stuff he had written himself. I've started to add to it, and there is a journal on the bottom shelf that is mine that I started right after I came here. Just please make sure to put them back before you go to sleep." Everyone stared at her, a little confused. "I have been doing everything here by myself for months. I didn't have time to take a day and clean the house, so I've been pretty picky about ensuring everything is where it goes before I go to bed." They seemed to accept this explanation. "If one of you could help me to the kitchen, I think I have everything to get dinner started. Nothing fancy, but I hope pasta and garlic bread are acceptable for everyone."

"You are not cooking. You are welcome to

come to tell us where everything is, but you are supposed to be resting." The older woman had stepped forward. "We will take turns, as there are only three showers anyway. Bobby, I, you, and your daddy will be in the kitchen with Shawn and June. Sarah, you and the rest get some fresh clothes and start working your way through the showers." The woman started to move to the kitchen and turned back, "And try to save a little hot water for the rest of us."

"No promises," the woman with the crazy hair Emily now knew was Sarah replied.

Emily watched the skinny man, the biker, and an older lady head into the kitchen. She knew one of the men was Shawn, and the other was Bobby's dad. Before she could overthink it, Bobby pushed a chair into the kitchen, obviously eager to help. Once inside, Emily told them where she kept the pots and pans and where to find the noodles and sauce. Bobby eagerly asked where to find the dog food, and he took care of Marley. Emily watched as the woman and the skinny man started cooking. She could tell right away that this man was Bobby's dad. Shawn, the biker, took the dishes that June was handing to him and carried them to the dining room table. Emily seldom came in here and had almost forgotten it was here. She ate all her meals at the kitchen table while Marley ate his.

Emily heard the front door open as some of the group returned from getting fresh clothes.

"I don't need your help, Uncle Jacob! I am almost ten years old; I can shower by myself!"

"I know you can." Jacob struggled with his niece, "I'm just trying to keep you safe, Tera."

The sound of Tera running told Emily that she most definitely did not understand.

"Ms. Julia, please tell my uncle I can take a shower alone!" Tera screamed as she ran into the kitchen. Bobby's mom turned and laughed as Jacob came into the room.

"I think you're just a tad overprotective." She said to Jacob.

"It's not that I don't think she can. I just worry." Jacob looked exhausted. He could not have been over twenty-one and was not ready to care for his niece like a father.

"Tera, why don't you use the shower in my room? Then your uncle can watch TV while you shower, and you guys can switch when you are done. You can shower alone, and he knows that you're safe. Does that sound fair to you?" Emily seemed to shock everyone in the room by speaking up.

"I'll take it!" Tera exclaimed as she took off for the stairs.

Jacob followed after mouthing a quick "Thank you" to Emily. The rest of the bunch was coming through the door, and the bathrooms were soon full. Those who had taken too long picking out their clothes waited for a shower to become available in the living room. Emily was beginning to enjoy learning their names by listening to them. It was like a living puzzle. She listened as the shower switches took place, and soon dinner was heading for the dining room. Bobby proudly pushed Emily to the head of the table, where someone had brought down the bassinet from her room, probably Jacob, as he and Tera were the ones to use that shower. Emily laid her daughter down in the bassinet for the first time in hours. When she turned back to the table, everyone was sitting quietly as if they were waiting for permission from her.

"Please, don't be shy. Help yourselves." Emily motioned for them all to start eating.

"We're not shy. We just wanted to say thank you," Bobby spoke up. "But then we all realized that none of us knows your name." Bobby seemed very confused about how none of them knew her name. "Mommy said it might be best for us to tell you ours first. I'm…"

"Your Bobby, your daddy, Sam, and your mama, Julia. Over here, we have Tera and her Uncle Jacob. This beautiful woman is June, and her husband, Howard." Emily felt proud as she worked her way around the table. "The gentleman over there with the plaid shirt is Derick. Next to him is Sarah, and beside her is Jessica." Emily motioned to the chair on her left, "This is Shawn, and that is Doc. Does everyone call you Doc, or do you go by something else?"

Everyone sat silently, just looking at her.

"How does she know our names, but we don't know hers?" Bobby was not shy and asked the question before his mother could stop him.

"Because little guy, unlike us, she has been alone a long time. She stayed alive by paying attention to everything around her." It was Shawn who spoke, and it caught Emily off guard. "She had to. There was no one else to depend on to notice what she missed. So, while all of us assumed at least one of us got her name, no one did. But she learned all of ours while we cooked dinner."

"Wow," Bobby gasped. "You are smart."

This finally broke the tension at the table as everyone laughed, even Emily.

"I do the best I can," she replied. "And you can call me Emily."

"What about her?" Bobby asked while motioning to the bassinet. Everyone started to go silent again, but Emily had had enough of silence.

"Hope, her name is Hope." Emily quickly replied. "Come on now, let's eat."

Soon, the sounds of conversation filled the air, and everyone was enjoying themselves. This reminded Emily of the family dinners when she was a kid. She barely ate that night but instead watched the scene unfold in front of her. She was never really alone; she always had Marley and Hope, but this was different. This was a complete family who laughed and enjoyed whatever they had together.

As the evening began to wear down, the next group headed out to get fresh clothes and start taking their showers. All of the rooms had been claimed, along with the couch. Emily grabbed Hope from the bassinet and turned to look at the stairs. She had not thought this plan through very well. She wasn't supposed to walk upstairs, but that's where her bed was, and there was nowhere left to sleep down there. She thought that if she went slowly, she could carry Hope up the stairs as someone stepped behind her.

"You're not planning on breaking Doc's orders and walking up those stairs now, are you, Ms. Emily?" Shawn teased behind her.

"No, I was just trying to remember how to fly from my days in Neverland." Emily teased back.

"Well, if I may be bold, I would be glad to assist you up the stairs, both of you." He nodded at Hope, fast asleep after another bottle and a diaper change.

"If it's not too much trouble." Emily wasn't teasing this time. She hated having to keep having Shawn carry her all over the place.

"It's none at all," he replied. Before Emily could speak, he lifted her out of the chair. He then began carrying her up the stairs. Once in the room, he placed her on the bed and returned downstairs to get the bassinet. "Is there anything else I can get you guys?" he asked after putting the bassinet next to Emily's bed.

"No, we are fine, thank you. You'd better hurry

before you lose your spot for a shower."

"Someone already took it." Shawn laughed. "I can wait for a while. How long can a married couple in an apocalypse take in a shower anyway?"

Emily could not help but laugh. "Well, the shower should be free by the end of next week, but only if they barely like each other."

"Well, shit. Between them and the teenager, I'm never going to get to take a shower."

"There's one right in there," Emily pointed at the bathroom. "I'm not going to be using it. Help yourself."

"Are you sure? I don't want to invade your space and all."

"Won't it be worse for me if you never shower and I have to smell you?" Emily teased.

"I can't argue that with you. I won't be long," Shawn stated as he closed the door.

"Take your time," Emily replied as she lay her head down on her pillow. A few moments later, she felt Marley jump on the bed and cuddle in close. "It's not just you and me anymore, pup. You going to be okay with that?" Marley wagged his tail, and Emily listened to it rhythmically hit the blankets. "Yeah, I thought you might." Emily heard the shower turn on, but she was fast asleep within minutes.

Chapter 23

Emily woke the following day and could already hear the sounds of people downstairs talking and breakfast being made. She leaned into the bassinet to find Hope still sound asleep. She thanked the stars for being lucky enough to have a baby who slept through the night. Without thinking, she pulled back the blankets and sat up. Her body was still sore today, but nothing she couldn't handle. She looked down to see that a fresh bandage had been applied to her lower stomach. Touching the dressing, she remembered that Doc had told her that she was not supposed to walk. She looked around the room but saw no way to get around otherwise. It was then that she noticed the note on the bedside table.

Everything is looking good.

You should be good to walk today

Just don't push it.

You can wear regular clothes if you want.

Just nothing tight over the bandage.

I'm sure you want to take a shower.

Just change the bandage when you are done.

Just call if you need help.

Emily focused on one word of the note, shower. She wanted one more than words could express and wasn't going to question the good doctor's judgment. She stood slowly, trying very hard not to wake Hope. Marley raised his head as she got out of bed, but lay back down, seeing that she walked into the bathroom. Emily left the door open as she turned on the water and slipped out of the hospital gown she had been in since the day before. She tried her best to keep the bandage out of the water but knew that she would change it by the time she was done. She tried to move quickly but carefully as she washed off the previous day's events. After she shut off the water, she stood for a moment to ensure Hope had not woken while she was washing. There was no sound from the bedroom, and Emily quickly changed her bandage, brushed her hair and teeth, and walked back into the bedroom to get dressed. Her only clothes were still the overalls that fit over her baby bump. They were not tight over the bandage and strangely made her feel like herself again.

Once dressed, she walked back to the bed to wake the sleeping babies. Hope woke very quickly and seemed to be happy about it. Marley turned on the bed, and Emily heard him snoring again as she changed Hope and put her in a fresh outfit. She opened the bedroom door and realized it was not locked for the first time since she had been there. Then she remembered that she had fallen asleep while Shawn was in the shower. Her face felt hot, and she couldn't understand why. She shook it off and walked out the door. Marley seemed to realize that there was no getting her to return to bed and jumped down to follow. Emily took the stairs slowly, one at a time, and Marley walked patiently behind her. When she reached the bottom, the children were watching cartoons and said a quick "Good Morning" as she passed. Emily made her way to the kitchen, where most of the group was either drinking coffee or helping to cook breakfast. Emily glanced over at the dog bowls and saw that they were both filled already, probably by Bobby. She made her way through the room to open the door for Marley.

Opening the door, she was frightened and did not realize that Shawn would be standing on the other side. Marley seemed immune to the shock and went out into the yard, pushing past Shawn. Emily felt her face turn red as Shawn moved aside for Marley. As he turned, she saw that he was holding a cigarette. As soon as he saw Hope in Emily's arms, he took a few steps into the yard.

"Bad habit, I know, especially around a baby, but I made sure to step outside."

Emily could tell he was trying to defend himself, but couldn't understand why. It had been years since she had her last cigarette. But the cartons in the store were tempting even her. Hope was the only thing that had given her the self-control to say no.

"It's fine, really," Emily tried to assure him. "It doesn't bother me, just as long as it's not around Hope."

"Thanks. I figure with everything going on, these things killing me are the least of my worries."

Shawn motioned at the cigarette.

"I understand that," Emily responded as Hope began to fuss in her arms. "Would you mind letting him in when he's done? I think she is done waiting for her breakfast?"

"Oh, no problem," Shawn said as he turned back to the yard.

Emily closed the door and looked back into the kitchen. The people were moving all over the place, but all seemed to understand the chaos. They were like a well-oiled machine working together, and everyone knew what they were supposed to do. Emily thought back to what Shawn had said the night before about her being alone so long that she learned to do everything herself. While having actual people around was a dream come true, Emily also wanted to scream because she could not do things as she had always done. Emily calmed herself before heading into the chaos to make Hope a bottle when Julia turned and handed her one. Emily forced a smile as she accepted it and left the room. The children were still watching the television, and Emily wanted to be alone. She headed for the study and breathed a sigh of relief at the empty room. She pushed the door closed behind her and went to sit in the desk chair.

She began to feed Hope and thought about everything that had happened. There were actual living people here now. Even Hope here felt overwhelmed, but adding in the others shattered her. She comforted that if anything were to happen to her, at least Hope would have someone who wasn't a dog to take care of her. But she didn't know how to adjust to life with other people after being alone for so long. She sat, rolling her thoughts through her head as Hope was nearly done with the bottle. A light knock at the door startled her more than she would have liked.

"Yes," she answered to whoever was on the other side. The door slowly opened, and Shawn stepped through.

"Sorry to bother you, but this poor guy has been pacing outside the door since we came in. Is it okay if I let him in here with you?"

"Oh my, yes, please," Emily had utterly forgotten about Marley in trying to sort out her thoughts. Shawn opened the door a little further, and Marley came bounding into the room. He sniffed Hope first and then Emily. Once he seemed convinced that they were both okay, he curled up on the floor next to the desk.

"They have breakfast ready if you are hungry," Shawn spoke from the doorway. Emily felt her stomach knot at the thought of going to the dining room. She feared being surrounded by all of them right now. "I know they can be a lot to handle all at once," Shawn spoke as if he could read her mind. "If you want, I could just fix you a plate and bring it here?"

"That would be great," Emily replied, breathing a sigh of relief.

Shawn nodded and shut the door behind him.

Emily did not know why he was so kind to her or seemed always to know what she needed, but she was thankful for him. A few minutes passed, and Shawn returned to the door with a plate. He set it on the desk in front of her without a word. He then smiled and walked back out of the room. Emily looked down at the plate and realized just how hungry she was. Holding Hope in one arm, she ate breakfast in silence while Hope began to fall asleep. Even when she finished, she sat with the empty plate before her for a long time. No one came knocking, and she heard nothing from the rest of the house. Emily realized that she could not sit here forever; her arm was falling asleep from holding Hope, and it smelled like Hope needed a diaper change.

Emily stood and walked to the door, turning back only once to ensure that Marley was behind her. She didn't want to scare him again, and Marley was not about to let her out of his sight. She opened the door to see that the living room was empty. In the kitchen, there was no one, and everything from breakfast had been cleaned up and put away. Emily began to fear that maybe she was going crazy. Was anyone here, or did her mind make it up to help her through labor? She turned and headed for the dining room, where she found everyone sitting quietly, talking. As she entered the room, the talking stopped, and everyone turned to look at her.

"Please, don't stop on my account," Emily said as she turned to leave.

"Wait!" Sam called after her as he rushed over to her. "We just wanted to ensure we were all on the same page before talking to you. I think we are ready if you are up to it?"

Emily nodded and allowed Sam to lead her to the empty chair at the table. As she sat, she remembered that her arm was asleep, and it was beginning to hurt.

"Not to be a pain, but this little one needs a change and an actual bed to lie in. I feel this talk may take more than a minute, so if you don't mind." Emily stopped as Doc stood up.

"We didn't want you to have to keep doing the stairs all day," he said as he walked toward her. He pulled forward a bassinet that Emily had not noticed was in the corner, but it was not the same one she had been using. "We hope you don't mind, but we went into the shop and found you another one to keep down here to make things easier. We also brought some of her clothes and diapers down here just in case you needed them."

Emily felt the tears in her eyes as she looked at the simple gesture. She could not help but feel guilty about her thoughts of wanting to be alone. Julia spotted it immediately and came over to Emily.

"If it's okay with you, I'll quickly take Hope into the other room and change her. I know Doc said you are good to walk, but it couldn't hurt for you to rest as much as possible."

Emily trusted Julia. She had since she met her. Emily nodded and handed Hope to Julia. Julia was only gone for a few minutes and returned with Hope. She laid Hope in the bassinet next to Emily and returned to sit next to Sam and Bobby. Emily looked at each of their faces and waited for someone to speak.

"We all know that you have been alone for a long time, and you told us about part of what happened to you the last time you were around people," Sam spoke. Emily saw Shawn clench his fist as Sam talked about what had happened to her. Emily tried to remain focused on Sam. "It makes sense that you would have wanted to keep everyone out to keep Hope safe when you found this place. I think any of us would have done the same thing." Sam finished and looked around at everyone, almost all nodding in agreement.

"Life is hard out there, not only because of the dead, but the living can be even more dangerous. And you don't know us very well, but we were hoping that maybe you would allow us to stay?" Sam looked down at the table as he finished. Emily felt confused by his question; there were more of them than her, and she was in no condition to force them out if she wanted to. Yet, they were asking her permission to stay, and she did not know how to begin comprehending that.

"We don't want to take over what is yours," Julia spoke. "Living here would be the miracle that most of us never expected, but it's not something we can just take because we want it."

"You know things about this place that would take us forever to learn, and some of it we may never learn," Howard said. "I have done some reading in the library, and it looks like you have reset all of the default codes, which was brilliant." Emily felt herself blush a little. "Robert may have built the town, but you are the lifeblood of it now. No one can make it work here without you."

Emily looked around at everyone and finally heard herself speak, "You all want to stay, but you want me to be in charge?"

"Well, we want to stay, but we don't all agree that you should be in charge," Derick replied. He hadn't said much since she met the group, and it caught Emily off guard.

"We've already been over this, Derick," Sam spoke up. "This is her place, and if we want to make it work here, we must do it by her rules.

"And what are those rules?" Derick sneered back. "Having a woman in charge is already asking for trouble, but asking us all to follow her rules when we don't even know what they are is suicide."

Emily realized that she had no idea what those rules would be. She had never planned to let anyone in and didn't think she ever needed them. The biggest thing she had thought about regarding rules was how much television time Hope would be allowed. She realized that Derick was now staring a hole through her. He expected an answer now.

"Shut the hell up, Derick!" Shawn yelled next to her. Emily looked at him as he spoke, "She doesn't have it all lined out how things should be done, and we are putting her on the spot. Give her a moment to breathe, dammit."

"Oh, just because Mr. Tough-Guy has a thing for the girl, we all have to be nice! Don't think I haven't noticed how you are around her, and I guess finding her pregnant just let you know she puts out!"

"You can shut the fuck up, or I will throw you off that fucking wall myself!" Shawn roared as he rose from his chair, slamming his hands on the table.

Emily glanced at the bassinet and was surprised to see Hope not stirring despite the commotion. She quickly looked toward the children and saw that they were not handling the situation nearly as well. Bobby had his hands over his ears and looked like he wanted to hide under the table. Tera's eyes were wide with fear, and she looked as if she might take off running at any moment. Emily realized this was her moment to prove whether she was supposed to be in charge. She would never have control; she let Derick bully her, and Shawn came to her rescue. She thought back to Chad and how he always made her feel powerless in her own home, and this was her home now.

"Enough!" she yelled over both Shawn and Derick. They both stopped and sat down in silence. Emily could tell that Shawn still wanted to throw Derick off the wall, and Derick was not nearly out of colorful insults. "I don't know how this is supposed to work, but I do know that screaming at each other is not going to help!" Emily took a few deep breaths and forced herself to calm down. "This is my home; I want this to be a safe place for my daughter to grow up without worrying about what she will eat, the dead eating her, or about rapists trying to make her a sex slave. I never planned on letting anyone in here. I vowed that I wouldn't. But now I see that I can't do this alone and need help to keep her safe."

Emily paused and looked around at all of them. Everyone seemed to be understanding and compassionate about her words, except for Derick, who appeared to have his face permanently stuck if he smelled something terrible. "Derick is right, though. You should know the rules before committing to stay." Derick let out a snort and smiled at Shawn.

"I am going to take today and think about this. Nothing this important should be undertaken without thought. I will have at least some answers for you all tonight." Emily knew that she had given herself a short timeline, but she knew she would have to make some decisions soon.

"That's more than we could have hoped for," Sam said. "Thank you."

Emily could tell that his words were sincere and simply nodded back. The room was silent for several minutes, and Emily knew she could not think. She stood slowly from her chair and reached for the bassinet.

"Here, I'll help you," Shawn said as he stood and gently picked up the bassinet with Hope sleeping inside.

Emily turned and headed back to the study.

Shawn followed with Hope and Marley right behind. Shawn gently set down the bassinet and stood quietly while Emily took the desk chair.

"I just wanted to say I'm sorry about all that stuff Derick said and how I reacted," he spoke softly.

Emily looked at him and realized that she would have been afraid of him just by how he looked before the flash. But now, she saw nothing but a gentle giant. He had been protective of her since before he knew anything about her. He had been the only one to notice her trying to talk, and he had done more than she could have asked to help her since Hope had been born.

"I've already forgotten it. It seems like Derick never has anything nice to say."

"You've got that right," Shawn laughed. "And just as a suggestion, you may want to include rules about how much alcohol one person can take in, or he just gets worse."

"I will keep that in mind." Emily smiled. She watched as Shawn turned and walked towards the door. "Shawn," Emily heard herself say. Shawn stopped and turned back to her. Emily knew that she had to talk now, "I just wanted to say thank you for everything. Without you, I wouldn't be here, and I don't know how to ever repay you for that."

"There's nothing to repay," Shawn replied, and then he turned and left.

Emily sat in the room with Hope and Marley and began to think. They expected her to have rules or some idea of how this place would work with more people, and she had no idea where to start. She wasn't a mayor of anything before this, just a glorified receptionist of a landscaping company. She knew how to keep work schedules organized and the payroll on time, but she was also useless. Robert built this place; he was the one who knew how to make it work. The thought of Robert reminded Emily of some of his books. She had said they were useless months ago when she found them because she was alone, but now, they were exactly what she needed.

Emily headed to the bookcase and began carrying the books to the desk. Once she had all the ones she thought would help, she sat back down and began to look through them one at a time, taking notes as she went. Robert had written out how work would be divided between the residents based on their skills and abilities. The only job that everyone shared was a guard shift on the wall. Since it protected everyone, it was everyone's job to protect it. Robert had even written out the currency form he planned to use inside to ensure that hard work paid off and those lazy were taught their consequences. Emily worked for a few hours, taking notes as she went through the pages one at a time. She only stopped when Hope woke and began to fuss for another bottle and a fresh diaper.

As Emily lifted Hope to the desk to change her, she noticed the pain in her lower abdomen for the first time. She then remembered the pills that Doc had given her and had yet to take one of them. Emily swallowed the pain, made it through the diaper change, and placed Hope back into the bassinet. She did not trust herself to carry her to get the bottle right now, so Hope would have to wait here.

"You're in charge until I get back," Emily said to Marley as she headed for the door.

Marley stood and went to lie down next to the bassinet. There was no way anything was going to happen to Hope while she was gone. Emily opened the study door and saw several group members in the living room, some watching television and others in small groups talking. The talking again stopped as Emily entered, but she paid it no mind this time. She spotted Doc and walked toward him as quickly as she could.

"I have a question, Doc," she asked as she walked toward him. "With everything going on, I have forgotten to take my medication. I'm going to take it now, but I just want to ensure that everything is going to be okay."

"Oh yes, there's no sign of infection, so the antibiotic is more of a just in case, and the pain killer is just to make you comfortable, so if you're not feeling any pain...." Doc stared at her for a moment, "But I get the feeling that the pain is what reminded you of them in the first place." Emily nodded as she placed her hand over the bandage. "They are probably still up on your nightstand. I'll run up and get them for you."

"Thank you," Emily breathed as she had been dreading trying to walk up the stairs. Doc took off for the stairs, and Emily made her way to the kitchen. Sam and Julia were sitting at the kitchen table talking as she entered, and again she ended another conversation.

"Sorry to interrupt, I just need to get some water, and Hope is already hungry again." Emily mused as she made her way to the sink.

"I have a bottle prepped for her. If you like, I can heat it and bring it in a few minutes." Julia smiled. Emily wanted to insist that she do it herself, but the pain got worse the longer she was on her feet.

"I'd greatly appreciate it," Emily replied as she tried to reach for a glass in the cabinet. However, the stretch only made the pain worse, and she abandoned the attempt and winced in pain.

Sam rushed to her side and asked, "Are you okay?"

"I'll be fine," Emily replied. "I forgot to take my pain meds." She could tell he was ready to rush off and get them for her. "Doc's grabbing them now. I was trying to get some water to take them with."

"I'll get it," Julia stated as she walked toward the sink. "You go sit down now."

Emily knew she needed to be strong and look like a leader, but even the most remarkable leaders know when to ask for help. Instead of protesting, she allowed Sam to help her back to the study and into the chair. He stayed with her until Julia and Doc arrived, and they all ensured she took the pills.

"See, I will be just fine. There is no need for you all to worry anymore."

"If you need anything, just yell," Sam replied.

'I will, I promise." Emily smiled at them.

She could see their hesitation, but they all left, leaving the door open just a crack so they could hear her if she yelled. Emily fed Hope her bottle in the bassinet this time, but Hope didn't seem to mind. Once the bottle was finished, the pain had subsided enough that Emily felt confident burping Hope and then placing her back down. Hope did not fall asleep this time, and Emily was treated to the sounds of Hope cooing and playing while she continued her work.

As she worked through the pages, she found a law that Robert had written about alcohol consumption that she made sure to write down. She continued to work, and it seemed to have only been minutes before Julia returned to the door with a plate of food.

"It's been hours since breakfast, and you must be hungry. Doc said you shouldn't need your pills again until supper. I wasn't sure if the little one was hungry, but I brought a fresh bottle just in case." Julia set everything down on the desk, and Emily smiled. She may have known her for less than a day, but Julia already felt like family to Emily. She watched as Julia walked over to the bassinet and talked to Hope for a moment. Hope had been lying there all day while Emily worked, and the poor baby was getting almost no attention.

"Julia," Emily spoke, "If it's not too much trouble, would you like to take Hope this afternoon? I'm sure she would like the attention, and lying there while I work all day can't be fun for her." Emily knew by the smile on her face that Julia loved the idea.

"Of course, I wanted to ask, but didn't want you to feel like I was trying to steal her away from you."

"It would help me a lot, and she seems to like you."

"We will just be in the next room," Julia said as she picked up Hope and walked towards the door.

"Thank you," Emily replied as they left.

Part of her hated handing Hope over to a babysitter so soon, but Emily had to figure this stuff out for Hope's future. She quickly ate the sandwich that Julia had brought her and went back to the books. She continued to write quick notes and was amazed by some of the stuff Robert had thought to write down. She found a list of all the possible jobs that Robert felt were needed in the town. Emily agreed with everything but added a few of her own to the list. She felt confident in everything she had and even planned to tell everyone that she was basing it all on what Robert had written. She then grabbed the census journal and drew a single line through the names listed. She added herself on the first blank line and the second, Hope. She had just finished when a light knocked on the door, and Bobby walked in.

"Mama asked me to let you know that supper is ready and to see if you need any help?"

"Just the man I needed to see," Emily smiled at him. "I need to move these books to the dining room for after dinner, and I think you may be the only one strong enough to help me. What do you say?"

"I'm really strong!" Bobby did not try to hide the excitement in his voice. "I will get them all moved for you!"

"Great, let's go eat first, and then we will move them after.

Bobby nodded, and Emily followed him to the dining room, where everyone was waiting. She took her seat and was happy to see that Shawn was still sitting beside her. Hope was fast asleep in her bassinet, and Emily dared not wake her. As soon as she sat, the table came alive as the food was passed around, and everyone began to eat. Emily ate her fair share and leaned back while everyone else was eating. Suddenly, two small pills appeared in front of her. Emily looked over to see Shawn pulling his hand back. He nodded, and she knew that the others had told him that she had forgotten about them before. She picked up the pills and took them with a sip of water. He smiled and then began to help clean up the dishes.

"Mama, I have a very important job, and I'm the only one strong enough to do it," Emily heard from the other end of the table. Looking up, she could see that Bobby was trying to tell his mom that he couldn't help clean up because he had another job.

"I'm sorry, Julia, that's my fault. I needed someone strong enough to carry my books in here, and Bobby was the only person I could think of. I hope that's okay?" Emily spoke.

"Oh, of course," Julia smiled at her. "You'd better run along then and consider yourself lucky." Bobby didn't hesitate and took off running to the study.

"I am sorry, Julia," Emily said once Bobby was gone. "I should have asked you first.

"No, I just thought he was trying to get back to the television. It's no problem." Julia seemed genuine, and Emily felt relieved.

Soon, the table was clear, and Bobby had stacked all of the books on the table for Emily. He sat proudly next to his mom, bragging about how heavy the books were and how no one else could have done it. Emily looked around at them and knew they were eager to hear what she had decided. They would want to know what she had been working on all day. Emily had never done a lot of public speaking before, but at this moment, she felt herself getting what she assumed was stage fright.

"Well, are we going to do this or not?" Derick sneered from the other end of the table.

300

Chapter 24

Derick's comment had silenced everyone at the table. It was like the man knew how to prey on a person's weakness. Emily felt that somehow, he knew she was afraid of speaking, and he jumped on the opportunity. He continued to sneer at her as everything fell silent, and everyone turned to her. The look on his face reminded her of Chad and how he used to talk down to her. There was no way Derick could have known that his comment, which was supposed to show her she was weak, would remind her of her strength.

"If you guys are ready, we can start," Emily said. "Before this happened, I was just a glorified receptionist for a landscaping company. I had a husband who viewed me as worthless and a family I didn't speak to because I didn't want to admit my awful life. I had just begun to find my strength when the world went to hell, and I lost everything again. The last time I saw my family, I insisted they stop and pick up my husband's lover because she was pregnant, having no clue at the time that I was pregnant. I was supposed to be with them, but a bite on the shoulder left me alone. I lived in my neighbor's SUV for months, searching for them with Marley as my only friend." Emily had not planned to give them her life's story, but it seemed to be coming out naturally, so she continued to talk.

"My plan went from finding my family to finding somewhere safe for my child when I learned I was pregnant. I learned to fight zombies, escaped a rape camp, and found this miracle in running from the rapist a second time. The man who built this place, Robert, knew he had played a role in making this terrible world. He knew that people would need this place, and he created something amazing. I have looked through his notes and decided it is his vision I will follow on how to run this town." As she spoke, she saw Howard nodding in approval. Emily remembered that he had been reading the books in the library and had probably seen Robert's notes about the town.

"For this to work, everyone has to choose to be here. In choosing to be here, you agree to work to help not only yourself but everyone inside the wall. I know that we cannot start where Robert had planned, but I know we can work up to it. Everyone will have a job. I have a list of jobs, and everyone will be placed in one based on their skill set. Anyone who chooses not to work will be denied access to the provisions. Even those of basic life, such as food. The town cannot take care of someone unwilling to care for themselves." Emily could see that this comment had upset Derick, but she was not about to let him take over. As he opened his mouth to protest, she continued.

"Everyone will be required to take a shift on the wall. They will monitor what is happening outside and warn us of any incoming dangers. It protects all of us, so we all will protect it. Everyone will be paid for their time in credits. Everyone will have the same base credit amounts for doing their assigned jobs, and extra credits will be given to compensate for the extra work. Anyone with children will automatically receive the credits for each child, as children will not work.

Education will remain important, and all children will be required to attend school and receive an education certificate. I know that we will have to work to get the school running, but we will still provide the best education we can."

"I plan to follow Robert's rules as closely as possible to start and make adjustments as needed. I can't say what will work for the long term and what will not. Robert did not include bringing people in because he planned to have the town filled before the outbreak. I will make suggestions and work with you to figure out the best plan to let more people into the town and increase our chances of making this work."

As Emily spoke, she felt her confidence growing, "I know that there are still a lot of specifics that I haven't mentioned, but we don't all want to sit here for the next week while I read them all aloud. I had the books brought in here so that if you want to know anything specific before deciding to stay, I can look at it for you, and we can decide together how to proceed."

"Wow, so that was a whole lot of nothing." Derick blurted out. "You were in there all day. I expected more information, but you have no idea."

"If you would like, Derick," Emily sneered at him, "I can read through the list of rules and laws that I wrote down, but I warn you, it's five pages long and will take a while." Emily could have sworn she heard Shawn snort in laughter next to her.

"That was more information than we could

have hoped for with giving her less than a day," Sam said.

"I looked at the books she had here and planned to reference," Howard spoke next, "Her planning to use them as a starting point and build from there sounds like the best plan to me." Howard took his wife's hand, and she nodded; Emily knew they were both on board with her plan.

"So, who gets the final say in everything?" Derick questioned. "If someone says a rule is unfair or if there is a dispute, who gets the final say?"

"I do," Emily replied without hesitation. She had been ready for this and was delighted that Derick had asked it. "I will pick individuals to be part of my council as I get to know people better. They will advise me on matters and help provide a perspective I may not see. While I will still be the one who takes full responsibility for any decisions, I will depend on those I trust opinions as well."

"So, whatever you say goes?" Derick said with disgust in his voice. "And if we don't agree with that?"

"Then I will open the gate, and you are free to find somewhere else to call home," Emily said with confidence that surprised even her. "I'm not forcing anyone to stay; you are free to go if you wish."

"And what if we do just take this place from you? We could throw you and that baby out the gate!" The agitation in Derick's voice was growing.

Emily saw that Shawn was about to lose his temper again. She began searching for a way to keep a repeat of this morning from happening. Before either she or Shawn could react, Marley did. He stood from his spot next to the bassinet and walked to where he could see Derick. His teeth were bared, and a terrifying growl bellowed from his throat. Emily smiled and seized the moment as this seemed to shock Derick into a passive moment.

"I said you do not have to stay if you don't like the rules, but understand that my kindness is not a weakness. I will do what I have to keep this place safe for my daughter, and anyone who threatens that will not be shown mercy." Emily watched as Derick visibly swallowed hard and lowered his head. "Marley, I think the message has been received." Marley walked back and sat next to her; he was willing to listen but not ready to relax.

"Well, how do I sign up?" The chipper in Shawn's voice was hard to miss. Emily grabbed the census ledger and held it out.

"Simply write your name on the next line."

Shawn took the ledger and the pen, flipped to the page, and wrote his name below Hope's. When he finished, he handed the book to Doc, who began to do the same, and the book started to work its way around the table.

"I'll also need to know what each of you did before and your skills to figure out how to break up the work around here. We will also pick each family a

home of their own based on family size." Emily
continued to explain.

"Yeah, because your family size explains why
you get the biggest house here," Derick muttered
while writing his name in the ledger.

"While it may seem too big for my family, you
can see that my house is where people will be
welcome to stay until they have a home of their own.
It will allow me to get to know them better and ensure
they are the kind of people we want to live with us."
Emily was proud of her comeback and had not thought
of that beforehand. Everyone around the table nodded
in agreement, and the journal continued to pass.

"I heard you say there was a farm," Jacob said.
"I grew up on a farm, as did Tera. We could help get it
up to par and get things running." Tera nodded beside
Jacob in agreement. "The two of us would not be
enough in the long term, but we could at least get it
started."

"That would be amazing. Buttercup would love
to have someone there more often." Emily grabbed the
list of jobs and filled in Jacob and Tess under the farm.
"I will talk to you guys more about what I've learned
there, and there is a farmhouse you can call home."

"Thank you," Tera and Jacob both replied.

"I taught in a college, and June was a retired
grade school teacher," Howard chimed in.

"Retired by age, not choice," June quickly

added. "We would be glad to educate the kids, and since there are only two right now, we can also help with chores on the farm until there are more students."

"Perfect," Emily replied as she wrote Howard and June down under education.

"I was going to be graduating from high school. I worked at a clothing store part-time," Jessica spoke in a timid voice. "I have no idea how I can be useful."

"Well, we need someone to run the stores in town. They will need to keep track of the credits, ensure everyone pays for what they get, and refill the shelves. They will also be in charge of keeping track of what supplies we have and what supplies we are running low on. It's a lot of responsibility, but I think you can handle it. When we get more people, you would probably move up and be in charge of overseeing all of the stores. Is that something you think you would want to do?"

"Wow, yeah!" Jessica seemed thrilled with the idea, and Emily promptly wrote it down.

"There are apartments above the shops. We can look at those and pick one out for you."

"I worked in construction mostly," Derick spoke in a husky voice. "But as everything here is built, I guess I'm out of work for now."

"There are a lot of unfinished buildings in half the town, and there are the remains of the ones who died here. I stacked them over by the construction area, but didn't know how to work the equipment to take care of them. There is plenty of work for someone with construction experience." Emily wrote Derick's name under construction.

"And which lovely house will be mine?" Derick asked with a smile on his face.

"Well, as you are single, it will be an apartment. I think we will use the left side of the main street apartments for women and the right side for men." Emily saw the relief on Jessica's face as she said this.

"So, you are telling me that the great Robert said anyone single had to live in the apartments?" Derick said with his stink face.

"Actually, yes. Would you like me to show you?" Emily replied, and Derick waved his hand, signaling he didn't.

"I was a paralegal, but I don't see much use for those skills here," Sarah said. "But I used to love to work with computers and electronics in my free time."

"We need to set up some system to communicate with those outside the wall to find more people we could bring in. Perhaps you could be in charge of our communications system?" This is one of the things Emily had added to the list that Robert did not have.

"Hmm, I would have to look through what we have, but I think I could handle it." Sarah looked at Derick and added, "I have no problem with an apartment."

Emily wrote down Sarah's name under communications and looked back at everyone.

"I was a stay-at-home mom," Julia stated, "But I loved to bake bread and different things."

"We have a small bakery, and I'm sure with all the work to be done, everyone would struggle to find time to bake their goods." Emily could tell Julia was worried, but this suggestion excited her.

"I can do it, thank you," Julia replied as Emily wrote her name under the bakery.

"I worked mall security," Sam stated as he stared at the table. Emily could tell that he was already embarrassed to say it out loud.

"Well, now our malls will be safe," blurted out Derick while laughing.

"I think we will all be safer," Emily quickly replied. "Law enforcement is something that we need. I think you would make a great police officer." Emily could see the joy on Sam's face. "Where there are so few of us right now, we may need you to help in different areas, as I don't expect a lot of trouble if that's okay with you?" Emily finished as she had already written his name down under the police.

"Yes, of course, thank you." Sam sounded thrilled at the new job title.

"That just leaves Shawn," Emily turned to look at Shawn, glancing around the table.

"Just write down a criminal and lock him up," Derick laughed again.

"Maybe I could talk to you about that one-on-one?" Shawn leaned in and said to Emily.

"Yeah, that's no problem." She then turned back to everyone. "Everyone not in an apartment, I'll go over the housing list and come up with some options for each of you, and tomorrow morning you will all get to pick your new homes."

Emily watched as everyone smiled and began to talk about how excited they were. Shawn stood and began to walk out of the room. Emily caught Julia's attention and pointed at Hope. Julia understood and nodded a yes to her. Emily mouthed thank you and followed Shawn out of the room. Shawn walked in silence as Emily followed to the study, and he shut the door behind them.

"Should I be scared?" Emily joked as she faced him.

"No, nothing like that. All of them know about my past, but if Derick had made another comment, I'm not sure if I could have controlled my temper." Shawn replied.

"Understandable," Emily replied. "So, what's the story?"

"At eighteen, I joined the Marines, served for six years, and then decided I was ready for civilian life." Emily felt confused about how Derick could have called a marine a criminal. "Civilian life did not come as easily as I thought, though, and I fell on my ass pretty hard. I joined up with a crew that had served like me. I've been running with them for the past six years." Shawn stopped talking, but Emily knew there was something that he wasn't saying.

"So, what did you do for a job?" she asked.

"On paper, I was a mechanic, but I only worked a few hours a week in the garage." Emily's mind thought back to all of the outlaw bikers she had seen on television. It was hard for her to imagine Shawn being a drug runner or selling guns. "You have to understand that this group of guys was the only one who accepted me when I returned. They were my family, my brothers. Just like any family, we had our issues, and part of those issues was that not everything we did was legal." The criminal comment suddenly made more sense to Emily. "I wasn't a serial killer or anything like that. Yes, I had killed people, but just like when I was in the Marines, only if I had to save myself or one of my brothers."

"So, you were an outlaw with a set of morals?" Emily didn't want to sound condescending, but the question still came out that way.

"It sounds ridiculous, but yes. I get it if you want to cross my name out and ask me to leave." Shawn looked defeated, and Emily couldn't imagine asking him to leave.

"Well, with your military background and experience with criminal activity, it sounds like you would make a great head of security."

"What!?" Shawn sounded both shocked and confused.

"Yeah, we will need someone to keep the watch on the wall organized, as well as the police force. Everyone will need to be trained with the firearms they will be using, and we will need someone to help lead groups outside the wall to hunt for supplies that we may have to get outside." Emily tried to sound confident and hoped that it would help reassure him that he was welcome here.

"You want me to stay, despite what I just told you?" He was looking at her with both confusion and amazement.

"What is that vest you're wearing?" Emily asked without hesitation.

"It's for the club I belonged to. They may all be dead, but I still wear it to keep them close." He looked at the vest while he talked.

"Upstairs, I have a photo album of my family. It has my parents, brother, and sister. It also has my dick of a husband. I keep it to hold on to the good, not to focus on the bad, just like you keep that to honor your brothers. It helps you to keep them close. We all have crap in our past that we may want to forget, but the bad stuff gives us the strength to move forward." Emily hadn't realized most of this until she spoke the words aloud.

"You are a remarkable woman," Shawn smiled. "I will take the job, boss."

"Good," Emily smiled back at him. They left the study, each still laughing, and found that everyone had moved to the living room. They joined everyone as they talked about how excited they were about what was to come. Derick sat silently in the corner and headed upstairs to bed without saying a word. Emily fed Hope once more before saying good night to everyone and heading to bed herself. She decided to skip the shower tonight instead of dressing for bed and sliding into bed next to Marley. Hope was asleep within minutes, and Marley was right behind her. Emily looked at the bedroom door and realized she had not locked it once again. Despite her dislike for Derick, she felt completely safe and couldn't remember the last time she felt like this.

Emily woke early the following day and got herself and Hope ready for the day. She remembered her pills and headed downstairs for a quick breakfast. As she walked through the living room, she found Shawn asleep on the couch and quietly made her way to the kitchen. She was surprised to see Doc was already there and enjoying a cup of coffee.

"Good morning," he chimed as she walked in. "You remember your pills this morning?"

"I sure did," Emily replied. "By the way, I realize I never said it was allowed yesterday, but I assume you are okay with being the town physician?"

"Oh yes," Doc laughed," I would be useless as a farmhand or construction worker."

"Great, I believe the clinic has a private apartment above it if that's okay with you."

"That sounds perfect," Doc replied. "I have one request, if it's not too much trouble."

"Of course. What is it, Doc?" Emily was opening the door for Marley as she spoke.

"The key code to the medication room. Are you able to reset to something that only you and I know?" Doc seemed embarrassed to be asking.

"I can. It's no problem. Is there something concerning that I should know about?" Emily felt that Doc would not ask if there was not something specific that worried him.

"I looked through the medications after your procedure, and the room is quite extensive in terms of what it has. I went back yesterday and noticed that some things were missing, and Derick went from being a loud jerk to calm and relaxed very fast yesterday. I can't be certain, but I would like to be certain that no one uses, abuses, or wastes the medication."

"I completely understand. As soon as I'm done feeding Hope, we will go change that code."

Doc seemed relieved that she understood. Marley came trotting back in and looked disappointed

at the empty bowls that waited for him. Emily shut the
door and knew that she and he would have to wait
until Hope was cared for. Emily fixed Hope's bottle
and sat at the kitchen table to feed her. Once Hope had
eaten her fill, Emily stood, and Marley was taken care
of. Emily said to Doc, "Let's get that changed quickly."

"Oh, I don't want to trouble you. Please have
your breakfast."

"It's no trouble, and the rest of the house is still
asleep. This way, we can be sure the code is secure."

After placing Hope in the bassinet, Emily
turned, walked to the study, and opened the panel that
hid the master computer. She opened the clinic and
went through the sequence to change the code on the
medication door. Doc watched as she went through the
processes. Once the screen flashed asking for the new
code, Emily moved to one side and motioned for Doc
to enter the code. He did it slowly as Emily watched,
and then the computer asked for it to be entered again
for confirmation. Emily entered it the second time as
Doc watched to ensure she got it right. The computer
flashed confirmation that the code had been changed,
and Emily closed the panel.

"See, no trouble at all." Emily smiled at Doc as
the panel closed.

"I have to say that felt like a science fiction
movie." Doc laughed.

"Yeah, Robert did have a certain flair, that's for
sure."

Emily turned and saw that Hope was already deep in her morning nap. She decided to let the babe sleep and leave the door cracked if she woke. She headed back to the kitchen with Doc. She poured herself a cup of coffee and made some toast. The toast had just finished as Shawn walked into the kitchen. He gave a quick "Morning" and walked half asleep towards the coffee. The house was awake not long after, and everyone grabbed a quick breakfast, eager to set out into the town for the day. None of them had a chance yet to explore, and they were anxious to see what was there.

Emily already had a few houses in mind for the families and was eager to set out. Once everyone was ready, she grabbed Hope from the study and walked to the door. She had not seen Shawn since his cup of coffee and assumed he was probably outside having a cigarette. Shawn was waiting outside when she opened the door, but not with a cigarette.

"I thought this might help with all your walking today." Emily looked down to see a stroller.

"It's perfect, thank you." Emily smiled as she placed Hope inside.

Hope seemed happy and was back to sleep in a few moments. Emily began her tour through the town, showing them the buildings and what she had found inside. She explained that everyone would be set up with a locker for their weapons and would only take them out while on wall duty. Shawn would be working on that schedule.

Right now, the only people allowed to carry a weapon inside the wall would be herself, Shawn, and Sam. Shawn and Sam brought the stroller upstairs to the apartments so Sarah and Jessica could each pick one out. They chose apartments across the hall, and soon it was on to the men's side. Shawn chose one towards the center of town, farthest from the wall. Derick looked in each apartment, complaining about what each one had to offer. Emily considered that maybe she should have let Shawn throw him off the wall when he finally chose one. A quick stop at the clinic, and Doc was able to look at the apartment and claimed it was perfect. She then took Bobby and his family to look at a three-bedroom house next to hers. Bobby picked out a bedroom within minutes, and his parents said they loved it. Howard and June liked the two-bedroom she showed them next to the school.

Emily then led them all to the farm. The group commented on how many houses there were, and the excitement grew. Once they reached the farm, everyone seemed in awe. Emily took them to the barn, where Buttercup was waiting as always. The cows were already inside and seemed very upset that she had not milked them the day before. After she finished the tour, Jacob and Terra seemed eager to get to work. Emily began the walk home, and everyone took off on their separate ways, eager to get to work. She needed to get everyone a locker set up and the cards to keep track of their credits. Soon, it was just her, Hope, and Marley walking down the road together. Emily turned to walk towards the wall instead of going home. Once she reached the wall, she picked up Hope and walked up the metal stairs to the top.

Emily stood looking out over the wall with the wind whipping around her. The change was definitely in the air, and she would stand here through it. She tried to remember the woman who just a year ago couldn't even stand up for herself. It was hard to believe that the same woman was now the leader of this town. Emily looked down at the baby in her arms and then at the faithful dog by her side. It was time for another new beginning, and Emily felt confident that she would handle it as well as she did the last.

****

The phone went straight to voicemail. The battery must have died months ago. Emily's voice rang through the speaker on the phone.

"This Emily. Leave me a message."

A dull tone followed her words, indicating that it was time for the caller to speak.

"Hey, Emily. I just needed to hear your voice. I hope wherever you are, you are at peace. I hope one day we get to see each other again." The sound of crying takes over for just a moment. " I love you."

The caller hung up, and the phone remained silent on the bedside table.